Paul and Millie get along like a house on fire and fancy each other rotten. They even like each other's mothers. But for Millie, convent educated, home counties reared, Paul has one major flaw. He is a football manager. She hates the cold, the boardroom snootiness, the noise and aggression of the crowd and she has no idea what is going on on the pitch. At her first game, she wasn't even certain which team it was her new found friend managed, let alone which way they were kicking. Worst of all, she sees little of Paul at games (being segregated with the Ladies) and then has to drive him home, reliving the highs and lows of the game which means nothing to her. Can their relationship survive?

Bryony Hill is married to footballer and broadcaster Jimmy Hill, and it was while helping him with his autobiography that she was inspired to start writing. She came joint second in the Harry Bowling Prize for new unpublished fiction in 1999. Bryony is now resident in Sussex, after spending some years travelling in France.

To dear Vronics —

PENALTY CHICK

*with fonder love,
Juny
B xxx*

Bryony Hill

The Book Guild Ltd
Sussex, England

First published in Great Britain in 2003 by
The Book Guild Ltd
25 High Street
Lewes, East Sussex
BN7 2LU

Typesetting in Meridien by
Keyboard Services, Luton, Bedfordshire

Printed in Great Britain by
Athenaeum Press Ltd, Gateshead

A catalogue record for this book is
available from the British Library

ISBN 1 85776 761 6

CONTENTS

ACKNOWLEDGEMENTS

If it hadn't been for Harry Bowling I would never have found myself in the position of being published. In his memory, his widow Edna, together with Hodder Headline and MBA Literary Agents, launched a competition for unpublished writers. Having recently joined the Romantic Novelists Association it was suggested that I enter. The long and the short of it is that I came runner-up and MBA took me on. Thank you, Edna, so much for having given me the chance. Over the years, as a friend, Carol Biss at the Book Guild devoted endless time giving me advice and encouragement in my writing and I am so proud that my story has found a home with them. I could not have done it without the patience, help and enthusiasm of my agent, Laura Longrigg from MBA, whose confidence in me never seemed to waiver. I also want to thank the following friends, in no particular order, who made the whole process fun from the start. Firstly, to Jim Estey, my indomitable trouble-shooter on call twenty-four hours a day when I had problems with my hard drive (the latest being when I had my mouse back to front...). Thanks go to Dave Woolf, comedian extraordinaire, for educating me on the finer points of the English Language and to Kelly Jane Noades for enlightening me as to the hidden delights of the Rampant Rabbit – less said here the better! Credit must go to Jan Campbell for having her ear bashed with monotonous regularity during our dog walks together and who gave me, in desperation no doubt, some classic expressions. Last but by no means least, my grateful thanks to my dear, long-suffering husband (and to the game of golf which kept him out of the house so that I could write in peace), expert-in-residence and technical adviser, to whom I am indebted for inventing the title, although he was heard to mutter on more than one occasion, 'thank goodness Jimmy Hill and Company aren't relying on you for income...'

PART ONE

TEAM SELECTION

1

'Lawksamussy, that'll be three points on my licence,' I bleated, praying that I wouldn't get breathalysed into the bargain. I had crashed my trolley into a display of baked beans, sending the tins flying. Pretending it had absolutely nothing to do with me I kicked a stray can to one side, hoping that I hadn't been spotted by the closed circuit cameras. Feeling hot and bothered, I gripped the handlebar for support and skidded over to the freezer cabinets. Lordy, I was tired. And rather drunk, having left a party at the house of someone I hardly knew. In the cab taking me home I hit on a brainwave – I'd go shopping. The taxi driver thought I was completely mad, but it seemed *such* a good idea at the time. Anyway, I was ravenous and a pizza wouldn't go amiss, whatever the time of day. We pulled in to a Tesco Express at a garage in Chelsea and I asked the driver to wait.

Swaying slightly I stopped to peruse the shelves in front of me. I had to squint in order to focus. Into my chariot I piled some *ciabatta*, then a microwave bread-and-butter-pudding. I meandered off to find the tea and coffee. Devoid of inspiration, suddenly I sensed a presence beside me. Crossing my fingers that it wasn't the store manager, I peered through my fringe and saw a pair of long legs wrapped in dark green cords, the turn-ups neatly breaking on polished brogues. I worked my way upwards. Definitely male. Yum yum. Hesitantly, I stretched to take a packet from the top shelf.

1

A hand brushed mine. 'I do apologise,' an agreeable voice said, 'There seems to be only one left of that make. Please, you have it.'

Flustered, I tried to speak but my teeth didn't fit.

He smiled. 'I insist. I'm more than happy with instant.'

I thought I had died and gone to heaven. In my inebriated state I dropped the packet. Bending down to pick it up, excitement rising in my throat, I cranked up my mega watt smile, which normally lights up half a street on the darkest day of the year, and waited. And waited. Power cut. By the time I had made sure that lipstick wasn't smearing my teeth and that my mascara hadn't run, he'd gone. Furious with myself, I forced my trolley into overdrive and charged up the aisle in the hope of catching up with him. Veering dangerously on two wheels I caught a glimpse of a tweedy elbow and a leg heading northwards only to find on turning the bend that he had vanished again, *pffft*, as if in a puff of smoke.

Oh vanity. Oh woe. Serves me right, doesn't it? I'd been bloke-less now for over six months and believe me, I wasn't enjoying my single status one iota. A furry hot water bottle in the shape of a cocker spaniel's all well and good, but no way does it replace a piping hot human in bed on a cold winter's night, nor a cool one on a hot one. It wouldn't have mattered too much if he hadn't been such a gorgeous hunk. I'm tall, over 5'8", well 5'9" really in my bare feet, so I need someone of above average height to feel remotely feminine and he looked just the job, with blond hair long enough to look sexy, curling over the collar. Almost edible. Oh well. Oh hell.

I trundled to the check out, cursing my rotten luck.

Out in the car park, depressed, and with tomorrow's headache beginning to bite, I remembered with a lurch that the cab driver would have kept the meter ticking. As I was calculating the price of delaying my departure in the pursuit of true love, I stepped to one side to let a snazzy silver car go past, the driver's face half hidden in shadow. My heart beat faster. It was him.

The next morning I made a telephone call. Susie Dalrymple and I were at school together, and along with Polly Farmer we're best mates. We are, to put it simply, joined at the hip.

'Catch ya at Floosie's at 8.30?' asked Susie.

'Yeah, great,' I acquiesced. 'Will you ring Poll?'

'No probs.'

So there we were, Susie, Polly and myself, ensconced in a wine bar in Wimbledon making, I'm afraid, rather a lot of noise. Susie is by far the prettiest and the possessor of glorious straight blonde hair, accompanied by wickedly intelligent, Icelandic blue eyes and pale lashes. She is also the richest, and as a child not only did she own a custom-built Wendy house with real tiles on the roof (her father is a building millionaire), but she also had subscriptions to several magazines. We loved nothing more than to congregate in her des. res. wading happily through piles of Bliss and Sugar (forbidden in our household), learning the gruesome facts of life which we subsequently passed on to our parents. She went off to study art in Florence for a year, losing her virginity the day after she arrived to an Italian Count up a watchtower in Naples. Then, to the immense astonishment of her family and friends (herself included), she secured a place at university and now works in the bowels of an auction house in London, running an expensive BMW and apartment subsidised by a comfortable trust fund.

Polly has brown hair like me, but hers is Pre-Raphaelite wild. She has a mouth like Juliette Binoche and her eyes are boot-polish brown. Her parents didn't seem to mind that they had spawned an intellectual airhead and she had been reared to do the season and little else, groomed for wedlock and a life in the shires with acres of parkland, wet Labradors and a brace of kids. Currently dabbling at earning some sort of a living, she works for a company called 'Presents of Mind' which requires her to seek out gifts for people (mostly men, naturally) with no free time and more money than sense.

We grew up, out and sideways, sharing our adolescent nightmares, spot-counting and boyfriends and I would happily swear under oath that the school gates sighed audibly with relief as we made our final exit. As for me, I'm ashamed to say that I didn't score any miracles academically. I was too bone idle. Also, my father having skipped off to pastures new, my mother's income wasn't exactly in the same league, and in an attempt at giving me some sort of qualification she forced me to take a secretarial course after which I hit the capital, where I have remained ever since.

3

'I've met someone,' I said, recharging my glass.

'What?' chorused the other two. 'Who?'

'*Someone*. Only I haven't. Not really, I mean...' I mumbled, feeling foolish.

'Stop rambling, woman. Explain,' said Susie.

'Well, I bumped into him. Literally. Our hands collided. I'd just knocked over a pyramid of beans.'

'A *what*?' asked Polly.

'Never mind,' I sighed, closing my eyes and trying to picture his face, 'it was *so* romantic.'

'Sounds it. What's his name?' asked Susie.

'What does he do?' asked Poll.

'Is he rich?' they asked unison.

'Oh heavens, I don't know. It doesn't matter as I doubt I'll ever see him again.' I told them what happened.

'You've got it in one, Mill,' Susie said emphatically. 'What d'you think, Poll?'

'Hmm, not exactly an ideal scenario.'

'Give me a break. I never said it was undying love,' I rallied, wishing I'd kept quiet. 'I simply said I'd met ... seen...'

'Someone,' they said together, Tweedledum and Tweedledee.

'What did he have in his basket?' Polly asked, leaning nearer and running her fingers around the rim of her glass, 'it can be *very* revealing.'

I drummed my fingers on the wooden table. 'Well, let me see,' I said, warming to the topic. 'Beside a giant sized pot of Marmite there were several packets of bran, three boxes of porridge oats, Bisodol and cat litter.'

Polly looked aghast. 'Ugh! Marmite? Get real, Mill. You don't think, with all that roughage, that he needs the cat litter for himself, do you?'

I burst out laughing. 'I was pulling your leg. His basket was empty – bit like this,' I said, waving the wine bottle. 'Time for another,' I suggested, grabbing a passing waiter, 'and anyway, I *like* Marmite.'

I thought a great deal about the perfect being in the corduroy trousers during the next few days and the missed opportunity. Please don't think I'm desperate, but when you actually do see someone you fancy as against someone to whom you would have to force yourself to give the time of day, the last thing you want is to let them slip through your fingers. Believe me, I'm not as desperate as *Mademoiselle* Bridget Jones, but as an unattached female you receive the inevitable invitations to dinner parties, knowing it's more to make up the numbers than for your vibrant personality and sparkling wit. If you are placed next to a married man, woe betide you if he ventures a minor flirt. Instantly, his wife will launch occular daggers with the precision of a circus act. The icy atmosphere at the door when you all stagger home hardly makes the effort of being there in the first place worthwhile, the only bonus being you are well fed and watered. Sounds cynical, but I've been there once too often.

The very next day I started my campaign – walking past the Chelsea Tesco's and peering in. I did this at lunchtime and repeated it in the evening. Two days later I opened an account at the petrol station where I spent a great deal of time closely vetting every silver car which happened to drive in. How I longed, yearned, wished to see his oh-so-lean-and-sexy figure. But no. The Gods weren't being kind. Serves me right. Hadn't my mother wisely told me never to force the issue? It's all about fate, you see. If something is meant to happen then it will, of its own accord, or not. However, these words of maternal wisdom didn't stop me stalking the place and it was only when I was beginning to get funny looks from the staff that I plucked up courage and went inside.

'This is a customer announcement. Will Rodney 'ackett please come to the service desk? Rodney 'ackett to the service desk. Tha-a-nk yee-oo.'

I glanced at the mêlée of vacant faces in front of me. Please don't let him be called Rodney Hackett. There's only so much a girl can take. I moved towards the flowers where there was no apparent sign of the elusive Mr 'ackett, discreetly rinsing my fingers in one of the buckets and wiping my hands on my pullover. My fingers were sticky as I'd eaten a sandwich in the car. Humming tunelessly under my breath I picked out a bunch of pink roses, reduced to half price, when I pricked my finger on a thorn. Only feet away were a pair of medium tan, polished brogues. I had only ever seen one pair of shoes like these. His. I couldn't believe it. In a state of blissful shock I stared at him. Clutching a basket, he was filling it with the sort of things I would have liked. Unaware of my existence, he toyed between selecting a flamboyant twenty pound mixed bouquet and white lilies. The lilies won and he snuggled three bunches against a bottle of pink champagne. Gently manoeuvring between a mother with two kids and a woman in a wheelchair, he headed off. I followed. Sensibly ignoring the pulses and pastas, he came to a halt at the chocolates. Then his hand hovered over the Ferrero Rocher. Perhaps he was Rodney Hackett after all? I stood far enough away not to be conspicuous and watched as he selected a conservative double box of Elizabeth Shaw mints. Adding it to his other purchases he walked purposefully towards the exit. Major dilemma. I didn't have a plan and in a matter of seconds I'd lose him for ever.

'Do you want your computer vouchers?' I shouted, although I was close enough to smell his aftershave.

'I beg your pardon?' he said, surprise written all over his face.

For the first time I saw the true colour of his eyes. Dark, dark brown. Almost black. With lashes. Oh God. 'Vouchers! Um, computer vouchers. For schools?'

His expression was more confused than ever. 'I'm sorry?'

'Um, I collect them. For my sister. She's got ten kids. (Where did they come from?) Seven, er, I mean twins. Anyway, I send them to her.' I haven't got a sister. I wanted to die.

A smile was beginning to grow at the corners of *the* most delicious mouth. 'Well, I don't see why not, only I'd better pay first. There won't be many, I'm afraid, but you're more than welcome to them.' He ran slender fingers through his hair and stared at me. 'I know it sounds corny, but don't I know you?'

Now what? Do I confess? Or pretend we haven't met? Faint? 'No, no, no, no, no,' I said, 'I mean yes, er, maybe,' I said, shaking my head and laughing uncontrollably. 'Hm, th ... the coffee?' He gave me a questioning look, which unsettled me further and scratching the edge of his ear discreetly, he turned as if about to go. Oh gawd, he thinks I'm trying to pick him up. Well, I am, but I don't want him to know. Don't panic, Mill. You're nearly in there, old girl. I drew in a deep breath and did a swift costing of the contents of his basket which resulted in sending me back a pace or two. I had serious competition. 'Nice flowers,' I said.

'Thank you. They are. I chose them carefully.'

'Party?'

'No.'

Oh.

'Gir-?' I stopped myself just in time before I committed social suicide.

The smile developed into a broad grin. 'Why don't you let me buy you a drink and we can discuss my shopping in full.'

'What can I get you? Cappuccino? Black?'

I was too in love to answer.

'Fine, er, cappuccino it is, then.'

I watched his long, straight back as he pushed the relevant buttons on the machine, placing each cup neatly under the spout. What am I doing? What's worse, what have I *done*?

'Here you are. Sugar?' he asked as he emptied two tubes into his cup.

Suddenly embarrassed, I blew on the frothy milk, watching the chocolate powder shiver. For want of something to do and having nothing brilliant to say, I picked at my chipped nail polish, checking my cuticles.

'You've got froth on your top lip.'

Before I could do anything, he wiped away the whipped milk. Then he licked his finger. Oh my God, Oh my God...

The brown eyes twinkled, creasing at the sides. What a cracker. What a humungous, humdinger of a dream boat. I was staring open-mouthed at a kaleidoscope of heaven. Fearing I was about to dribble, I zapped around the cafeteria to see if I was being watched by the dozen or so marauding females who usually frequented the place – this is Chelsea after all. Ha! Look what I've caught in my fishing net my beauties, my eyes said, my claws extended. Watch it. Paws off. He's mine.

'Have you got time for another?'

'Have you?' I parried, hoping I might still have a chance of unearthing who the goodies were for. This time I was going to try and get froth on both lips.

Stirring to dissolve the sugar he said politely, 'My name's Paul, Paul Campbell.' His voice was soft, slightly hesitant and classless with neither the twang and strangulated consonants of *sarf* London, nor the clipped tone of the Home Counties. It was deeply alluring. He put out his hand.

7

Grinning stupidly, surprised and inspired by his formality, I shook it – rather too forcefully – increasing my embarrassment as I watched him massage life back into his fingers, the nails of which, like me, he evidently chewed. Second observation: perhaps he's shy, and definitely sensitive. Things looked better and better. I slid my chair further under the table, shuffled my feet and shoved a wodge of wayward hair behind an ear. 'I'm Millie Palmer-Ede,' I rattled off as fast as possible. I mean, really, what a mouthful. What's worse is that 'Millie' isn't short for Camilla. That would have been tolerable. It's a diminutive for Millicent and I certainly wasn't about to reveal this piece of information in a hurry.

'I'm delighted to meet you, too.' Oh Christ, what a crappy, stupid thing to say. What a complete turn-off. I've never said, 'I'm delighted to meet you' to anyone in my entire life. Why start now, for goodness sake?

He was apparently undeterred by my formal reply and he laughed nervously, showing immaculate teeth. 'It's weird. I don't normally shop here and haven't been back since the other night but I was desperate for petrol and needed the other things, so it couldn't have been more convenient. Then I bump into you again. You have to admit it's a bit of a coincidence.'

I wasn't about to disillusion him that I had practically moved lock, stock and barrel into the place in the hope of setting eyes on him again. All I could think of was thank heavens Polly and Susie weren't in harness, as I wouldn't have stood a monkey's with Paul, if either of them had been around.

'Not exactly what you'd call top drawer, darling,' I could hear my ubiquitous mother hiss in my ear, 'but he scrubs up well.'

'Um, important date, have you? The flowers I mean, and the champagne?' I persisted, my guts knotting with the rudeness of my questions.

Throwing back his head with laughter, he put both hands flat on the table in front of him. 'Me?' he said, his eyebrows shooting up in mock horror, 'you've got to be joking.'

'But I don't understand. Surely they're not for yourself?'

'No, Miss Sticky Beak,' he said with no hint of irritation, 'as a matter of fact, they're for my mother.'

I nearly wet myself with relief.

We exchanged telephone numbers. In one oyster in a

hundred you may tumble across a pearl. Had I found that lucky shell? But hang on, remember this is me we're talking about here, and naturally there had to be a flaw.

It took precisely one week to find out what it was.

2

For my sins, I am a member of that dreaded breed – the lowest of pond life – an estate agent. Our office is north of Ladbroke Grove Underground, beyond the Westway. We like to consider it a reasonable area, but it's more Kensal Rise than Holland Park. 'Up and coming' the blurb says. Our premises have room only for two negotiators with a miniscule kitchenette and loo at the back – definitely not in the bracket of the Big Boys. Having said that, I'm happy there and we run it more or less as we like.

I crossed my fingers, toes and anything else to hand and prayed Paul would ring. He did, an agonising week later, during which time I was consumed with insecurity, fears I had gone over the top, been boring, talked too much, or not talked enough. On Wednesday morning I had eventually resigned myself and given up all hope of hearing from him. Feeling dejected and thoroughly miserable, even the chance of checking out a new instruction did nothing to lift my spirits. Three quarters of an hour later I trudged back to the office.

Mary McCarthy, the girl I work with, said gaily, 'A chap phoned for you when you were out. Sounded rather nice.'

I swallowed with excitement, thrilled that it might have been Paul. I fiddled with my folder in an effort to appear cool, calm and collected, none of which I was. Also I was beginning to feel slightly sick, that *nice* sick feeling if there is such a thing, you get when you first realise you fancy the pants off someone. 'Did he leave any message?' I asked, my voice noticeably wobbly. 'I don't suppose he said he'd ring back?'

'Nope.'

'Are you sure?'

'Yep.'

I looked at the telephone, sitting silently amongst the debris on my desk and wondered whether to return his call. Generally I am not backwards in coming forwards, but I do draw the line at ringing a man when I hardly know him. It could give the wrong impression – no – it would give the right impression and *that* would be wrong. There. Do I make myself clear? I would simply have to sit tight and pray that he would ring me again. I thought of cancelling everything in my diary for the rest of the afternoon to be on standby.

I needn't have worried, as by tea-time he had telephoned again and we'd fixed up to see each other. Only there was one problem. Today was out of the question, so were Tuesdays, Wednesdays, Thursdays, Fridays and horror of horrors, so were Saturdays. Sundays could be available, though. With such flexibility we were bound to get a relationship off the ground.

'Sunday would be great,' I said, too enthusiastically for my liking, wondering what was the hitch with the other days.

'It's the only time I'm free, I'm afraid. I'm caught up the rest of the week,' Paul said bluntly.

Now, strange as it may seem, in all the time we had spent drinking coffee, we hadn't broached the subject of his employment, or mine for that matter. Maybe he had mentioned it *en passant*, but I had been too engrossed in scrutinising his face at close quarters to notice. Then the awful truth emerged and a bigger bombshell than any cruise missile despatched to Iraq dropped between us.

'Why? You're not in the police force, are you?' I asked, thinking sneakily that a pair of regulation handcuffs could come in useful.

'No, grief, nothing like that,' he replied, a hint of humour in his voice.

Mentally I flicked through a list of likely careers. 'What then? Are you a doctor? Prison officer? Please don't tell me you're a social worker.'

He laughed loudly. 'No, none of those. I manage a football club.'

Shit. I groaned inwardly, in total despair. Euphoria disappeared with that one word comprising eight menacing letters. This was serious. What on earth was I thinking? I needed my bumps felt. *Moi*, who has always hated sport with a vengeance, was hoping to tackle the most unlikely pairing this side of Stamford Bridge. Games never were my strong point. Although blessed with height I possess flat feet and no spring, added to which I simply don't have an eye for the moving target. I make an even poorer spectator. I'm good at feminine things, like retail research. It was my typical bad luck and small wonder he had little, if any, free time. I soon discovered that if he wasn't training with the 'lads', he was watching a new talent somewhere in the wilds of Birmingham, or travelling to an away game, which explained why Tuesdays were out. Even an ignoramus like me knows about Saturdays, but I'd never thought to consider the possibility of an overnight stay in Rochdale before the second match of the week. It was a recipe for disaster and it would be best to be the first rat to jump ship. Then I imagined his sexy eyes, his adorable face, his long legs and I decided aganst my better judgement not to blow the whistle on this one.

'Millie? Are you still there? I haven't put you off, have I?'

I scratched my head. 'Heavens no. What can have given you that idea? It sounds, er, fascinating.'

'Well, it was the tone of your voice. You didn't sound too pleased.' He paused. 'It's not as bad as that, I promise.'

I knew I'd hesitated a moment longer than I should have. I wish I could learn to hide my feelings. Taking a deep breath, I made a valiant attempt at showing some sort of interest, mostly to convince myself that I should continue my attack. 'Which team are you with?' I asked, not knowing my Arsenal from my elbow. A premiership club would at least have some clout with my mates, except they'd all want tickets.

'Not a premier league one, I'm afraid. I hate to disappoint you again, but we're in the third division. Netherfield Town. It's an old club,' he said proudly, as if to up the ante, 'we've recently celebrated our centenary.'

There was a brief silence during which I could hear paper rustling.

'Hmm, I can squeeze in a few hours on Sunday. What's your diary like?'

Squeeze? Sunday? He made it sound like the last slice of treacle tart left on the plate that would be a pity to waste. Shamelessly

11

I abandoned all pride, relieved that we had some small patch of common ground. 'Yes, I'm free *all* Sunday. That'd be great.' I wondered again whether I should have accepted, having half an inkling of what I was letting myself in for.

Mary was staring at me, with a naughty smile on her face. 'Well,' she asked, 'and who was that?'

I didn't feel like a cross examination as my mind was already in top gear thinking about what I would wear as bottom gear on Sunday. Trousers or skirt? Short or long? Jeans or combats? 'Uhm, what?'

'It was him, wasn't it?'

'Him? I don't know what you could possibly mean,' I said flippantly.

'I saw your face. It was lit up like a beacon. And you were doodling. You never doodle when you're talking to someone you don't like. Take a look at your message pad.'

Mary was absolutely right of course. As a match to a touch paper, a full bottle of meths to a wino, whoosh! I was away and there was simply no stopping me. When I eventually finished (purely because I had run out of info not oomph), having circumnavigated his career prospects, bank balance and even the unlikely prospect of Netherfield Town FC going up a division, I stopped, exhausted to see that Mary had fallen asleep at her desk somewhere between the Cup run and Mansfield Town.

'Lost you there for a moment, Mill. Sorry.'

I have a feeling she was a teensy, weensy bit jealous.

I had six whole days to fill before Paul and I could see each other again. The long wait was aggravated by the fact that for some inexplicable reason in this day and age of space travel and 'Always' (with wings), he never managed to get near a telephone. I began to suffer from further self-doubt.

Being female I have always considered that a newspaper finishes at the start of the business section, but all of a sudden I began to cast an eye over the sports pages of my *Daily Mail* (which every girl should have and hopefully I was about to). Rather than skip through to read Lynda Lee-Potter and my horoscope, I found myself turning immediately to the back page like a bloke, in order to scan the football section for a few column inches on the Nethers, as I had taken to calling them. This isn't their real sobriquet, which happens to be the Miners, something to do with the fact that they come from Kent. Are there still mines in Kent? Anyway, they'll remain the Nethers to me. Surprisingly, there wasn't any press coverage for three days, until whoopee! a mention on Friday, tucked away in a corner between an advertisement for a royal commemorative plate and one for mobile phones.

> *'Netherfield Town FC's ambitious manager, Paul Campbell, has a daunting task in front of him. Floating around in the bottom rung of the division, this head on clash for survival with equally vulnerable Torquay United should prove a battle indeed. Etc. etc. etzzzzzzzzz...'*

3

It was my turn to do the solo Saturday stint at work and I nipped into the newsagents to invest in copies of *Four Four Two* and *Loaded* in the hope of finding a colour pic of Paul, arriving with my usual punctuality at twelve minutes past ten. This can be a hazardous process, as it's often an obstacle course dodging the tramps and drunks comatose on the pavement, having enjoyed the liquid benefits collected courtesy of the DSS the day before. Our office unfortunately is equidistant between the Social Security and the cheapest cider in town and it's inevitably our doorway into which they slump. Stepping over one somnolent and very dirty pair of legs, I unlocked. It was extremely cold outside, but thankfully the night storage heaters had made the room nice and cosy. I switched on the lights and ran the answerphone in case Paul had left a message. Some hope. I opened the meagre post, which produced one or two properties on half commission and a clutter of junk mail. I went next door to buy a king-sized Twix and settled down for breakfast. With no appointments so far in my diary, it was going to be a tedious three hours.

About half eleven, when I was three quarters of the way through a second filthy cup of black Nescaf in order to stay awake, Arthur, our local keeper of the peace, put his head round the door.

'Any chance of a quick one, Millie?' PC Arthur Malone, endearingly handsome, all springy red hair and freckles and a face all mothers would love, stood blocking the doorway, grinning. He really did look as though he had never put a razor to that sweet face of his and yes, his feet were at least size twelves. He lolloped in without waiting for a reply, as ever the clever detective he had already observed that I wasn't exactly rushed off my feet and plonked himself at Mary's desk. Thinking this might be bad for business having six feet three of boy in blue perched on my colleague's executive leather swing chair, I nearly asked him to move, but since Joe Public seemed to have vanished off the face of the earth and the phone was equally silent, I let it ride. I was glad of the company. As I've explained, Arthur is our resident plod and I have a strong suspicion that he has a soft touch for me. He's very protective of us girls and makes sure we don't go to certain areas unaccompanied and certainly not after dark. I'm not sure if he is a very effective policeman, but he is a big one and that's an advantage and he has bailed us out efficiently on more than one occasion.

'Arthur,' I asked as I handed him his mug, into which I had piled four sugars at his request, 'do you like football? I mean, do you have a team you support?'

'Me? Football?' he asked, surprised, as he dipped into the digestives. 'The only football I've had time for is having to be on duty at Wembley.'

'Yes, but when you were a kid you must have followed one team in particular. All boys do ... don't they?' I asked, feeling ridiculous. 'Ahem, what's your view of, um, of Netherfield Town?'

Arthur bit into his biscuit and a stray crumb went down the wrong way. 'Netherfield?' he choked, extracting a freshly laundered handkerchief from his trouser pocket and wiping his mouth. 'I don't follow the lower divisions much,' he replied, before chomping the remaining half of biscuit. 'I'm more of a Leishter Shitty man.'

As it had been exceptionally quiet, I felt I could justifiably lock up half an hour early. Stuck firmly on the windscreen was a parking ticket. I hadn't seen a warden all morning. Why hadn't next-door warned me? We run a network of spies as we all systematically park on yellow lines and at least three times a day we play musical cars as we drive round the neighbourhood, racing to find an official parking space. Crossly I scrunched up the Cellophane envelope and threw it on the floor which was carpeted with at least two dozen such others, mingled with Twix and Mars wrappings, a Kentucky Fried Chicken box (empty) and a can of Coke (half full), which had fizzed all over the rubber mat. I catapulted out of Westbourne Grove and headed for High Street Ken.

I had a serious decision to make. What does one wear on one's first date with a budding football manager? I'm a fairly conventional sort of dresser, but looking through my dismal wardrobe that morning before work, I found nothing that would impress. I'm fairly big you see. You know I'm tall, but I'm heavy boned and when I was three my father said Wales should sign me up as a prop forward. With my height, my mother (her again!) says I'm lucky and can carry it off, but I know differently. There's no getting away from it; I'm galumphing. Like many a slave to fashion before me, I've spent agonising moments flat out on shop floors, struggling not only to get the zip done up on a pair of jeans, but trying to get them above my knees in the first place. No matter what size I request in an embarrassed whisper to the charming (sadistic) assistants (all size 8 – and that's just the men), they invariably produce a pair to fit an elf, not a giant. Also, tell me, why do they have to shout out your knicker size at the till in M & S for everyone to hear? *I* know I've taken three pairs of size 16–18 from the rack because, as I've tried to explain, they shrink in the wash. Don't everybody's?

My saving grace is a reasonable face and long, mid-brown hair. Nowhere near supermodel status, but relatively well put together and, as one boyfriend once said to my moth— ... once said to me, if I took the trouble to learn to flirt I could have any man I wanted. Having always thought that I could actually flirt for England, this remark was most damaging to my ego. I like to think he meant it kindly.

Only last week I bumped into Meredith Winkleman, an old

school friend – I use the term loosely. We all thought she was a nerd because she passed exams, partly because she was very bright but mainly because she did something we didn't – work.

Trundling her push-bike along the pavement in a dreamlike trance, she stopped and stared, having not seen me for at least a decade. Her expression was one of a bulldog chewing on a wasp. 'My God, is it you? *Millipede?*' she screeched at the top of her voice so that the whole of W11 could hear. (Thank you, parents, for giving me such an easily ridiculed name.) 'It's not really, is it? You look so, sort of different.'

'What exactly do you mean, Meredith?' I enquired, wanting to scratch her.

Unaware of the offensive nature of her comment, she carried on. 'Well, it's your face. It's, um, it's kind of settled,' she replied, whinnying hysterically.

What an extraordinary thing to say. She hadn't changed, I might add and she still looked about fourteen and a half. Swamped by a long skirt (Laura Ashley *circa* 1975), flat Jesus sandals and an Alice band tightened vice-like on her head, all that was missing was a pair of ankle socks. The missionary position was her stock-in-trade. You might be surprised to learn that I didn't invite her in for a coffee and as soon as she had departed ('I can't stay Millipede ... I'm frightfully late for choir practice at the Brompton Oratory'), I rushed into the loo and looked at my mug in the mirror. Perhaps she was right after all, the cow. The single eyebrow which had haunted my early adolescence, along with a splurge of volcanic acne, had experienced miraculous binary fission in my mid-teens and I now sport two expensively plucked numbers above a pair of hazel eyes. Admittedly they are slightly lopsided and one lid is thicker than the other, but if you don't look too closely you mightn't notice. My nose is average and so is my mouth, but I do have good teeth and neat ears. I've learned to live with my short-comings, with one exception – the size of my backside. I am also endowed with an enormous pair of bazookas. I suppose it's God's way of keeping me to the perpendicular and where they came from I shall never know. They mystify my mother, as she was the proverbial ironing board and while I was at school they produced plenty of teasing but also a certain amount of envy, although I would have willingly swapped them for a pair of bee stings any day. They sprang into action when I was eleven, as if inflated overnight, and once unleashed are uncontrollable.

'Blimey oh bloody riley, Mill! You were definitely at the front of the queue when they were doling that lot out,' a previous boyfriend observed when confronted with their magnificence for the first time. 'Thank God I don't have to lug them around all day. They wouldn't half get in the way of my golf swing.'

The relationship landed in the rough shortly afterwards.

Let's return to the shopping expedition. After much deliberation, I decided on trousers. The weather was typical for the time of year, no longer deep winter but not yet spring. Hope was in the air. Snowdrops pierced the tired grass in Hyde Park, the ground iron hard, as was my will to purchase something special. Aggravatingly, in spite of a comfortable bank account for once, it was one of those depressing days when nothing looked nice, felt nice or did anything for me. Yet again, diet on Monday went through my mind when I put back another size 14 which strained at the seams. Where had it all come from? I asked myself pathetically as I replaced three rejects on the rails. Eventually I admitted defeat and, having bought a tuna sandwich (full fat version) and a bottle of freshly squeezed orange juice from M & S, I went back to the reassuring solitude of my one bedroom flat.

Yippee. The red light on the answerphone was blinking at me like a cyclops on speed. I pushed the rewind button, then 'play' and listened, my heart in my mouth.

'Millie? Is that you? Hello? Oh sorry, it's your machine. It's Paul here. Erm, oh yes, about tomorrow. Something's cropped up and I'm really sorry, but I've got to cancel.'

I don't believe it. I could kill him.

'I've got to work, I'm afraid. Sorry. I'll give you a ring later.'

My second reaction was to think, thank goodness I hadn't wasted any money on a posh frock. I flumped in the chair. Disappointed, furious, let down, hurt, in despair, I was bordering on suicidal. I added insult to injury by ringing Ma. If all else fails, go back to home base. Heaving myself up, I stomped crossly into the bathroom and taking my sponge bag, threw it into a case, along with a change of underwear, nightie and bed socks and left the Smog for some decent cooking and a bit of TLC.

PART TWO

TRAINING

4

Ma has long since given up quizzing me about prospective sons-in-law since I am as likely to produce one as take a photograph of a leprechaun. Having got hitched herself at eighteen, the mere fact that at twenty-four and heading for my third decade as a confirmed spinster is enough to give her the collywobbles, considering I'm left with a limited on-the-shelf life. I arrived some time before supper, to find that she had already attacked the sherry with more than a degree of enthusiasm. 'Shluvly to she you, pet,' she shlurped.

Not wanting to be a spoil-sport, I went to the drinks cupboard and poured myself a stiff vodka and tonic and wandered into the kitchen to fetch some ice and lemon. I felt I might as well do things properly as it was a sort of celebration after all and although I didn't exactly have a man in tow, there was one on the wing.

The television was droning away and, judging by my mother's expression as she blinked adoringly at David Attenborough on the small screen, I sussed accurately that I would be doing the remains of the cooking. Half an hour later I carried trays into the sitting room piled high with comforting stew, dumplings (made prior to the opening of the medium dry Amontillado) and two veg. We spent a happy evening together ensconced in front of the fire like Darby and Joan. Ma has lived on her own since Dad did everyone a huge favour by doing a bunk with his dippy New Age secretary five years ago. Caught up in a six-ties time warp, they live with the great unwashed in a com-mune in a confusion of ley lines in the west country.

It doesn't seem to worry Ma in the slightest, as she loves her cats and garden far more than she ever did him. 'Blessed release,' she calls it, 'if only from all that ironing.'

After a disgustingly late morning where I caught up on a month's sleep, I came downstairs wearing my father's old dress-ing gown which he had generously left behind, to find Ma busy building breakfast. It was well after eleven, but as it was the first meal of the day, we reckoned it to be an appropriate time to stuff ourselves on eggs, bacon and beans. Bang goes the diet. If a size 14 is well cut, it shouldn't look big, should it? Hey ho! Might as well be hung for a sheep as a lamb.

I kissed Ma goodbye on Sunday evening as the organ struck up on Songs of Praise, hitting the M25 hopefully before the bucket and spade brigade. My little car buzzed up the motor-way, Dire Straits playing at full throttle and I thought about Paul. To my horror I found I couldn't remember exactly what he looked like and here I was thinking I was falling in love. Each time I tried to conjure up his face, the edges blurred and he turned into a giant football.

I reversed expertly into the last space of Respark, leaving myself not too long a walk to the flat where I have lived on my own for just over a year and lugged my case and a carrier bag of vegetables my mother had harvested for me up the front steps to the top floor. The detached, double fronted property is situated behind the Portobello Road 'within easy walking dis-tance of the District and Circle lines at Notting Hill Gate'. Forgive me, it's all too easy to slip into estate agentese. I dumped everything on the landing and went into the sitting room to see if there were any messages and hell's teeth, I hadn't switched on the wretched thing. Paul could have been trying to reach me and I'd never know. I sat down, debating whether or not to fight the habit of a lifetime and ring him myself, when I jumped out of my seat as the phone rang of its own accord. In the rush to pick up the receiver I dropped the whole contraption and got ensnared in the cord.

'Hello? Hello? Millie? Are you there, Millie?'

As I was disentangling myself, I said, 'Oh, Paul, hi. I've been at my mother's.' Now why did I have to say that? 'Um ... actually, I've been away for the weekend,' I said more calmly than I felt, snipping the apron strings, the butterflies in my stomach in danger of flying out of my mouth. 'How did the team play on Saturday?' I asked, regretting it instantly, realising that if I was interested I should know. Black mark to me.

He didn't seem to notice and launched into a blow by blow description of their win – and away what's more. Enthusiastically he continued, 'Oh, Millie, I wish you'd been there to see it. We really needed the three points. It was fantastic. Everyone played well and all the hard work paid off. We were one nil down two seconds before half time and we were about to equali—'

In danger of nodding off, I butted in ignoring the fact that he hadn't finished his sentence, let alone word. 'Doing anything tonight?' I asked, amazed at my brazen nerve, my heart pounding.

There was a moment's silence. 'Well, nothing as a matter of fact. How about you?'

The thought of sticking four (for heaven's sake, be honest for once, six) fish fingers under the grill to be knocked back with a cheap bottle of plonk wasn't something I was about to reveal. 'Me? Nothing either,' I said nonchalantly.

'My place or yours?'

When I had picked myself up off the floor having already hit the ceiling, I suggested nervously, 'Let's meet half way,' fearful that I might have landed myself in it as it was possible he lived somewhere ghastly like Crouch End.

'I'm two minutes from Redcliffe Gardens.'

My fears were instantly quelled.

'That's not far from you, is it? I could always drive over to you, if you'd prefer.'

Thinking perhaps it would be rather nice to let the mountain come to Mohammed for once, I nearly relented, but aware of my reputation I told myself play hard to get. 'How about Finnegan's, behind Holland Park? It's a sort of bistro, and I know it's open on Sunday. Have you been there?'

Unfortunately he hadn't, but I gave him long and detailed instructions of how to get there, naming each street he would drive down, past how many letter boxes, even the telephone number and grid reference. I wasn't going to take any chances

20

of him getting lost. 'See you there in half an hour,' I spluttered as the butterflies finally made their exit.

Never has a person bathed, changed, pampered and preened as fast as I did that night. I tugged on a pair of jeans (clean) and a white shirt (not quite so) and stuffed my feet into a pair of suede boots which had seen better days, but which I loved. As there were no plans for *La Grande Séduction* that night, I threw caution to the wind and pulled on odd pop socks, one black and one brown, as I couldn't find a matching pair without holes in the heels. I changed my knickers but not my bra as there wasn't a clean one within a five mile radius, sprayed a squirt of 'Tommy Girl', grabbed my jacket and bounced down the stairs.

I was able to park outside the café and sat for a moment, too excited to move. The anticipation was thrilling. The restaurant was busy for a Sunday night and dimly lit and I couldn't see if he'd arrived before me. I confess I find it intimidating going into places on my own, even worse, sitting on my own. People might think I'd been stood up. It was now or never and I had to make a move. I checked my make up and sniffed under my arms. So far so good.

As I was in the process of locking the car, someone came up behind me and pulled my hair away from my neck. I spun around and there he was – all seventy four inches of drop dead gorgeous male.

'Hi!' Paul said, kissing my cheek swiftly enough not to be too familiar, but kissing it nevertheless.

Overcome with last minute nerves, flushing pink to the gills, I fumbled with my keys, promptly dropping them in the gutter, two inches from a drain.

'Here, let me get those,' he said, bending down to pick them up for me. He was wearing jeans, an open-necked shirt (thank God no medallion), and the same tweedy jacket. He must have had a shower or washed his hair, as little damp curls stuck endearingly to his neck, making me want to reach out and touch them.

My knees went weak and my mouth dry.

'Let's go in shall we?' he said, casually draping his arm around my shoulders, a simple gesture which made me feel a million dollars.

We were shown to a small round table at the back.

'Oh, sorry. Just remembered,' I said, as I was about to sit down. 'They don't have a licence. I'll get something from next door. Be back in two shakes.'

Paul felt instantly for his wallet.

'No, no, please, it's my treat. I'm already in debt to the tune of three coffees as it is,' I said hurriedly and before he could protest further, I was out of the café and into the off licence. Blinded by the exotic labels, I picked out a Chablis way above my normal range, but as this was an investment, he was worth every wicked penny. As every girl knows, if you don't speculate you can't accumulate... Back at Finnegan's the waitress took it from me with a knowing smile and pulled the cork. Mine was popping too.

We talked and we talked, we drank and we drank. At some stage during the proceedings some food appeared but I can't remember what and I have to confess that I observed that Paul held his knife properly and not like a pencil. I am beyond hope. Egged on by the alcohol (Paul bought another bottle) we held hands.

'Time to be off,' he said.

'Wha'? Can't be. Already?'

He looked at his watch and laughed. 'I'm afraid so. It's getting on for twelve and I've got an early start.'

We had been sitting there for five hours and it felt like five minutes. I tried to stand up and promptly had to sit down again. I had drunk too much and had done the unforgivable and got utterly, shamefully pissed.

Paul helped me to my weary feet. 'I've phoned for a taxi as neither of us is in a fit state to drive. We'll leave the cars here and collect them in the morning. Come on. Up you get. We'll get you home first.'

All sense of coordination had disappeared. I wanted to curl up in a teacup like a dormouse and sleep. With both hands under my armpits, he yanked me out of my chair, propping me up against the counter as he signed the credit card docket. Whoopsadaisy, here we go again and I began to slide down the woodwork. Catching me deftly he led me hazardously between the tables, which thank goodness, were empty. We managed to get outside when, hit by the blast of cold night air, I was

22

luxuriously sick in the same drain where I nearly lost my car keys earlier. Oh dear, oh dear, oh dear. That was it then, wasn't it? A thoroughly revolting, inelegant end to what could have been the love affair of the century. I sat on the pavement and cried.

Paul put his arm around me and uttered words of comfort I knew I didn't deserve, 'Better out than in, eh?'

I remember precisely nothing about the journey home, nor being carried upstairs. The time lapse between total unconsciousness and when I woke at three in the morning in a cold sweat, remain a blank. I opened a bleary eye to find the bedroom littered with items of clothing and touching and looking for tell tale signs, I wondered whether or not we had performed the dreaded deed. I had so wanted it all to be perfect and above all, to be fully *compos mentis* so that I could enjoy it. My pillow was dented, but not the one next to it, the blankets neat and tucked in. Hardly evidence of unbridled passion. It took a moment more before I realised that I wasn't actually in bed, but on it, covered only by the bedspread. I lifted the quilt. My knickers were firmly clamped in place and my feet remained locked in the ill-assorted pop socks. It had to be one of the most horrendous moment of my life. I stifled a sob.

Trembling, I went to fetch a glass of water from the kitchen. God, I felt awful. The inside of my skull was thumping as though occupied by a headbangers' rave, my tongue as thick as a layer of carpet underfelt. The demon drink. Never again. I put down the tumbler, unable to finish the water and tried to remember what had happened. The sequence of events began to collapse into place and I shuddered with horror as the last part of the evening came to mind. Paul will hate me and will never want to see me again. I'm a disgrace. Can you imagine anything more awful than being sick – in public? The stigma of it all. I'm a social pariah. I stuffed my head between my knees as I thought I was about to pass out, droplets of sweat falling to the floor, splashing onto my carpet slippers, which I was sober enough to notice I had put on the wrong feet. When the nausea subsided, I staggered back to bed, my heart pumping like a steam engine about to burst out of my chest. Palpitations and a vacuum where my brain used to be were not conducive to a deep, relaxed sleep and I lay there, conscience ridden, seeing the evening events flicker behind my exhausted eyelids like the images from a child's magic lantern. I turned on the bedside light, hoping to find a stray aspirin in the drawer. Propped up against the lamp was a small, folded piece of paper, torn from a Filofax. It was a note from Paul. My fingers shook with anticipation, or was it *delirium tremens*?

'Dear Miss Pie-Eyed, I hope by the time you read this you'll be feeling yourself again. By the way, you're a very lucky girl that I'm a gentleman. Your honour is preserved.
P.
XXX'

PART THREE

FIRST HALF

5

Oh lordy. I didn't hear the alarm go, it's already ten to nine and I've got to go and pick up my car from outside Finnegan's before going to work. Ohhhhh, the lead weight inside my head clunked to the left, then to the right, reverberating against both eyeballs. No time for a life-saving shower, only a quick scrub of the teeth and to slap on some lipstick and blusher to make me look less like a white-faced clown who's been dead a week. I crawled out of the flat, only to return ten seconds later to collect my car keys when chunderland swamps me again. How I hate hangovers.

Mary, all freckles and frills and annoyingly pretty, watched me as I struggled through the door, as though it was perfectly normal for me to appear every day after ten thirty. She swivelled from side to side in her chair, her elbows resting on the arms, her fingertips touching. 'You look frightful,' the tone of disapproval in her voice sobering.

I grunted incoherently and hung up my coat in the back room.

'I trust he was worth it,' she ventured, her voice saccharine sweet.

'Don't – shout – at – me,' I whispered. 'I'm ... I'm not actually feeling very well, if you really must know. Probably something I ate.'

'Bad prawn? Come off it, Mill, I wasn't born yesterday.'

Mary eventually got the message and mercifully had to shut

up as the phone rang. Not wanting to run the risk of my answering it and possibly losing a client, she leapt on the receiver as though her life depended on it. I sat and stared vacantly at the room in a daze. There was no point in buying a paper from next-door as I wouldn't have been able to read it: merely looking down at my desk gave me the dizzies. I sat corpse-like while Mary's soft gentle Scottish tones floated over me as she dealt expertly with anyone who walked through the door. By eleven I was feeling even worse, by twelve death offered the only release.

'Millicent, this simply won't do,' she said bossily. 'This calls for drastic measures and you need some urgent survival gear. Back in a tic and don't you dare move a muscle.'

She need have no fear, *rigor mortis* was advancing like hemlock, from the feet up. Six minutes later she deposited a greasy paper bag on my desk. I opened it and nearly fainted. It contained a bacon buttie.

'This should do the trick, kill or cure, eh?' she said merrily. 'I asked Pat to splodge on a double dollop of brown sauce to pep it up a bit. Always works. Now, eat up!'

Life is full of surprises and nausea was now fighting a losing battle with greed. Bearing in mind that although I had eaten last night, to put it delicately, I hadn't actually benefited from it and hunger pangs were starting to gnaw. Tentatively I unearthed the gourmet treat and grabbing it in both hands, took a cautionary bite. Wonders will never cease, and in precisely two point six minutes I'd knocked it into touch.

In the meantime, the darling girl had been into the kitchen and made a pot of builder's tea.

'That didn't half hit the spot,' I said satisfied, feeling half human, my hands clasped on my stomach.

'Welcome back to the land of the living, Millicent. Now, do you think you could do some work?'

The rest of the day was so hectic that I didn't have a moment to think of Paul. The phone never stopped ringing. We put three properties under offer, took on a massive new instruction in one of the best streets and couldn't find the keys for love nor money to a house which was completing at 5 o'clock. These eventually turned up mis-filed in the petty cash box. At twenty past seven I'd had enough.

Mary turned off the lights and locked up. 'I'll take the post,' she said charitably. Pausing before going on her way, she took hold of my hand. 'We didn't have time to talk about last night. You did see Paul, didn't you? Did everything go all right?'

Tears pricked at my eyes. I felt such a clot. I didn't want to tell her what a fool I'd been and that I had made a complete pig's ear of the whole evening.

She gave me an affectionate peck on the cheek. 'Never, mind, we'll talk about it tomorrow, that is if you want to. Have an early night. Byee.' Off she trotted to her car, whistling Scotland the Brave slightly off key.

Before going home, I went to the Europa in Queensway to buy ballast in the form of milk and Mother's Pride. Back at the flat, the first thing I saw was that the friendly little cyclops wasn't flashing, but I ran the tape just in case. Only an old message from Ma. Deflated and tired, I found homes for my shopping and wondered what to do next. Perhaps a therapeutic – and necessary – hot bath would help. I turned on the telly. Depressing news as usual about floods in the Far East, hurricanes in the Caribbean and Tara Palmer-Tomkinson's new boyfriend. The sound of the telephone ringing made me tip nearly a whole bottle of Penhaligon 'Bluebell' into the water. Leaving the taps running I covered the ground faster than the speed of light and panted into the mouthpiece. 'Hello.'

'And how's the head today?'

Oh, to hear the rumble of that dark, chocolate-brown voice. I slumped into the sofa, pulling my dressing gown over my legs, the towelling catching on the stubble. Lowering my pitch to what I thought was a sexy level, I rasped, 'I'm fine, thank you.'

'Are you sure? You don't sound it.'

I sat up and cleared my throat, wisely returning to my normal dulcet tones an octave higher. 'Paul, I'm so embarrassed about last night. I can't believe what happened. Never in my entire life have I done anything so revolting and throughout the night I kept on waking up in a cold sweat praying it wasn't true.'

'I wouldn't give it a moment's thought,' he said, laughing. 'It was quite funny, really and it's ages since anyone's been sick on my shoes.' He chuckled again and proceeded to give an account of how he got me into bed. 'I did the necessary and made you comfortable, that's all and I didn't look, I promise.'

Hmmm.

'Glad that you're taking it the way it was intended and that you're not upset. I wasn't in the best of shape, either, to be honest. Cor, you didn't half rabbit on, though. Chatter, chatter, chatter. I couldn't understand half of what you said, but you found it very funny.'

'You don't, um, happen to remember exactly what I said, by any chance?' I asked, full of dread.

'Oh, you kept on muttering a load of nonsense, about droops was it, or droopy? Something like that, which I thought was quite unnecessary, considering the circumstances.'

A trickle of icy sweat ran down my spine. I had a feeling it wasn't his physical state of affairs to which I was referring. I wouldn't have been aware of it had it hit me in the face. Did he say *droops? Droopy? Please* don't let him mean Rupie. Oh no. I could really have blown it this time. I must have been talking about Rupert Holland. Why would I mention him when I was hoping to be seduced by the man of my dreams? Freud has a lot of explaining to do. 'Oh,' I lied, 'it didn't mean anything, honestly. I was drunk, that's all.'

There was a pause. 'When can I see you again?'

Was I hearing right? As I was about to ask him to repeat his question I remembered something. Something very important – *the bath!* Without explanation I dropped the phone and bolted next door. Steam masked my vision and I tripped on the mat and searching anxiously in the mist I managed to find the taps. Thank heaven I had caught it in time, half a millimetre from disaster, the poor old overflow pumping for all it was worth.

'Hello, Millie, are you there? I'd really like to see you again, that is, if you can bear to.'

I gulped and tried to control my breathing. If he still wanted to take me out after last night's spectacular performance I had to be onto a winner. 'Erm, yes, I'd like that very much. Thank you,' I said, bewildered that I had been given a second chance.

'Great. Ever been to a football match?'

Deathly silence.

'We're at home to Scarborough on Saturday. Like to come?'

Never in a million years would I have believed that I actually made the following answer. Before you could scream 'offside', out of my wider than wide goal mouth popped, 'Yes.

28

That'd be lovely. Why not?' *Why not?* Even if you gave me a hundred k I couldn't think of two reasons why. One was obvious. If it wasn't for Paul, root canal treatment would have been preferable.

'Fantastic. I'll pick you up at ten. By the way, the forecast's cold, so wrap up.'

As I listened to his proposed arrangements, I sat like a prune on the sofa. A *football match*. I know that football is the new sex and all that, but, just because everybody else is going crackers about it, doesn't mean I have to. My father would bust a gut if he knew. My mother would think I was away with the fairies and as for Polly and Susie, well, I could hear their guffaws from here. They preferred the oval ball and Polly had once been engaged to a Rosslyn Parker whatever that was. Douglas Maitland, the RP, was a six foot five monster with a squashed nose, missing front tooth and the hero of the squad. He was also a selfish, egotistical pig and forced Polly to take driving lessons, at her own expense, purely so that she could pick him up half cut after the post match celebrations. Astute enough to see the warning signs written in flashing neon lights, she chucked him. Terrified that history might repeat itself, she has stubbornly refused to pass her test ever since.

We said our goodbyes. I sat plugged in the armchair, relishing the exquisite feelings of sheer excitement, the first wonderful flutterings and stirrings of an imminent affair on the horizon. People say it's like riding a bike. I hope to God they're right. I hugged myself smugly, realising that I could delete the Rampant Rabbit from my Christmas list and fold away my unicycle.

Acknowledging that by now my bathwater would be luke-warm, I knotted my dressing gown firmly around my waist and skipped into the kitchen. I retrieved the fish fingers which I never got round to eating last night from the icy confines of the freezer and chucked them under grill and switched on the radio. With Capital Gold at full tilt, I lobbied some equally petrified peas into a saucepan, missed and sent half scattering all over the kitchen floor. They scampered across the linoleum and ended their days in lemming-like fashion under the fridge, never again to see the light of day. Fish fingers sizzlin', peas a' poppin', Cap'n Birdseye has a lot to answer for. I poured myself a mammoth slug of white wine and thought, ain't life grand?

6

Saturday, home to Scarborough. Tickety boo. A force ten gale was blowing, rain imminent, visibility poor. How pleasant. There was going to be no gentle introduction into the water, no first tentative tip of a toe, then an ankle, ending up with a terrible, icy grip around the waist. No. This was going to be straight into the deep end. Splosh! What could be better than to spend a winter's afternoon stuck outside for two hours at a football match?

Taking Paul's advice to heart, before leaving the cushioned comfort of my flat, I raided the cupboards, digging out every chunky pullover on which I could lay my hands. Thinking I'd need half the stock of Damart to keep anything like warm, even if I didn't actually have to suck on a fisherman's friend, at least I could borrow his wardrobe. The damp and the wind had made my hair an area for national concern, making me look as though I had been plugged into the mains. On the brink of selecting a jaunty bobble hat to squash it, mercifully I remembered in the nick of time that I was trying to impress Paul and not put him off for life, and whipped it off, ramming it swiftly back into its hiding place.

My darling arrived on the dot of ten. When I opened the door, to my horror his face became distorted, his eyes half shut and he was biting his tongue as if in the throes of a fit. He turned away, hunched over the threshold, snorting and coughing. I could have sworn he was laughing. Tempted to slap him heartily between the shoulder blades, I told myself I must be mistaken as two shakes later he was in perfect control. He gave me a friendly peck, but continued to stare at me oddly, a final snigger escaping adding to my insecurity.

'Have we got time for a coffee before we go?' I asked, thrilled to see him again.

'I might give it a miss, thanks,' he answered, swallowing another giggle.

He must be psychic. I make even Harrods beans taste like dishwater.

He looked at his watch. 'I'd rather leave now, if that's okay, as you can't guarantee the traffic and I mustn't be late,' he said amicably.

I grabbed my coat and he led me to his car, parked nearby. Once on the open road we talked away nineteen to the dozen, the ghastliness of last Sunday evening's events pushed to the back boiler, arriving at the HQ in Kent in under an hour and a half. I think this is an opportune moment for me to tell you the good news: Paul and I get on famously. We are as Pyramus is to Thisbe, Noddy is to Big Ears and Tesco is to a wobbly trolley. Now for the bad: football and I don't. *Voilà la différence.* I hate it. I loathe it. Frankly, tell me who in their right minds would travel two hundred miles (each way) to sit on a punishing plastic seat in the freezing cold for three quarters of an hour, only to get your chilblains trodden on as you clamber through the crowd to get a cup of tea, then traipse back into the cold for another forty-five minutes of torture, plus injury time – for *pleasure*? Don't forget there's still the return journey home and after a two nil hammering not a great deal of conversation takes place down the M1 to while away the hours. I reckon if the Spanish Inquisition knew about the agonies of watching a football match, it could have become their most effective weapon. Thumbscrews would be a picnic after this.

'This way, please, Madam,' a uniformed commissionaire said authoritatively.

I imagined I was going to suffer further indignity by having to mix with the throng in the stand, when to my surprise – and momentary delight – I was shown a place in the Directors' box. I sat between a chain cigar smoker in a Crombie and a spotty girl in an anorak. Earlier Paul had said a hurried 'goodbye' before he disappeared into the subterranean lock-up for the pre-match talk, warning me that I wouldn't be within spitting distance of him until after the game was over. Terrified at the prospect of sitting on my tod for the next forty five minutes, I tried desperately to look interested. Not an easy task. The two teams were in the traps, champing at the bit. The whistle blew. They were off.

The crowd erupted. 'Poorcamborsbloonwhyarmy! Poorcamborsbloonwhyarmy!'

What on earth was that? Not a glottal stop within miles. Finally, the penny dropped.

'Paul Campbell's blue and white army!'

What a philistine I am. I was being exposed to another language, another culture.

Whoops! Someone did something to someone and there was a lot of heaving and rolling around on the ground and a yellow card was produced. Things were really hotting up and the crowd changed up a gear to a more joyous mode (I think) as it was one of the other side who had been a naughty boy. For the whole of the first half all the kissing and cuddling had been in the opposition's camp, leaving us three nil down to a non-league side and I was frozen rigid. Either I had lost the plot – or the team had – or both. A red card was brandished high in the air, the offender despatched when the ultimate in verbal abuse ricocheted around the stadium.

'Cambor ow!'

Oh deary me. My poor darling Paul. My powers of interpretation were improving rapidly and sadly I got the gist of this immediately, 'Campbell out!' being the insult.

Though he must be suffering from being so publicly barracked, I did have one redeeming thought – praise the Lord his surname wasn't Dicks. The ref gave a couple of bursts on his whistle and a surging mass exodus removed everyone from the stand confirming that it was half-time.

'Hello, love, you look lost. We're in here. Come with me and get yourself warm. Cuppa tea?'

I looked gratefully at the kindly face in front of me, iced lips preventing any form of speech. I nodded acceptance and followed her obediently.

She chivvied me into a small room, where a long table was decked with sandwiches and cakes.

'I've not see you here before, have I? I'm Veronica Thornton. My husband's the Chairman.' She smiled. 'It's nice to see a new face.'

I was unable to shake her hand firmly as my fingers were in a similar state to my mouth. 'Sorry, my hands. Cold you know. I'm er, Millie. A friend of Paul's, er, Paul Campbell,' I stuttered.

'A friend of our Paul's? Oh lovely. Now let me get you that tea.'

There was something a trifle odd about the place, on which I couldn't quite pin a finger. Then it hit me. There wasn't a pair of size eleven shoes in sight, nor a whiff of glorious testosterone in the entire room. I was being introduced to something which has outlived the dinosaurs, defying time, women's lib, political correctness, *et al.* – The Ladies' Room. Allow me to elaborate. At certain football grounds – not everywhere it's true – but more than you would care to believe, the female of the species high up in the club's hierarchy are segregated away from their male counterparts. This chauvinist practice enables the men to discuss in private and in immense detail any topic which provides subject matter for this particular breed until the cows come home, or their wives drive them. Paul hadn't thought to warn me that I would be sequestered with a load of ball-obsessed (the vynil variety), tactic-fluent, referee-hating women. In this rarefied environment the home crew set about clinically dissecting every second of the first half, from this foul to that, So-and-so's brilliant left foot and why Thingy got a red card when obviously it wasn't his fault. I was rendered dumbstruck by the sheer depth of knowledge they possessed.

To one side of the room was the impenetrable vanguard of the club (Chairman and Directors' wives). Facing them sat two of the perma-tan, mohair-sweatered (with bits attached), leather-trousered brigade (guests of the manager). Disturbing the peace was a smattering of unruly children clambering over the chairs and one babe in arms, all sporting team colours. Cowering in the corner away from this indomitable group sat two timorous visiting directors' wives, who wisely kept their own counsel. As a new girl in town there was no way I could join in. Nearly choking on my tea as I smothered a yawn, being exposed to the elements once more was beginning to hold some attraction.

7

'After the Scarborough game I hardly dare ask, but can you bear to come to another match, Mill? It should be exciting as we're in the Worthington Cup and we're playing Gillingham away.'

'Which day is it?'

'Saturday. You can get time off, can't you?'

'Well, I'm not sure. It's a bit late notice.'

Paul said nothing.

Back-pedalling furiously I said, 'I'm sure I can sweet talk Mary into swapping with me. Yeah, okay, I'll come.'

'Great. I promise it won't be as boring as before. Unless something unusual occurs, we should be able to get away quickly.'

Famous last words. You can imagine what happened and if anything, the scenario was worse than the first time. I sat alone in the Ladies' Room for over an hour and a half with only a few cheese and tomato sandwiches for company as the natives had long since departed. They were friendly enough but they didn't have a clue who I was and didn't include me in their conversation.

It took a superhuman effort not to be crochety when Paul's angelic face eventually appeared round the door. 'Ah, Millie, good, you're still there. Okie doke? We're off now.'

I didn't have it in my heart to get cross with him. As we walked to the car I couldn't help thinking what a thorough waste of an entire afternoon it had been and certainly not one I wished to repeat ever again. But this was no doubt the pattern of things to come and the gulf between us appeared huge. More doubts niggled. There was no way I would ever understand the finer points of the game, let alone the basics. I didn't want to and knew I never would. Was there any real hope for us?

On the way home Paul launched into infinite detail about the whole ninety minutes, pleased, I suppose, to have a pair of semi-attentive ears beside him. Poor disillusioned man.

'...Didn't he?'

'Wha...?' I said, a million miles away, mentally half-way through my shopping list.

'The ref. supported Gillingham. How the hell they got a penalty when Leclerc made contact with the ball first, God only knows. Eh? What do you think?'

Oh 'eck, crunch time. Here comes the acid test and knowing I would fail miserably, I cleared my throat, buying time. 'Well,' I started, 'I suppose instinctively they try not to favour the home side in case they get accused of partisanship.'

Terrified he'd rumble me as soon as look at me before you could say, 'Take an early bath,' he burst out laughing. 'Oh Millie, you're amazing. I thought you couldn't care. Shows how wrong you can be. But I have to say, you're absolutely right. Sometimes shrewd referees do lean a touch towards the home team because of the crowd, but not today.'

I decided to quit while I was ahead.

As we were driving through nocturnal Greenwich, the Georgian houses and shops lit up and merry, Paul looked at me. 'It's too late to go out for something to eat. Fish and chips do you?'

Has there ever been an occasion when I have been known to refuse where my stomach is concerned? He pulled over. 'Shall I put some vinegar on yours? What about a wally?' he shouted as he dodged the traffic.

Not waiting for an answer I stared at him as he stood in the queue, totally besotted. Taller than anyone else by at least a head, slim, good looking – and mine, well, nearly, if I played my cards right. My mind boggled as to what a wally might be.

'Don't mind if we sit and eat them here? I'm famished.' He banged shut the door and, not standing on ceremony, he passed me mine and unwrapped his.

We stopped talking and started chewing. Mutual mastication. The car windows steamed up as the engine had been off for ten minutes, and I was beginning to feel chilly and damp.

'Right. That's that. Hmm, delicious,' Paul said, smacking his lips, wiping his mouth and hands energetically on a tartan hanky. 'Your place or mine?'

My heart began to beat faster.

'It's probably best if I drop you off at your flat first.'

Lust was stirring in loins which, with the aid of the fish and chips, had also had the chance to thaw. I am a devil to convention and would never dream of making the first move, particularly after my misdemeanour the first time Paul invited me out, so I wasn't prepared to take any risks. I couldn't wait to get into his Calvins. 'Thanks,' I said with baited breath. 'You can come up for a drink if you want.'

'I'd love to. All that vinegar's made me thirsty.'

YeesssSSSS!

We drove back to Notting Hill, unbelievably getting every green light from SE whatever to W11. Paul slipped the car expertly into the same space where funnily enough, he had parked that morning when he came to fetch me. I took it as an omen. Rummaging around in the dustbin at the bottom of my bag, my keys unfortunately had hooked themselves onto a spare pair of tights, only revealing this when I extracted them with a flourish. The tights remained attached and flapped like dead man's fingers as I tried to insert the key in the lock. To hell with laddering them, I yanked them off and stuffed them in my pocket hoping he hadn't seen. The flat was warm and I turned on the table lamps in the sitting room and drew the curtains. In the soft light everything looked cosy and reasonably tidy. The daffs I had bought in bud yesterday off a barrow in the Portobello Road had opened and were bright and bonny on the coffee table. 'Paul,' I said, his name sounding strange and wooden, 'would you like a glass of wine? I can make tea, or a coffee if you prefer,' I offered, my mouth parched and my heart thumping so loudly I was sure he could hear it. I was suddenly very frightened of what might, or might not happen. All my confidence flew out the window and I turned my back to the door to plump up the cushions on the sofa in a nervous frenzy. I didn't know what to do with my hands, which had developed a life of their own and were flailing the air like a windmill when, whoa! two strong arms halted me in my tracks and wrapped themselves around my shoulders.

'Stop fussing and come here,' Paul said, his voice soft and low.

He spun me around and I found myself inches away from a pair of almost jet-black eyes, the pupils completely dilated as they peered deep into mine. I blinked. Then he kissed me. From

36

the first hesitant touch of lip on lip, tongue on tongue, I knew he meant business. It was like gobbling a Crunchie bar and lemon sherbet at the same time, fizzing, salty, sweet and delicious, leaving me wanting more. It was perfect.

Pulses racing and having rapidly reached first base, we bypassed second as Paul steered me expertly straight for the bedroom for phase three. Real panic set in. Even though he had already seen me virtually starkers, albeit in an alcoholic haze that first Sunday, I was petrified about presenting him with the whole hog and that, sober, he might find me unbearably ugly, but I needn't have worried.

'Of course you're not fat. It all looks soft and cuddly to me.'

'But I'm huge and my tummy shakes when I clean my teeth, my thighs are gross and...'

'Will you shut up for a mo'? It's your body. It's unique and beautiful, believe me.'

At that particular moment, I would have believed anything.

Dear Reader, this is where I have to make an apology, probably not for the last time in this story. I have been advised by the powers that be not to draw a spinsterly veil over what happened next, so sensitive souls, either stop now, or be prepared to take the consequences. What followed between Paul and me was a night of the most wonderful, chandelier swinging, orgasmic lust. In short, it was emission accomplished. To hell with riding a bike, this was being astride a 1000cc Harley and I can honestly say, hand on heart, that it was the best fuck I have ever experienced in my sheltered life. I hope to goodness my mother never reads this but there is simply no other word in our vocabulary fit to qualify such sublime delight. Only a genuine Anglo-Saxon expletive will do.

It was ace.

It was the biz.

It was lip-smackin', finger-lickin' good.

Yee-ha!

8

My spare time spent scanning the pages of footie mags had paid off, so much so I didn't realise how much of the jargon I'd taken on board. I shall proceed to give you a full match report.

Although in the opening two minutes Paul nearly gave away an own goal, I have to confess that his ball skills were exemplary, his dexterity on the touch line received a standing ovation and as for positional play, well, definitely my man of the match. There was one minor hitch when he came down in the penalty box, where I had to give him a helping hand – we all know about that single swallow – but after a serious head to head in the early hours about certain moves, miraculously we came to a satisfactory conclusion.

Planet Football was blissfully lost in space, as I lay back and thought of Ingerland.

Later, we lay in each other's arms, amazed that everything had worked out so well.

'Well, thank you very much, Millie. That was very nice indeed. Yes, very, very nice,' Paul said, nuzzling my neck.

Oh yes, it was, wasn't it? Please can we have some action replay? Three points for a win are nowhere near enough!

Exhausted, we shared a deliriously lazy Sunday surfacing only to renew supplies of food, a trail of breadcrumbs leading from the kitchen to the bedroom giving the game away. My larder was half empty, or being the eternal optimist, half full, so improvisation was the name of the game. Breakfast was hot buttered toast – no problem, since I had bought ample supplies on Friday night. Lunch required a pinch more of imagination and scurrying around in the fridge we found some vintage (in that it was past its sell by date) mousetrap and a jar of chutney, courtesy Mama. Two minutes under the grill and hey presto, Welsh rarebit. This was washed down liberally (but not excessively, as hopefully I had learned my lesson) with a bottle of fine red which I had been given by a girl friend when she came over to supper one night. Far too mean to open it with her, as I recognised it was of considerably better provenance than the exotic Algerian I had bought, I'd squirrelled it away. Tea? Who needs tea when you are living off love and fresh water? Unfortunately, as luck would have it, the telephone rang persistently during one extremely intense moment and annoyingly, the efficient secretary in me made me answer it.

'Millie darling? Is that you, dear? My, you sound quite out of breath. Been out jogging? Oh, the exercise'll do you the world of good.'

As we hadn't had a proper square meal all day and you will appreciate that we did burn up a hefty few calories between us, Paul nipped out to purchase a gargantuan deep pan pizza. This, naturally, was consumed in bed whilst watching the Antiques Roadshow, endeavouring to beat the experts at their own game.

My lover skulked off at midnight leaving me with more than a satisfied smirk and rumbling indigestion. I knew I could help the latter and after swigging some milk of magnesia straight from the bottle, I dropped off into a blissful, dreamless sleep of the innocent.

9

Having turned over a shiny new leaf, the next morning, miracle of miracles, I arrived at the office before Mary.

The dear, sweet girl scuttled in at thirty seconds past 9 o'clock, pink in the face, a puffin' and a pantin'. 'Och, I'm sorry I'm so late. I couldn't get my car to start and I know it's a terrible excuse, but please forgive me.'

I would forgive Mary anything, even to her eating the last bit of Twix, if ever there was an occasion when I left any. She went to hang up her coat and having brushed her shiny coppery hair, she mounted her swing seat all of a bother. I've already told you that Mary is vertically challenged, but she also has the tiniest pair of feet I have ever seen on a human being. If I said they were size three, it would be an exaggeration. Size two and a half and as wide as they are long, they are like little chunky bricks. She finds it impossible to buy normal shoes, waiting until the sales when she can buy the samples from the top houses at drastically reduced prices. Even then she has to stuff the toes with Kleenex. She is so embarrassed by her lack of height that the pumps she purchases are usually tart's trotters with the highest heels in the business and she teeters around the office like the Christmas tree fairy.

The dear also suffers from some sort of word blindness. I discovered this one day when she proudly showed me a 'Confirmation of Sales' sheet she had typed soon after I joined Wallis's. Listed under 'Vendor's solicitors', she had correctly written the name of the firm, but their address took some deciphering. Typed out in caps were the words: 'HOBAN VIA DUCK'.

I tactfully suggested that I would do all the correspondence in future. There has been another occasion when her Pitman's also let her down, in a very big way. Prior to joining Wallis & Co., Mary was PA to a financial adviser in the West End, who had a propensity for what he referred to as 'Director's lunches' on the company.

'I'd have to go every day to the local deli to buy whatever we needed, entering every item afterwards in the petty cash book. One day, Robin, my boss, decided he wanted to come with me. We drove down the King's Road in his old Bentley, with him dictating what he wanted, like tomatoes, pork pies, things like that. It was very embarrassing being in such an ostentatious car and everyone stared at us. I was still trying to spell *dolcelatte*, ending up writing 'cheese', when he said something which made me snap the very lead in my pencil.' She looked positively flustered at the memory.

'What did he say?' I asked, as I scrunched up a Mars bar wrapper and chucked it at the bin – and missed.

'Well, it was after he asked for bread. He wanted some, um...' She cleared her throat and said under her breath, very quickly, 'French letters'. She shuffled the papers on her desk, her long lashes brushing soft, freckled cheeks.

'He didn't! The bloody nerve of the man. What on earth did

you do?' Intrigued, I unpeeled a second *bogof* Mars (buy one, get one free).

She looked up, her eyes as wide as saucers. 'There wasn't much I could do in the circumstances. I didn't know him well enough to refuse and thought I'd better do as he asked. I was extremely miffed, I can tell you, getting me to do his dirty work. The thought of him in bed with some poor unsuspecting girl was revolting. He wasn't exactly my idea of the romantic hero. He was fat – and short. Anyway, I bought all the other things he wanted and stood outside the chemist for what seemed ages, unable to pluck up enough courage to go inside. Then I saw him drive up a bit further along the road and park, so I dived in. In a line behind the counter stood three generations of the Patel family. One look at them and I'm afraid I panicked and bolted.'

I burst out laughing. 'I don't blame you. Was he furious when he found out you hadn't bought them?'

'Well, not exactly, but he could see I was out of sorts and asked why. I didn't beat about the bush and told him straight that I simply couldn't buy his hateful French letters. And do you know what he did? He laughed until he was practically in tears. Oh, Millie, I've never felt more embarrassed in my life. Can you imagine it? With your boss of all people? When he eventually managed to speak, do you know what he said? He said he'd only asked me to buy some fresh lettuce. How stupid can you get? I thought I'd get the sack.'

Whatever her shortfalls may be as far as her secretarial skills are concerned, she does have something I don't – a husband. He is a great big bear of a man called William and adores the very ground she walks on. He was in the army stationed in Germany when mutual friends who lived in Berkshire introduced them one spring when he was home on leave. They fell a over t in love and in a matter of weeks he'd packed her off to Baden Baden to start what seemed to be a perfect marriage.

William's army career over, he now works as a head hunter in the city and if he telephones her once a day, he rings twenty times. They're little clucky phone calls which some might find nauseating, but to witness them is rather enchanting and restores your faith in human nature. Desperate for a baby, for ages they've been trying every conceivable method. A semi-vegetarian, eating sausages and smoked food for a boy made Mary sick and sweet, sugary things to produce a girl made her pile on the pounds.

'Following the old wives' tales in one book, we've tried it pointing south, north, east and west, but nothing's worked so far,' she said sadly. 'One weekend we were staying at William's parents in the country and I knew the timing was perfect, only we didn't know which direction his bed was. Guess what? Darling William shot out of bed at one o'clock in the morning to look for his old school tuck box. It was hidden at the back of his wardrobe and seconds later, he fished out his pocket compass!' Mary looked even more downcast. 'Nothing happened then either. Maybe the compass was broken.'

Poor duck.

A couple of weeks after my blissful Sunday with Paul, Mary announced, 'We've planned a trip to Cerne Abbas to lie on the giant's dewberry firkin on the night of a full moon. You're really meant to do it, you know, properly, but there's no way I'm going to do that in public.'

Watch this space.

She rummaged in her handbag and took out her mirror to check her lipstick. Her green eyes looked at me expectantly over the top of the mirror. 'How's Paul, by the way?'

I realised she wanted to change the subject.

'I meant to ask earlier and forgot. Sorry.'

I thought it was time to check my make up, too. 'I've heard precisely nothing, not a squeak,' I said as I removed a smear of eyeshadow from my cheekbone. 'He's got a heavy week, travelling across England, seeing this player and that.' I clicked shut my compact. 'Oh, Mary, it gets so lonely when I don't see him or hear anything, sitting at home, waiting for the blasted phone to ring.'

'Stop it. You'll make me cry. Why don't you give him a ring? You can, you know. We're no longer in the Dark Ages.'

'I could, but it's not worth it. If I ring him at the club, he's either in a meeting or not at his desk and if I try him on his mobile, he's most likely at the training ground and has switched it off.'

Mary clambered down from her chair, giving me an odd stare.

'I'm going to make us a coffee. You look as though you could do with a dose of caffeine.'

I called out to her, shouting over the rush of water from the tap and the clinking of cups. 'He's off to Darlington on Saturday. Thankfully I have to work and I've got a built-in excuse as I know he was about to ask me to go too. Can you bear the thought? Where in heaven's sake is Darlington?'

Mary's head peered round the door, smiling. 'Who cares?' Seconds later, she put a steaming mug of coffee on my desk. 'Here you are, you stupid old bird. I'll go and buy a couple of duffnuts to go with it. They'll cheer you up.'

'No, please, not doughnuts. They're the worst.'

'Millie,' she sighed, 'I'm fed up to the teeth with you going on and on about your wretched weight. For the last time, there is nothing wrong with your figure. It's fantastic. You're a dream machine and if you really want to know, if I had half your boobs, William would be a happy man.'

'But I'm huge,' I wailed, 'I'm immense. I'm deformed.'

'For God's sake, shut up. No you bloody aren't. All right, have it your way, I admit you're not exactly a stick insect, but you're nothing like the elephant you think you are. You're in perfect proportion – all over. So there!' Holding the office door with one hand, her money in the other, she said, 'Now, shall I go and get those doughnuts, or not?'

'All right, you win and make that two – each!'

10

So formed the pattern of my relationship with Paul and I was sorely tempted to purchase an office planner to mark the squares when our paths might cross. In spite of these complications, we managed to settle into a routine and I was coping with our some-what unorthodox union. My emotions remained as if on a helter skelter, one moment filled with self-doubt, then with sheer joy when he rang and despondent once more when I put down the receiver, not knowing when we might speak again. The truth is

I knew so little about him. He'd told me virtually nothing about his past. The longer I spent on my own, his imaginary wife became one ex-wife, then one current wife and six kids. When could I talk to him properly, at length, with no interruptions? Time was so precious when we were together that the serious side of life, apart from problems at the club, rarely had a look in.

I think Paul got the message that although he and I are, football and I never shall be bedmates. Even so, he succeeded in dragging me, reluctant as ever, to a couple more home games, including one on a Tuesday night. My, it was painful stuff. There was no prospect of an early night, as the kick-off wasn't until 7.45pm and since I hadn't eaten anything more substantial than a sandwich at lunch, I was ravenous. It was also the coldest February night since records began.

Predictably, Paul was delighted I had accepted to accompany him. 'Thanks for agreeing to come, Millie. As a special treat, I'll take you out for a Chinese afterwards, on the way home,' he offered as a fitting reward.

Coming from anybody else, I would have considered his remark thoroughly patronising, but with him it was different. He meant every word. I should have known better.

The game was appalling and my opinion wasn't based entirely on ignorance. Even Paul found it so. Both teams played like idiots, fouls left, right and centre, the ref. strutting about like a prize cockerel. After the final whistle, I returned to our Ladies' Room (we were no different), my blood sugar level at an all time low, grumpy and irritable. Not feeling in the slightest bit sociable, I rudely ignored the clutch of visitors on the other side of the room and sat and stared longingly at the assorted food which grew more delicious-looking as the minutes ticked by. I resisted all temptation, looking forward to the promise of spare ribs, sesame prawns and banana fritters. I pulled back the sleeve of my jacket to see what time it was: just gone 11 o'clock. I'd been at the ground for over four hours, bored out of my skull, when I could have been curled up at home with a giant pot noodle, glass of wine and *EastEnders*.

The cleaning lady poked her head around the door, expecting the room to be empty. 'You don't mind if I whisk me 'oover round, d' you, love? I'm runnin' lite as it is. Time I should be back 'ome in bed. You too, by the looks of fings.'

Resigned to my fate, I nodded and lifted my legs as she dragged the vacuum cleaner noisily under my feet. Then, humming tunelessly, she turned off the telly and switched off most of the lights. At a quarter past twelve I woke with a jolt.

'Oi! Wakey wakey!' Paul said, shaking my shoulder. 'I'm really sorry about all this, Mill, but JT called an emergency board meeting. Hope it hasn't been too tedious sitting here alone.'

Bored? *Moi*? Just downrightbloodystinking bored, that's all.

'Did you grab something to eat?'

I waited, timing my reply. 'No, I didn't, as a matter of fact. I was saving myself for the Chinese.'

At least he had the courtesy to look guilty. 'Ah, yes, well,' he said, looking at his watch, 'it's a bit late for that, I'm afraid.'

Gritting my teeth, I unfolded my coat from the adjacent chair.

Ignoring the fact that I couldn't find the right armhole, he said, 'The girls produced some smashing scampi and then a plate of steak and kidney. Did they bring any into you?'

You are probably aware by now that I am the world's worst moral coward. I could have raged at him, called him every name under the sun as any normal human being would have done in the circumstances, criticising his lack of consideration, his selfishness, the fact that he was a man with his brains in his underpants, but oh no, not little old me. Would it have been a touch churlish and unreasonable to mention the hours I had spent watching the crusts curl on the sandwiches and the marzipan fall off the Battenburg? I peered at him through narrowed eyes. 'Scampi, did you say? Steak and kidney? In a word, no. They didn't.'

Avoiding any direct looks, he said, the relief in his voice that he had got away with murder almost tangible, 'Oh, well, Mill. Think on the plus side – you wanted to lose a bit of weight, didn't you? I've just given you a kick start.'

AAAGHH...

Small wonder he had never considered a career in the diplomatic service.

A mid-week appearance at a match wasn't all I had to subject myself to. I don't know why I said yes, but I did. I'm actually taking part in the Supporters' Club Quiz Night at the ground tonight. What on earth made me accept? Lord only knows and I will end up looking a complete prune.

'You don't have to be a genius,' Paul said encouragingly when he put the proposal to me in bed last week after a magnificent bit of hunga bunga. 'It's mixed – there are four couples. They've called it a "Game of two halves". Wives and girlfriends are taking part and I've got to set a good example so I've said yes, which means you're roped in as well. The questions won't be difficult, but we might have to do some extra research...' He sat up and leaned on his elbow and stroked my hair. 'You'll be fine. If you're stuck I will send the answer by telepathy.'

I was trembling like a frightened rabbit and had been to the loo four times already. The bar where the quiz was being held was full of people, smoke and spilled beer. My body as usual, was caught in an awkward little place and the poppers couldn't stand the strain. I could feel them dangling which meant another trip to the cloakroom. Five minutes later, trussed and ready, I saw Paul wink at me in the far corner, near the bar. He was talking with the team captain and his girlfriend.

'Hi, Mill. Come over here and meet Dave and Mandy. This is Millie. She's been swotting up on the *Rothman's Year Book 1960–1984* every night, haven't you Mill?'

Dave the goalkeeper grinned broadly, swamping my hand in his huge mitt. He towered over Mandy, a fluffy, very pretty blonde in stilettos, ankle chain and a skirt up to her armpits. 'Here, let me get you a drink,' he offered. 'Can I get you a glass of white wine? Rum and coke for you, Mand?'

Mand stood on tiptoe and kissed his cheek, standing aside to let him push his way through to the counter.

Paul smiled. 'Calm down. We're on the same side, you and me. We'll thrash 'em. What with my knowledge of the game and your stunning good looks, we'll destroy the opposition.'

As Dave returned with our drinks, someone tapped a microphone, which hissed and squeaked. 'Ladies and gentlemen, to your places. Let battle commence.'

'Have I got time to go to the...?'

'Hurry up then. That's where we're sitting, at that table on the right. Don't worry,' Paul whispered in my ear, squeezing my hand.

The room settled, some leaning against the bar, others at tables around the room. Dive 'n' Mand, a terrifying combo, were deep in conversation, if that isn't a contradiction in terms. The quiz master interrupted. Mandy was first on and the firing of questions began.

'Mandy, welcome. Here's your starter. Who was the first £100 a week player?'

'Johnny 'Aynes!' she said, triumphant, flicking her hair with victory before he had time to finish.

'That's the right answer. Give her a cheer everyone.'

Everyone clapped enthusiastically, banging their feet on the floor.

'Next question, this time to Vickie. Now Vickie, who is the current most expensive player?'

'Rio Ferdinand!' she shouted, doing a little wriggle in her seat, applauding herself.

Oh help, it was my turn. I felt sick.

'Millie. This shouldn't be too difficult for you. Who scored the winning goal for England in the 1966 World Cup?'

World Cup? England *winning*? Help, help, help... A cold sweat broke out and I could feel it trickling, an icy cascade down my back. I shuffled in my chair. Now I felt burning hot.

'Shall I repeat the question? Who scored...?'

I was completely deaf.

'Time! Sorry, Millie, but can anyone here tell us the answer?'

'GEOFF HURSSSST!' the audience screamed.

I didn't dare look at Paul, but I could feel his eyes boring into me. I want to go home. I want my mummy.

Minutes later it was my go again.

'Now then, Millie. Who plays at White Hart Lane?'

The only White Hart I've ever come across is the pub down the road. I mumbled and hid behind my hair.

'Sorry. Time up. I have to pass it over.'

'Spurs,' was the correct answer given by the player to my left.

For some inexplicable reason, Paul and I were in second position, though heaven knows how. Apparently he'd earned a couple of bonus points, no conferring (no point).

'Now, Millie, here's your final question. Good luck. We're all rooting for you.'

Failure had never seemed more certain and I felt like Dirk

Bogarde going to the scaffold in 'A Tale of Two Cities'. I drank some water and it went down the wrong way. Paul thumped me on the back and tears poured from my eyes.

'Millie, who hosted the 1994 World Cup, and for a bonus point, who won?'

The room fell silent. Then someone laughed. That made me very cross. The entire competition was in my hands. I began to panic. Another World Cup question? Who do they think I am? Gary flipping Lineker? 1994 ... *1994*. What the heck was I doing in 1994?

'Time's nearly up, Millie.'

I looked anxiously at Paul's face. It was very white. Think, girl, think. Hang on a mo', there's something familiar, I'm sure there is. Cogs and wheels began to whir. Think, think, *think*. Yes! Oh, oh, OH! YES! I know it! I know the answer!

I jumped out of my seat as though the ejector button had been pushed. 'It was ... it was in America. Yes, yes! Italy v Brazil and, and ... Brazil won on penalties!'

'Congratulations, Millie! I don't believe it, but you and Paul are the winners!' the quizmaster said above the roar. 'Let's hear it for Millie and Paul!'

Paul hugged me until I thought I would burst. 'Oh, Millie. You're fantastic. That was the hardest question in the whole competition for you and you knew it. How in heaven's name did you know the answer?'

'Promise you won't laugh?'

'Course, but just tell me how you knew.'

'Well, I was on my first holiday abroad on my own in Ibiza and I'd met this bloke on the beach. He was from Essex and much older than me. And four days later I, er, we ... well, guess, only it wasn't quite how I'd imagined it would be. He'd turned on the telly in his room to watch the final and it was on when we, er, when we ...'

'You're great, Mill. The best.'

PART FOUR

HALF-TIME

11

I couldn't help but realise we'd reached a milestone in our affair. We'd known each other for two months now and it was make or break: we were going to spend the weekend with my mother, although Paul, at this point, was unaware of the situation. Netherfield Town were due to play their league game on the Friday night, unexpectedly televised by SKY, which meant – bliss oh bliss, or so I thought – that Saturday would be a football free zone. On the Monday before, Paul was free and we walked to the pizzeria around the corner from the flat. I picked up the sticky, laminated menu and studied it thoroughly. Somewhere between the antipasto and the pizzas I suggested, 'How about coming with me to Sussex for the weekend?'

'That's really weird you should say that. I was about to tell you, but I've got to be at Brighton on Saturday to watch a player and I was going to propose a dirty weekend by the sea. Maybe we could find a small hotel, or a b&b outside the town, if you like.'

My heart sank to my boots. How could I be so naïve? Every Saturday for Paul was a busy, normal, working day. Because the team had played the day before didn't mean he had a day off. I gnawed at my thumb nail, terrified that the close proximity of a predatory parent might give him second thoughts. 'Actually, a hotel won't be necessary. My mother lives only half an hour from the ground,' I added tentatively, a sprat to catch a mackerel.

His eagerness caught me by surprise. 'What, stay at your mum's? Why not? And a hell of a lot cheaper. With any luck, I can still claim expenses.'

Now I had to tell him the hard part. 'Er, there's something I should tell you, and I fully understand if you want to back down. You see, she's a bit old-fashioned about me sleeping with anyone, so you'll be in the spare room.'

This did nothing to dampen Paul's enthusiasm. 'That's the least of my worries. I haven't done any corridor creeping in years. It could be fun,' he said, with a wicked grin. He looked at his watch. 'Gotta go, sweetheart. I've just got enough time to get to the reserve game. I'll ring you in the morning.'

With a hurried kiss, he was off. I paid the bill. Emmeline Pankhurst has a lot to answer for.

I rang Ma pre-prandially the next day from the office to find her reasonably sober, having had time to recover from the lunch-time intake.

'Darling, what wonderful news. A new boyfriend. How simply marvellous. What's he like? Is he good looking? I do hope he's single – this time,' she said ominously.

Straight to the point, that's Ma.

With a shiver, I realised I'd never asked Paul that question. It had simply never arisen. What if he was married? He didn't wear a wedding ring, although not all men do and he didn't look married to me, whatever that is, but the silent ones are often the ones to watch. My confidence flickered again.

Ma continued down the line with her relentless cross examination and I guarantee that within ten minutes of my call she had already chosen her hat, booked the church and iced the cake.

We decided to leave very early on Saturday and to ensure a good start, Paul stayed with me, arriving at the flat very late after the Friday game. Inspired by playing in front of a televised audience, Netherfield had pulled out all the stops and had beaten the others 1-0. It was an encouraging result, as the club lurks in similar fashion to lees in a bottle of port, at the bottom of the League. They float to the surface every now and again, but their usual position is not one to be envied. There are frayed nerves at the end of each season as the team plays devilish cat and mouse with the Conference. High as a kite on adrenalin, Paul rattled on about what a great bloke Richard Keys was and as for Big Andy... It fell on deaf ears, I'm afraid and I was spark out as soon as my head hit the pillow.

At daybreak, after a cup of tea, we left London and flew down the motorway. Paul looked in the rear view mirror and indicated left when I pointed out the turning off the A23.

'I'd better warn you,' I said anxiously, 'everyone in the village knows Ma as the "Wild Woman".'

'Wild Woman?'

'Well, you see, the poor thing suffers from chronic insomnia and she has a habit of wandering around the garden in the middle of the night, so she can check up on her plants for slug damage. All this done by torch light.'

'I have a sneaking feeling there is something else.'

'Hmm, I'm afraid there is. She talks to the birds.'

'She's not, er, you know, a bit ... er, doolally?'

'No she jolly isn't, thank you very much. She's merely a trifle eccentric and likes to commune with nature, that's all. She got it from my father, only he did it with no clothes on. You'll see what I mean when we get there. It's nothing to be frightened of,' I said, as I saw Paul frown. 'It's not hereditary either – I hope.' I thought it best to tell the whole story, so that there wouldn't be any surprises. 'As soon as Ma puts a foot outside, the birds come swooping down: chaffinches, blue tits, even a thrush with a limp she's nicknamed Dook Dook. She feeds them Sainsbury's crunchy nut cereal, and they won't touch anything else. She's weaned three generations of chaffinches on the stuff and one or two of the tits eat out of her hand. Oh...' I chirruped, 'it's the next on the left.'

12

'Why, hello. You must be Paul,' Ma purred, blushing coquettishly as she threw crumbs on to the terrace, confirming my predictions and wiping her hands on her apron (a Cath Kidston pinnie, a present from me last Christmas). She preened her pepper and salt hair as she gave him an expert once over, accidentally dislodging a hair band made from an old stocking. If I didn't know her better, I could have sworn she was flirting.

'Thanks so much for letting me stay, Mrs Palmer-Ede. Millie's told me so much about you.'

'Oh, good heavens, dear boy, please call me Daphne. Mrs Palmer-Ede makes me sound so old,' she said, beaming and becoming increasingly skittish, giggling like a teenager.

Emergency, emergency. *Du calme, du calme.* There's no need to go overboard.

She linked her arm through Paul's.

He winked at me over his shoulder. 'I understand from Millie that you are a passionate gardener. Perhaps you could give me a guided tour?'

Once this button is pushed there is no stopping her.

'Oh, yes. How wonderful. You're interested in gardening, are you? Come and see my babies. I've got some seedlings growing in the green house and I haven't a clue what they are,' she said, laughing. She leaned nearer to Paul and whispered conspiratorially, 'You'll never guess what I did. I culled them from the garden centre. I pretended they had dropped off. I hope they didn't catch me doing it on the closed circuit thingy,' she added mischievously. 'I might end up in prison.'

I left them to it and carried our cases upstairs. My single bed looked lonely and pathetic, my moth-eaten bear slumped on the pillow. There was hardly enough room for me, let alone the two of us. There's a small double in the spare room, so no doubt I'll be the one to do the orienteering. I went downstairs and put on the kettle. As the water was coming to the boil, Titchmarsh and Dimmock reappeared, twittering away like starlings.

'My, what a wonderful invention. Does it really work?'

'It most definitely does. That's the miracle of under soil heating,' Paul replied, holding the door open for her.

What on earth were they talking about?

'But what if there's a very heavy frost, or snow? Surely it can't function then, can it, as it's outside?'

'Oh yes, that's when it's at its most effective. You see, there are miles of electric cable underneath the turf and not only does the pitch remain in perfect condition, but the grass continues to grow, even in January. I only wish we had the funds to install it at Netherfield.'

They were talking football. Was there no escape?

Paul looked up at the kitchen clock and frowned. 'I'm going to have to leave you in an hour and a quarter. You don't want to cook lunch, Mrs Palm... er, Daphne. I'll take you both out for a bite. Is there somewhere nearby I can take you to? Any ideas?'

In spite of her protestations, we managed to bundle Ma in the back of Paul's Alfa and headed off for a favourite pub of mine down winding country lanes, ten minutes away, where I used to drag all my past boyfriends. I prayed none would be there today. The car park was full of heavy metal: three Porsches, a filthy old Land Rover, a Mini Cooper and a whopping great black 4WD with tinted windows which had never seen a bale of hay in its life.

Inside, the low-beamed bar was blissfully uncontaminated by repro horse brasses and the ubiquitous trappings of a modern boozer, with only a few carefully chosen hunting scenes which decorated the smoke-stained, plaster walls. Although the food was unforgiving, the beer was out of the cask and I loved the old place. Ma and I sat companionably on an oak settle by the inglenook in which a roaring log fire blazed, while Paul ordered our drinks.

She had a whimsical look in her eyes. 'Well done, Millie, I have to say. Ten out of ten. He's quite smashing. Where on earth did you dig him up? He's got to be the cat's pyjamas, hasn't he?'

This had to be the understatement of the year and before I could comment, the cat's pyjamas returned, clutching a pint and a half of Badger's Bottom and a sherry. We spent a happy hour bent over the *Telegraph* crossword which Ma had thoughtfully remembered to bring, stuffing our faces with toasted ham and tomato sandwiches.

'I'll drop you two off and then you've got the afternoon free,' Paul suggested, as he helped Ma into her seat, this time in the front.

'We could go antique hunting, darling, the way we used to.'

That evening, I offered to do the cooking, leaving Ma to watch the goggle box. It was dark outside and the long case clock in the hall sounded the half hour. I was peeling the potatoes when I heard a car in the drive. I put down my knife, dried my hands and went outside to meet Paul, hoping to catch a surreptitious snog.

'Player any good?' I asked, as the security lamp switched on, putting me in the spotlight.

'No, complete waste of an afternoon,' a voice answered in the undergrowth.

Where was he?

A shadowy figure emerged from behind a rhododendron bush. Swiftly zipping up his flies, he smiled awkwardly and walked round to the boot of the car. 'Here,' he said, handing me a massive bunch of white lilies. 'I've bought these for your mum. Do you think she'll like them?'

They were an extravagance she would never permit herself. How could she resist?

After a supper of Ma's fabulous home-grown veg and organic lamb from the farm down the lane, we collapsed in the sitting room to watch the news over a cup of coffee.

''Nighty 'night you two,' yawned my mother half an hour later, as she forced herself up from her armchair. 'I'm up the wooden stairs to Bedfordshire. Turn off the lights and shut in the cats, would you Millicent, there's a dear? See you both in the morning. Sleep well.'

One glance at Paul, and I could see sleep was the last thing on his mind.

The cold woke me early on Sunday, as Paul had pinched most of the blankets. Resisting the temptation to snuggle up, I went downstairs. It was five to seven. As I was pouring myself a cup of tea, the newspaper dropped through the letter box in the hall and I sat down at the old pine table for a quiet read.

Twenty minutes later Ma, also an early riser, appeared in the doorway, comfortingly tousled and sleepy. 'Any cha left in the pot?' she asked amiably, touching it to see if it was hot, and flinching when she discovered it was. 'Had a good night, darling?'

Her bedroom was at the other end of the house and with any

54

luck, her hearing being a touch below par and further dulled with sherry and a glass or two of wine, she wouldn't have heard the floor boards creak.

'Yup, there's some left, but I'd better add some hot water. I was about to take one up to Paul, if that's okay.'

Three quarters of an hour later, dressed and shaved and smelling divine, he drove into the village and came back with the rest of the papers. By mid-morning I had put together a cholesterol overdose of scrambled eggs, bacon, sausages, tomatoes and baked beans, a mountain of toast and fresh orange juice for the three of us. Needing some fresh air and exercise after such a feast, Paul and I opted to go for a walk, after having dealt with the washing up. Actually, I will clarify this: I did the washing up, while Paul and my mother sat in the sitting room, no doubt to continue their discussion on the whys and wherefores of the offside rule.

We came back a while later somewhat flushed, though not I hasten to add from pedestrian exertions, but brought about by a nifty bit of alfresco fiddling up against a fir tree. The fire was crackling in the sitting room and on the low stool in front of the sofa Ma had laid a tray, decked with a Victoria sponge of skyscraper proportions

'Saint Delia's all-in-one,' she said proudly as she cut a death-defying slice for Paul. 'Never known to fail.'

Full to bursting, we were in danger of falling asleep, when Paul glanced at his watch and fidgeted on the sofa. 'Erm, Mrs Palmer-Ede, sorry, er, Daphne, you wouldn't mind very much if I put on the telly would you, so I can have a quick look at the half-time results?'

I cringed. I have always been brought up that when you were a guest in someone else's house, there were one or two rules to which one had to adhere, or risk being drummed out of the Brownies. Namely, one: you never put a log on the fire or play with the poker unless you have known the people for at least fifteen years, twenty if you really want to be on the safe side and secondly, you never, ever touch the television clicker, no matter how long you have been acquainted.

'Of course you can, dear. Make yourself at home.'

Oh crumbs, 'ere we go.

Paul perched forward on the edge of his seat, watching the

screen intently. 'Torquay are one nil up... Grimsby and Blackpool nil nil... Blast, Lincoln drawing away...'

I looked across at my darling mother who was gazing at him gooey eyed, as if each word he uttered was a pearl of wisdom. I could see she was already dandling two, if not three, blond grandchildren on her knee.

The afternoon passed all too quickly. Approaching six o'clock, Paul said, 'I think we ought to be heading back, to try and miss some of the traffic?'

I agreed and went upstairs to throw my things into my case, while Paul did the same.

Ma called from the kitchen, 'Yoohoo! Millie! I've put together a little smackerel before you go. You don't want to suffer from night starvation.'

I appeared on the landing, trailing my case.

'I'm sure you've got time,' she insisted.

Far later than we intended, my mother said as we were about to leave, 'It was lovely meeting you at last, Paul.' She kissed him affectionately on the cheek. 'I do hope you'll come again soon.'

'Oh so do I, Daphne, so do I...'

13

The traffic was awful and I didn't speak much so as to avoid distracting Paul and to reflect over the happenings of the week-end. God willing he seemed to have taken all my mother's oh-so-unsubtle hints at marriage and babies in good heart, brushing them off with polite charm. I could see she was totally bewitched by him and in fact, looking back over the last forty eight hours, they had got on remarkably well.

Surprising though it may seem, I had absolutely no idea she was in the slightest bit interested in anything athletic and little did I know that since my father had left her, when she wasn't in the garden, Ma watched sport on the telly. Not only an avid snooker fan, she adored tennis ('All those strapping mid-Europeans and their long hairy legs ... and that's just the girls!'). What's more, she followed football. She knew more about the Nationwide League and the Cup Winner's Cup than I could muster in a month of Saturdays. Too wrapped up in my own life, I'd never bothered to ask.

Paul deposited me outside my flat nearly two hours later. He stifled a yawn, rubbed his eyes and gave me a wonderfully lingering tongue sandwich. I stood on the pavement, watching as he drove off.

There was one message on the answerphone.

'Darling, hope you've got home safely. It was lovely to see you both, and *so* happy. He's simply divine. Bring him down again as soon as you can. I'm hopelessly in love. He said he'd take me to a football match if I wanted. Can you believe that? Kissy kiss, darling. Byee!'

14

Later that week I met up with Susie and Polly in our usual haunt. We hadn't seen each other for ages, although we had spoken heaps on the phone. Pre-Paul, we used to meet two or three times a fortnight to compare bloke notes, but what with Mary away on her all-important holiday in Cerne Abbas, and the resurgence of a man in my life, the days had flown past with ingratiating speed. The girls were in fine fettle, but Susie was terminally single and very much on the prowl, hence the choice of rendezvous.

As for Polly, she had found herself a fellow, but had promptly lost him. It was a tragic story of Greek proportions. The temporary lightness in her step, the spring in her heels were caused by a chap who was high up in a merchant bank. She was in love. Poor, pretty Polly. When she falls, she tumbles like a sky diver without a parachute. Her love life has been a series of such disasters and this latest foray into the realms of romance proved no exception.

'He's called George,' she said, blinking back tears. 'We hit it off instantly.'

'Then why the long face?' I asked.

Polly ignored me and, with her eyes out of focus, she put one hand to the double rope of pearls at her throat. 'He's gorgeous, tall, good-looking and totally charming.' Embarrassed, she said, 'He's quite old-fashioned, actually.'

'Sounds too good to be true,' interjected Susie.

'He is, that's just it.' Her face lit up. 'Imagine a mixture of a young Gregory Peck, you know, when he was in *To Kill a Mockingbird* and Keanu Reaves, but more mature. That's what he's like, well, a bit,' she said, shyly.

Susie nudged me under the table. We both felt that something was amiss.

'You haven't seen much of me over the last week or so, as George has invited me out to dinner every night. He's also taken me to the cinema twice – not the local fleapit, but the Minema in Knightsbridge and we were going to Covent Garden next month, but...' She bit her lip and looked down at her lap, a fat tear glistening on her eyelashes.

'He doesn't sound short of the odd spondoolick, so what's the prob?' Susie was brave enough to ask.

'In all the time we spent together, he didn't lay a finger on me. Okay, he kissed me goodnight, but it was only a peck on the cheek, not the real thing. I thought I had bad breath.'

'Silly moo, of course you haven't,' I said, encouragingly.

Poll was on the verge of breaking down completely. It was too sad to watch.

'Last night I learned the truth.'

She looked at us in turn, her eyes welling. 'He'd booked a table at the Ritz. I was so excited, as I'd never been there before. We were getting along so well, honestly and I thought he might want to ask me something – something serious, you know. It was as though he had been courting me, like in the old days. I pretended I was in an old film. I felt special, precious...' she tailed off. The fat tear fell, swiftly followed by a second, like the first heavy raindrops of a summer storm. 'I imagined I was Greer Garson.'

Who?

I touched her arm. 'Go on, Poll, if you want to, that is. You'd better tell us the rest.'

She wiped her nose on her sleeve. 'Yes, well, I had to go to the loo. You know what it's like and we'd drunk nearly a whole bottle of champagne and I was bursting. I was so happy and everything seemed to be going so well. I sat down and waited and he just looked at me. Then he took my hands in his.'

'What happened next?' The agony was excruciating. It was like pulling teeth.

'Sorry, both, I can't stop filling up simply thinking about it. He said in a very serious voice, "Polly, darling, there is something I should tell you".'

She sniffed again, more loudly this time, almost enjoying the drama. She brushed away the snot. 'Either of you got a tissue?'

Susie handed her a clean one from her jacket pocket.

'Thanks.'

'Well?' we both said, unable to bear much more agonising suspense.

'Little did I know it, but my bubble was about to burst. I was convinced he was going to own up to a wife and three kids in Buckinghamshire...'

I picked up the bottle of wine and emptied the contents into Polly's glass. 'I'm ordering another one. I think we're going to need it.'

'He's not married, is he?' whispered Susie, voicing our mutual doubts.

Polly stopped breathing and went red in the face. 'It was far worse than anything you could ever imagine.' She fell silent, unable to speak as she struggled with her breathing, which was coming in huge, choking gulps.

My patience was rapidly running out.

She wiped her eyes with the back of her hand, smearing her mascara. 'Oh, Millie – Polly, he told me he was ... he told me... He's g-g-gaaaay!' She pleated folds in her pullover, snorting up a huge filbert.

In desperation, I passed her a second Kleenex.

'Then I did the most awful thing. No sooner had he told me, when I started to laugh. I couldn't stop. I went on and on until it hurt. People understandably were beginning to stare at us. It was awful and I felt so ashamed. There I was, in the middle of the Ritz dining room, with, as I thought, the man of my dreams, in hysterics. I wanted to die.'

'Surely you must have had some clue, some hint that he

might be, er, that way inclined? You must admit that it is a bit odd if a man doesn't pounce after the first time he's flashed his credit card,' Susie said. 'It's not called American Sexpress for nothing.'

'No, I didn't have any inkling whatsoever. Anyway, they don't always pounce with me straight away. We were having such a wonderful time. I thought he wanted to take things slowly and I was enjoying being treated like a Jane Austen heroine. I'm pathetic and a stupid fool. I'm doomed,' she wailed.

Neither of us knew what to say or do to comfort her. She sat in her chair, exhausted by her confession. It was the longest speech either Susie or I had heard her utter at any one time since we had known her. Totally downcast, another large tear splashed onto the table.

'Come on, Poll, don't blub. We can't bear to see you like this. You'll be fine. Give it time and we'll find you someone else, won't we Millie?'

Polly looked up gratefully. 'I'm all right, honestly, don't worry about me.' She clenched her teeth with determination and frowned, anger taking over. 'It's bloody sod's law that something like this happens to me every time. What have I done to deserve this? It's not as though he's a flipping Catholic and I'm C of E. At least then I would have half a chance of converting him. But this... Fuckity, fuckity fuck. Oops,' she said, clamping her hand over her mouth, 'I've actually said it! Fuck! There, I've said it again.'

The wine was having a slightly different effect from the one we intended.

'Oh, you've done me the world of good, you two,' she said, smiling. 'Hopefully men are a bit like buses. None comes and then three trundle along at once. The first two might be full, but you can always hop on the third.' She removed a trace of mascara from the corner of her eye and smiled bravely. 'Well, that's me sorted, now what about you, Mill? I feel selfish having hogged all the conversation. How are things going with Paul? Are you madly in love?'

Much to their disappointment I spared them the more intimate details although I suffered a cross examination in stereo worthy of the Old Bailey.

'When can we meet him?' they begged in unison.

Never, if I had my way, knowing that the words 'scruple' and 'honour' don't exist in either Susie or Polly's vocabulary. So I decided to throw up a challenge, which would give them plenty to think about. 'If you're prepared to come to the Netherfield Town v Chesterfield game on Saturday, you'll get your chance.'

There was a sudden deathly hush.

Ha!

Called their bluff.

15

Mary came back from her jaunt to the West Country and began to study her calendar religiously. Each morning it was the same and this continued diligently for two whole weeks. On the fifteenth day, she paused in mid-count, her index finger pointing north. She turned very white making her freckles stand out as though her face had been splattered with brown paint. I watched, fascinated, as she bent over her diary, scribbling notes in the margin, counting and muttering to herself.

'Oh my goodness, Mill!' she shrieked. 'I think it's worked! The Giant's thingy's worked. I'm pregnant.'

'Now calm down, don't let's get too excited,' I said. I so wanted it to be true and I knew what effect it would have on her if it was a non-starter. 'First things first. Have you done a test?'

Mary shook her head.

'Right, would you like me to nip over to the chemist for you?' I hesitated. 'Out of interest, my sweet, exactly how late are you?'

She shot me a beaming smile, almost splitting her angelic face in half. 'I reckon at least three hours. I've got to ring William and tell him the wonderful news.'

'Ah, I think it might be wise to wait a day or two, don't you?' I suggested, erring on the side of caution.

Although she agreed with me in principle, she was absolutely no help to me all day. Wrapped up in a whirl of apoplectic excitement she spent the entire time on the telephone to her husband, who of course was told within the time it took to dial his direct line. I buckled down to some long overdue envelope stuffing and looked at her indulgently, praying as I never have before that this time she'd potted the black.

After an uncharacteristically long lunch hour, she returned laden with shopping. I feared the worst.

'Guess what I've done?' she grinned. 'I've opened an account at Mothercare.'

PART FIVE

TEAM TALK

16

In life, there is a rule. What comes up must come down and the state of euphoria I have been enjoying in recent weeks plummeted to earth faster than a pair of whore's drawers. I thought I was able to cope with the long absences between seeing Paul, believing that I could put up with his anti-social hours. I kidded myself I might, just might, one day surprise myself and everyone who knew me by ending up liking football. Fat chance. And here was I thinking that Father Christmas and the tooth fairy existed. The demons had it in for me and Paul and I had our first row.

The day started well and I went along with him to Netherfield to watch a reserve game. That's really what I call love. It was against Brighton & Hove Albion and I suppose I was one of only two or three hundred people who had turned up. There was no proper catering and the boardroom was open to all and sundry, male and female and on this occasion even I was allowed into the holy of holies. I didn't know anyone there, as Veronica Thornton, the chairman's wife, not surprisingly restricted her attendance to the real thing. Stranded on my own, I got to know the trophies in the glass cabinet intimately. I learned the names of the teams who had played for Netherfield Town FC from 1900 to the present day. Not one of my most entertaining of days, as you can gather. What's worse, one of our talented young players on whom Paul was relying heavily to boost the fortunes of the club, broke his leg badly in two places. We ended up drawing with Brighton 0-0. They were the stronger side and clearly deserved to win.

Paul was angry, surprisingly so I thought, for a reserve game. 'We've been hoping to promote two or three of the lads into the first team, but they played like prats, except for young Robbie Green. We're going through the worst time in our history,' he said, his head hanging, as we walked to his car. 'If things don't improve, not only will we be in the Conference, but I'll be on the scrap heap.'

'Surely not,' I offered. 'They won't let you go. They can't. They need you.'

'Ha, dream on, Mill, if that's what you think. It's not like that in real life. If you lose more games than is acceptable, you find yourself on a tightrope. Relegation, my darling, is the path to the nasty little door marked "good bye". Points count and losing costs. Supporters are fragile creatures and only come out in numbers when their team's winning. Take today, for example. Okay, it was a reserve match, but it still merits support. Fans are as fickle as a bloody weather vane on a windy day and vanish into thin air if the team's losing.' He stopped and pointed the clicker at the car. A vein pulsated in his neck. The locks clunked emphatically. He knew he was walking on a knife edge, his career on the line, and I tried to sympathise.

We travelled back to London in virtual silence. I was feeling extremely off, a bumper attack of PMT on its way and, like most men, Paul doesn't fully understand the intricacies of a woman's complex psyche.

He overtook a caravan, which was wobbling dangerously in the middle lane. 'Bloody contraptions. Shouldn't be allowed on the roads,' he growled. 'Would you come with me on Saturday? It's your day off, isn't it? I could do with the company, as it's a hell of a long journey on my own. The team's leaving on Friday night, but I've got to watch a player in Bristol. I could pick you up early on Saturday morning.'

I looked out of my window and sighed. Not another trip to Lancashire. Why are football clubs situated in such godforsaken places? You can travel across England till you're blue in the face, glorious countryside as far as the eye can see, but set foot within half a mile of a stadium and it's like the Devil's armpit.

All right, I know I'm exaggerating. The Yorkshire Dales are glorious, the Pennines awe-inspiring. Oh, how I moaned. I went on and on and on. I kept it up, virtually non stop, for thirty minutes, hardly pausing to take breath.

Paul drove mechanically and was unusually silent.

I saw his jaw tighten, but he didn't rise to the bait and bait him I did. No salmon in the Dee would have been safe with me on the banks. Talk about change the record, I covered more ground in that half hour's soliloquy than Netherfield Town's captain's boots on a match day. 'And as for the unbelievable Ladies' Room ... blah blah blah ... the women are ... blah blah... Never get to see you ... blah...' I launched salvo after salvo, Motor Mouth in Olympic gold medal form.

Paul ground the gears fiercely. 'Will you be quiet for one second – please?'

I was ranting and raving so loudly at this point about hanging around for such a long time after the game was over, that I nearly didn't hear him speak. 'What d... did you say?' I stammered.

'Shut your rattle for two minutes, will you? I'm trying to drive.'

I gulped. I should have listened. Things went from bad to worse. 'Why should I shut up? Why should I always be the one to give in? What have you given up for me, huh? Answer me that, if you please.' I clamped my arms across my chest and sulked. Would I ever learn? No, not me. I attacked again, both barrels this time. 'No woman in the world puts up with anything like the things I have to. Do you realise that most *normal* men see their wives or girlfriends at *normal* times, like evenings and weekends? Is it too much to ask? I'm lucky if you can deign to see me for half an hour mid-week and half the time I have to book an appointment. I really don't know why you bother to take me to a match. We're never together. I'm locked up with all those stupid women with whom I have absolutely nothing in common, for hours on end, waiting for his lordship to finish gossiping in the boardroom before taking me home. And more often than not, I have to drive.'

Well, I couldn't believe what I'd done. Did that mouth really belong to me? Was it in any way connected to my brain? All the hours of frustration waiting at the end of a telephone, appointments cancelled, dinners forgotten, exploded to the surface. You could have sliced the atmosphere in the car in two. I began to shake.

Paul drove off the dual carriageway. 'I'm going for a pee and a coffee. If you want one, you'd better hurry.'

He slammed the door. I sat in my seat, horrified at what was happening between us and tried to cry, to winkle my way back into his affections. Nothing came out. I squeezed my eyes, desperately trying to squirt out at least a couple of tears, but not one came. I thought of the day our dog died. That didn't work either. In disgust, I opened my door and called out. 'Please, Paul. Wait for me, please.'

He ignored me and strode angrily through the doors, turning left to the men's loo.

I walked into the cafeteria and sadly picked up a tray. I have never felt so sorry for myself – and frightened – in my life. I had doubtlessly destroyed the most precious thing I have ever been close to and there seemed no way back. I took two mugs from the stack and placed each one under the tap and pushed the button for black coffee.

The steam hissed and spat at me, as though criticising what I had done. 'SSSSSsstupid ... sssstupid .... ssstupid...'

As I was grabbing six mini cartons of cream from the basket, I felt a hand on my shoulder.

'I'm sorry, Mill. I've been a shit, but it's a shit job. I told you right from the outset that it wasn't a belly load of laughs and never going to be an easy ride, but you can be so bloody stuck up at times that if you shoved your public school nose any higher it'd fly into orbit.'

Instinctively I touched the offending object.

He sighed. 'It might help if you liked football or at least attempted to understand it, so that you could appreciate the problems I'm facing. I can't force you to, but if you showed the slightest interest it might help.'

The girl at the till, eye lashes like girders, looked at us, then at the tray, riveted by our conversation. 'That'll be £1.75 please,' she honked in a flat, nasal voice.

I gave her two quid and waited as she laboriously counted out the change.

'Here, let me take this,' Paul said, removing the tray from my trembling hands. He put the mugs onto the formica table. 'I can see you've got the cream.'

Was that a glimmer of humour?

'I'll fetch some sugar.'

I sat down miserably and tried to rub the stress from my forehead.

'Cheer up, Millie, it's not the end of the world.'

His grim expression didn't convey that sentiment. I'd never seen him like this before and my heart sank. Where did I go from here?

Stirring his coffee as though mixing concrete, he said, 'I never kidded you it would be a bed of roses. We're worlds apart, you and me. You can't stand what I do and I don't expect you to like it. Fair dos, I know nothing about your world. But all I ask is that you show some sensitivity. I don't ask you to go the length and breadth of England without a valid reason.' He put down his spoon and ran his fingers, which were shaking, through his fair hair. 'I ask you to come with me because, strange though it may seem, I enjoy your company. You're a beautiful, sexy, gorgeous girl and I want you with me.' He looked down at his cup. 'I'm proud of you...'

'Paul, I'm so sorry,' I whispered. 'I couldn't work out why you ask me to come as we're never together, except for the journey. You're either in the dressing room, or with the Chairman and Directors in the boardroom. There doesn't seem any point. Surely you can see that?' I was treading on dangerous ground again. Why didn't I button it?

Pouring a second sachet of sugar into his coffee, he looked up at me, as intense as I had ever seen him. 'What you fail to understand is that I ask you to come because ... because I like to know you're there.'

That was enough. I burst into tears. I'd never had such a hateful time, never been so frank with anyone in my life and now I was paying for it. 'I didn't mean to be so foul. I'm due my period and you know what a vile cow I turn into. Don't take any notice. Just *please* forgive me,' my voice pathetic and pleading. I tried to shift a huge lump in my throat. 'There,' I said, clipping my bag on my lap, 'You see, look it's all over, I'm smiling again.' I waited for his reaction, crossed my fingers under the table, praying for all I was worth everything would be all right.

67

He looked at his watch. 'We'd better get going. There's still a good three quarters of an hour to go. I'd rather not be late, if you don't mind.'

He put his jacket on and walked ahead, me following meekly two paces behind. Had I succeeded in patching things up? On a scale of one to ten, I reckoned it was only about three and a half. Paul's back was rigid, his head stiff and what's worse, he didn't take hold of my hand. I felt awful.

He sat in the driving seat. 'I'm going to fill up. I won't have time tomorrow.'

Changing gear viciously, he headed for the pumps. There seemed little point in continuing the conversation, as I knew it wasn't going to diffuse the situation. The tank full, he drove fast making me feel carsick. Paul had promised we'd have a proper meal together that evening, the two of us, no fish and chips, no take away, a proper, elegant meal, with spanking white table cloths, candles and I'd blown it. Atomic bomb blown it.

I was so wrapped up in my guilty conscience that I hadn't been paying attention to the route we were taking when I began to notice territory not a million miles away from my flat. Within ten minutes we were driving down my street. Paul swerved into an empty space, scraped back the handbrake and turned off the ignition. He sat in silence, his knuckles white. I didn't know what action to take and sat there, miserable as hell, longing to say something, but nothing appropriate sprang to mind. His body was ramrod straight, the vein on his temple continuing to throb alarmingly.

'Paul, we're being...' I said.

'I'm sor...' he said.

'No, after you,' we said together.

He released his grip his head flopping forwards. 'I'm sorry, Millie. I've been thinking the last half hour about what you said. You were right, on nearly all counts. Why do you think I was available when I met you? No one can stand my life style. I thought you might be different. Maybe you are. Only time will tell.' He brightened. 'Come on, cheer up. Let's go and have that meal, shall we?'

Only time will tell. How prophetic those four words turned out to be. I wasn't sure if I'd won the battle or lost the war – it wasn't exactly a case of forgive and forget.

He cranked up the engine. 'What you have to realise, Millie, is that if we're going to continue together – and I hope we do – there is one thing you must get into that thick head of yours – I'm only joking, but it's no good taking the good moments only to opt out when it doesn't suit. You have to take the whole package. It's that or nothing, right? Do I make myself clear?'

'Yes,' I gulped barely audibly, feeling knee high to a grasshopper. Crikey. I'd never met anyone who had put such a proposition to me. I'd let him down big time. They say the truth hurts and by gum, it did. I knew I'd been at fault, selfish beyond words, unsympathetic, unreasonable. I didn't want us to bust up. I love him for goodness sake. I took the opportunity while he drove to study his profile, his head held high, proud and beautiful. Oh Paul, I love you, I love you, I love you. I thought it diplomatic to keep schtum. It had been a perfectly ghastly moment and although the tension was dissipating, unfortunately, so was my appetite. There was still some way to go before the status quo was back on course.

By the time we reached the Italian restaurant in Shepherd's Bush I was beginning to feel better, nothing that a good measure of 13.5% white couldn't fix. The ambience between us was perceptibly lighter. Paul once more took my hand as we walked into the restaurant. The waiter, a football fanatic, recognised him instantly and showed us to a table in the corner, with soft lighting and gentle classical music. I said a silent prayer.

We sat down and minutes later a bottle of chilled Frascati was placed between us. Having poured two glasses Paul picked up his, clinked mine and said, 'Let's put all this down to experience. Let's forget this afternoon. I have no excuse for being a bum, but you know only too well that I've been under a lot of pressure recently and I'm afraid that you're on the receiving end. I've used you as my punchbag. I'm sorry.'

There is a God. 'Thank you for putting up with me,' I said, hope rising, 'for putting up with my horrible moods. I'm not normally like this and I'm sorry too.'

'Right, we've got that sorted. Now, for heaven's sake, behave yourself.'

He sounded like my father!

We ate our meal in perfect harmony and as I licked the last

of the cream off my pudding spoon, I gazed at his wonderful face, the candlelight flickering on his features, strong and masculine. His square jaw shone, with a hint of 5 o'clock shadow, straight nose and full, sensuous mouth. Oh, that mouth, weaver of spells and enchantment... Ahem. I continue, his eyes, velvety and intelligent, but why go on? You can see I'm on the mend emotionally.

Then he said something which had me instantly awake.

'Mill, don't get up, please. We can't go – not yet.' He looked at me imploringly. 'Erm, I – I've got a hard on. It was seeing you lick your spoon,' he said, his cheeks flushed with embarrassment. 'Could you sit tight for a mo'?' he begged, as he struggled in his seat.

The thought of a great big stiffy was too much for a girl to bear. Quick as a wink I dropped my bag on the floor and bent down under the covers to take a thoroughly long, lascivious look. Wow! It was a big one and no mistaking. I gave it an encouraging flick with my finger and popped back to the vertical. 'I think we ought to get you home as soon as possible, don't you? I'll pay!' I said joyfully, giggling at Paul's discomfort. By the time I was back at our table, Paul was back to normal and standing up, as against the other way round. I was still feeling somewhat guilty about having dug in my heels over the trip north, realising that it might end up being fun. I faced him bravely. 'If you still want me to come with you, I will. It's a sacrifice beyond the call of duty I know, but seriously, I'd love to. If you'll still take me, that is.'

'Thanks, Millie, it would mean a lot to me. Of course you can come,' he said, giving me a hug by the car.

We trundled off to my flat for some further hands on discussion on the problems of the diminishing rainforests in the upper – and lower – regions of the Amazon and if you believe that, you'll believe anything.

PART SIX

SECOND HALF

17

On Friday afternoon I embarked on some necessary research and studied Mary's road map of England. I scanned the bit at the top, near Scotland. I went through Carlisle once with an old boyfriend on our way to Skye. Now, where had he said? Top left hand corner, ah yes. Running my finger along the blue lines of motorway outside London I read, Birmingham ... Derby ... Sheffield ... Chesterfield ... passport country if ever there was one.

Paul picked me up, as punctual as ever, me armed with case, warm coat and a woolly hat, for it was a romantic trip after all. Lots of girls get taken to a football match with their beloved as a treat, but it was still a relatively new experience for me. We were held up getting onto the M1 due to sheer volume of traffic, as most of London appeared to be taking the same route as us. We passed towns the names of which I knew but hadn't a clue until today where they were, like Luton, Dunstable, Milton Keynes. Goodness gracious, so that's where Milton Keynes is. Well I never.

An hour and a half into our journey, the petrol light flickered ominously and somewhere between Newport Pagnell and Northampton we pulled into a service station to fill up. I sat tight in the warm and Paul returned a few minutes later laden with Twix, Mars bars, Walkers crisps and two cans of coke, which I noticed with amusement were the low cal variety. We crunched and chewed and slurped the miles away. Wiping a salt 'n' vinegary mouth, I cast a sideways look at Paul. He was concentrating on driving, the conditions having deteriorated and it was now raining hard. Cars flashed by, their lights blazing, but it didn't seem to have any affect on Paul. Everything he did he did precisely, neatly and deftly. I thought, cor, I'm a lucky girl. Without taking his eyes off the road, he put his left hand on my knee. I could see he was smiling. I turned round as well as my seat belt would allow me and snatched the rug from the back seat and snuggled up. Within minutes I was asleep.

I was woken with a kiss.

'Millie, wake up, darling,' a soft voice said inches from my face. 'We're here. Up you get,' Paul said, touching my cheek gently.

Our hotel was a typical sales reps' horror, low built, made of red brick and girders, like a Tesco on steroids. One consolation, the carriage sweep up to the entrance was covered and I was able to get out without getting wet. The rain plays havoc with my hair.

Paul said, with relief, 'Oh good, I can see the coach. I'd better check they're not in the bar.'

He took our cases and I followed him inside. We were very late and the journey had taken longer than Paul had hoped, what with the rotten weather and the fact that it was Friday night. Too late to eat and too tired anyway, we walked round endless miles of swirly-carpeted corridors to our room. The slut in me took over and I was so sleepy I didn't bother to take off my make up and got straight into bed. I never heard Paul join me.

The next morning I woke feeling miles better, to find my lover, stark naked, messing with the electric kettle. What a body. The complete antithesis of yours truly. It's lean, without a spare ounce of fat and his hairless torso (our only similarity) curves proudly above a nicely sized six pack.

I studied his backside as he bent over to plug the kettle into the socket above the skirting board. It was a tight, wonderfully firm little bum and it was all I could do to stop myself leaping out of bed to bite it. His legs are long, hairier than his arms and very muscular, brought on by years of training. For a man, his feet are surprisingly small. They're a bit battered from playing football and he has a black big toe nail on his left foot. But when I think of his skin ... it is the softest I have ever touched. Softer than a baby's, it's like satin and I could spend my life stroking it. I've never known a man who smells as nice as Paul, either. It's a mixture of warm, clean skin, a hint of soap and shampoo. In one way it's a clinical scent – but with earthy undertones, a bit like bracken when you squash it with a gumboot. He also tastes sweet, better than the best vintage champagne.

'Tea?'

'Hmm, love one,' I said, punching the pillows to fluff them up as I stretched and yawned. I sat up, covering my chest with unprecedented modesty, as he padded over carefully carrying a steaming cup, trying not to slop in the saucer.

'Shortbread?'

Ridiculous question.

Scratching his head and still as gloriously naked as nature intended he opened the door and picked up the huge bundle of papers on the mat which he had ordered the night before from the hall porter.

Paul turned automatically to the back page, while I sifted through the dross to get to the mags and thus ensconced, we spent a delightful hour reading in bed.

He tweaked a nipple which had escaped from its hiding place. 'Time for breakfast.'

I went into the bathroom, attempting to do so with some grace, wishing I had taken the complimentary robe with me the night before to cover my cellulite, but Paul was looking in the *Mirror* and getting a bit of *Sun*. The modern shower was wonderfully powerful and I had great pleasure in using every one of the free samples laid out on the marble-topped basin. As I took a clean towel from the rail, Paul came in and sat on the loo. What, are there no mysteries left?

Ten minutes later we were in the queue for breakfast. As soon as we entered the dining room I saw the entire squad. A wave of knowing sniggers swept round the long table and a nudge-nudge, wink-wink produced a 'Morning, boss!'

It was acutely embarrassing. I went to the end of the brass trimmed buffet and poured some orange juice into a glass and piled some fresh fruit onto a plate. We sat down at our own table, not because we didn't wish to be with the others, but because there was no space. I found it intensely awkward being scrutinised at such close quarters.

'Coping okay, Millie? It's a bit of an ordeal, isn't it, having twenty virile young men know exactly what you've been up to? Imagine what it's like for me. They'll calm down once the novely has worn off. You sit with your back to them, so they won't bother you.'

Wiping his mouth on his napkin, he folded it neatly beside his empty plate. 'I'm going to have to leave you, as I've got to work to do. Will you be all right on your own?' He fumbled in his breast pocket. 'Here, you'd better have our room key.'

'Thanks. Yes, I'll be fine,' I said, 'I've got all the papers to read and I'll be more than happy.' I turned to see we weren't being watched. I blew him a kiss discreetly. 'See you later.'

Paul walked over to the team table, said a few words and they followed him out like baby ducklings behind their mother. I stayed long enough to absorb two more slices of toast, then returned to our room. I leaned on the sill of the wide picture window, thinking how ghastly and anonymous modern hotels are. They're constructed with no soul, simply dormitories for businessmen. Vast expanses of tarmac car park spread before me, liberally dotted with selected trees, beyond which lay the motor-way. Mercifully, with the double glazing you couldn't hear it.

I knew Paul would be tied up for a couple of hours, so I put the 'do not disturb' sign on the door handle and went back to bed. I was woken by a discreet knock on the door. It was already twelve o'clock. I must have been tired.

'Coming for lunch, sleepy head? We're eating in ten minutes.'

Help. Baptism by fire. 'Uh, yes, thanks,' I said nervously, 'give me five minutes.'

'Okay, but get your skates on. Chop chop!'

A separate room had been put to one side for the club's use and was now laid for lunch. I walked cautiously behind Paul and as we entered the dining room the chattering and laugh-ing stopped.

'Right, everyone, we might as well get this over and done with as painlessly as possible. I'd like you to meet Millie.'

There were a couple of knowing snorts at the back of the

room, but they were in fact a friendly lot, and not as intimidating en masse as I had feared. After the initial curiosity, they settled down to eat plates of pasta with tomato sauce and ignored me, which suited me fine.

Paul stood up. 'I've got to get this lot ready and into the coach. They'll be leaving in ten minutes and we'll follow on in my car.'

The team filed out, jostling each other with good humour, nerves taut.

I picked my bag up off the floor.

'There's no rush. We've got time for a coffee.' He went to the far side of the room, where a percolator bubbled away and poured two cups.

I contemplated the extraordinary situation I found myself in. Less than two months ago I knew absolutely nothing about our national game and here I was at the hub of things, an hour before a make or break clash in the third division. It felt rather odd.

'Here, take this. I've put in some sugar.' He stirred his vigorously. 'That went off all right, didn't it? I mean, meeting the team. Not a bad bunch, aren't they?'

'I'm glad it's over. I could tell what they were all thinking. I hope they won't give you too much stick.'

'Good God, no. They'll make the odd comment I don't doubt, but once they've got the ribbing off their chests, they'll settle down.'

I giggled. 'I fancied the tall one sitting on the end.'

'Oi, don't you dare. He's married with two kids.'

He couldn't have been more than twenty.

When we reached the ground, the place was teeming with a faithful clutch of Netherfield's fans who had travelled all this way to support their team.

'Hello, Mr Campbell,' called out a fresh-faced boy. 'Can I have your autograph, please?'

Paul signed his match day programme.

Within seconds a group of people, both young and old, gathered round to do the same. The atmosphere was friendly and so different from how I imagined it would be. There were no drunken yobs, no fights, merely families and friends of all ages, walking in harmony to their seats. Paul led me to the directors' entrance, guarded by a uniformed steward and we went inside to relative peace and quiet.

We'd had a discussion in the car on the way up from London about where I would be before and after the match.

'Don't worry, Mill, course you won't, not here. I've been before,' he insisted, when I said I was bound to be shoved into a Ladies' Room.

'I'm more than prepared to swear on the Bible that it won't be the case and that you'll be with me. We'll be together, I assure you. Last time I was here they'd disbanded their Ladies' Room.'

'I'll bet you my last sixpence that you're wrong.'

On arrival, we were taken upstairs to the first floor by the commissionnaire. The corridor was narrow and we stepped aside to let a girl past carrying a tray of sandwiches.

The steward turned and said to me over his shoulder, 'Madam, if you'd be kind enough, this way please. Straight on, Mr Campbell, please. To the boardroom.'

I looked questioningly at Paul, but before he could say or do anything I was guided through an open door. Judging by the apologetic expression on his face, he accepted the fact that he'd lost the bet.

'You owe me one,' I mouthed.

18

The room was small, rectangular and with no windows. It was lit from crystal wall lights. The gold-metal framed chairs were upholstered in red brocade and were parked around the walls with regimental precision. Set in the middle was a table covered in a white damask cloth, laden with food. I was the only person there. For want of something to do, I unzipped my coat to hang it on the stand behind the door. As I was doing this, it opened. I stepped back quickly and an expensively dressed lady, comfortably the other side of sixty, confronted me.

76

She was decked from head to toe in camel, her face smothered in a matching foundation, with no trace of eye shadow nor lipstick, a veritable stick of fudge. 'Hello, love,' she said kindly, as she placed an impressive lizard handbag on one of the chairs. 'Like a cup of coffee?'

My voice cracked. 'Actually, I'd rather have a cup of tea, if that's all right, please.'

Unbuttoning her coat, she sucked in her breath. 'Well, I'm not too sure about tea. I'll have to go to the Boardroom. We've only got coffee in here.'

Before I could say that coffee would be fine, she bustled out.

Fixed to the walls were framed photographs of the past chairmen. On a table in the corner were some artificial flowers arranged in a Crystal d'Arques vase, the label still stuck to the glass, next to a couple of bottles of Blue Nun and an opened bottle of Bristol Cream.

Mrs Fudge came back and handed me a cup of tea.

'Like anything to go with it, love?'

I looked greedily at the spread in front of me. 'Thank you. I'd love some of that meringue, please. It looks delicious.'

She placed her arms under her substantial bosom and said in all seriousness, 'Oh no, sorry love. It's sandwiches for now, gala pie at half-time and meringue nest when t' game's over.'

Put firmly in my place, I retreated behind my teacup only to be saved by the arrival of a noisy brood bursting into the room as two more women made their entrance. The first had to be the north of England's answer to Kate O'Mara, tall, painfully thin and clad solely in green, from her suede boots to her knitted coat, pullover and leather skirt, the only problem being they were of different greens and didn't match. She had lavishly peroxided hair and an unnaturally tanned, heavily lined face, evidence of having spent too many hours under a sun lamp, to the detriment of her skin. She clinked and clanked as the jewellery on her person fought for space. A guess made her age hover around a leathery fiftyish. Her companion however, and in complete contrast, was short and mumsy, sporting a tartan skirt and comfortable oatmeal twinset. Her natural hair was pepper and salt and she wore sensible lace-up brogues and I deemed was of roughly the same vintage as Mrs Fudge.

They completely ignored me. They were like busy little chickens, peck, peck, squawk, squawk, hardly pausing for breath.

Mrs Green (as I shall call her) flicked open a gold Dunhill lighter and lit up a Silk Cut tip. 'Did you hear about Rosemary?' she inquired between drags, studying the scarlet ring of lipstick on the filter.

'No,' said the other two in unison. 'Why?'

'She's only had an abortion.'

'No,' they squealed, cups poised in mid-air. 'She couldn't have.'

'How do you know?' asked Mrs Fudge.

'Well, you'd heard she'd gone into hospital last week all of a sudden?'

'Ay,' came the reply.

'Well, don't kid me that in twenty four hours courtesy of the National Health Service she went in to have her teeth capped!'

'Ooh!'

Mrs Tartan piped up. 'Well, since we're talking medical matters here, I've been suffering from,' (and this was uttered Les Dawson fashion) 'vaginal dryness.'

I couldn't believe my ears. I perched on the edge of my seat, transfixed, trying not to laugh.

'It got to such a point that I went to the doctor as I thought the whole lot had caved in.'

The peals of laughter from the other two women nearly prevented them from hearing the buzzer for the match to begin and in a uniform rush which would have made Pavlov sit up and take notes, they donned coats 'n' 'ats and disappeared into the cold. It's immaterial what happened during the first forty five minutes of the game and I can't remember anyway. It was only when someone scored a goal that I realised which half we were defending. The whistle blew and we shuffled hurriedly down the corridor as best we could, standing to one side to let the male contingent pass us to go to their inner sanctum.

'You could do with putting on some weight, hen. Just look at you. All skin and bone. You really should eat more,' Mrs Tartan said to Mrs Green.

'Well, things have improved since I went on,' (once again a delivery straight from the Les Dawson Academy of Drama) 'hormone replacement thera-*peh*. I'm a different person now, I

78

can tell you, but my Derek's the same as ever. By the time he's collected the kids from school, fed the cat, caught up with the sport in the evening *Pink*, he's gone off the boil. Come to think of it, so've I.'

The other two commiserated with knowing nods.

'Mind you, I'm relieved real*leh*, as I never understood what all the fuss was about. All that jigglin' around endin' up with what is tantamount to a great big sneeze and about half as much fun beats me.'

Bell. Scramble. Whistle. Yawn.

Yet again, history repeated itself and it was a disastrous result for us, losing 2-0. We never looked like winning, let alone scoring. The team played like a load of silly girls' blouses, but I have to confess that I did rise on my seat at one point when the tall bloke I spotted at lunch hit a blinder from the corner flag, the ball curved beautifully and I thought it was heading for the net. No such luck. The goalkeeper literally flew into the air and punched the ball over the cross bar. Two minutes later, the other side got the second goal. With such a dreadful result, I realised that Paul was one step further from the boot room and two steps nearer the boot. I returned despondent to the Ladies' Room to wait patiently. Being the only visiting 'wife' I felt isolated.

'Like a glass of dry white, pet?'

'Huh? What? I'm sorry. I was miles away. Er, no thank you. I'm probably driving.'

Blue Nun, *dry* white?

Mrs Tartan poured two glasses, one for herself and one for Mrs Fudge. Mrs Green helped herself to a healthy schooner of the Bristol Cream. With a victorious home win under their belts, it was party time.

In spite of the journey home that would take at least four hours, Paul still had to have his chat with the Chairman. At a few minutes after six thirty he came to fetch me, his face grey and tense.

I saw the warning signs and hastily collected my things together. 'Would you like me to drive?' I asked by way of comfort.

'No, Mill, thanks. I'm fine. I might hand over to you in a while, though. See how we go.'

I suppose we spoke all of ten words to each other during that first hour. Paul was deep in thought and concentrated on getting us back to London as quickly and as safely as possible. He's an excellent driver and I felt completely relaxed and, I'm ashamed to say, that yet again I fell asleep. It was only when I heard through my dreams that I realised the car was stationary. I was disorientated and my body ached from having been in one position too long. I tried to sit up, but the seat belt held me back. 'Oh God. I didn't help with the driving. You should've woken me. We're not here already, are we? I am so sorry.'

He took hold of my hand and put it to his lips.

'It's all right, Millie. I didn't have the heart to wake you. Mind if I don't come in tonight? I'm shattered.'

I hid my disappointment and undid my belt as he walked round to the boot to fetch my case.

'I'll give you a ring in the morning. Thank you for coming with me. I really appreciated it.

I could see under the street lamp that he was worked up.

'They've called an emergency board meeting first thing on Monday and I can tell you that I'm not looking forward to it.' As we were climbing the steps to the front door he said, trying to be cheerful, 'Made a hit with the team. They thought you looked great.'

Thank heaven for small mercies. I kissed him goodbye on the doorstep and watched him return to the car. He was deep in thought as he drove off and didn't look back.

'Good luck tomorrow,' I whispered.

19

No announcement was made at the meeting on Monday.

'They've been chewing the fat and haven't exactly given me an ultimatum, but it's not difficult to read between the lines. Things couldn't be more serious and it's obvious to anyone what the board is considering. I can't believe they've kept me on as long as they have. Probably the cost of terminating my contract early, I shouldn't wonder,' Paul said, unable to hide the despair in his voice.

'When can I see you again?'

'I don't know. We've got a home game on Tuesday and somehow I've got to reshuffle the team and make sense of it by Saturday, if only to reassure the directors that I'm still in the driving seat. What's more, the press, bright lads that they are, are sniffing around like vultures waiting for me to be turfed out.'

'I know. I've read the articles.'

'Have you? You didn't tell me,' he said, surprise in his voice. 'I didn't think you read beyond the television page.'

If I'd been within a foot of him, I would have kicked him – and then kissed it better. 'Don't be so patronising!' I said. 'You'd be astonished how much knowledge I've accumulated over the last few weeks. You can test me on it, if you like.'

His voice lowered a tone and he said quietly, 'I know I've got the Chairman technically on my side – for the moment at least – but even I'm not crazy enough to believe it can go on for ever. I'd better get my c.v. in order. I don't fancy being on the managerial merry-go-round,' he added prophetically.

20

The following Sunday was Valentine's Day and I was hoping that Paul and I could spend it together. He rang to say he was free and we arranged to go to Hampstead Heath. I woke with a shock to find it had been snowing during the night. At least four inches must have fallen and London was shrouded in silence, except for the soft hiss of an occasional car slipping and slithering. I love snow. I love the feeling of being cocooned in a muffled, unreal, white world. Excited, I stepped into the pile of clothes at the foot of the bed, taken off all in one last night and went out to buy a Sunday paper. The crescent looked magical and I experienced a childish thrill as my footprints were the first to make their mark.

As soon as I was back the flat, I turned immediately to the back page. Shouting at me in thick, black print was the headline:

'CAMPBELL SACKED'

My heart thumped, my mouth dried. I read it again, hoping it wasn't true. He couldn't be. What was he going to do? I rushed to the phone. It was engaged. I sat perched on the arm of the sofa, pushing the redial button every two seconds. Eventually, it rang.

'Thank God I've got you,' I said, panic-stricken. 'Are you all right? I've read today's paper. Please don't tell me it's true. I've been so worried about you.'

'Hey, calm down, Millie. I'm okay. They haven't sacked me – not yet. Don't get in a state. It's merely a rumour some clown thinks it's funny to run.'

His voice sounded tired and he spoke in disjointed phrases. 'You couldn't go and buy all the other papers for me? I can't go outside. There are journalists all over the place. I'll try and make a dive in half an hour and come over to you.'

I picked up my purse and returned to the newsagents, grabbing everything off the shelves and the floor, from the *Independent* to the *News of the World*. Worried witless, I made myself a bowl of porridge and read all the sports pages. Not only was Paul supposedly sacked, but Netherfield's place in Division Three was teetering suicidally on a cliff edge. With a dozen games to go if they didn't pull up their little blue and white socks, they would tumble into the Conference. It didn't make for jolly reading. No wonder Paul was depressed. I couldn't be bothered to wash up and deposited my dirty plate in the sink, along with others from the night before, throwing the porridge crumbs I had spilt on the floor out of the window. Domestic science never was my forte.

I jumped when the entryphone buzzed in the hall and I pushed the button to let Paul in. He looked pale and drawn and ten years older. As I opened the door I said, 'You look awful.' Blast, damn and blast. Couldn't I have said something a little more sympathetic and understanding? Why does my mouth go into gear before I engage my brain? He looked more crestfallen than ever. He is such a proud man and having failed affected him badly. There were snowflakes on his hair and eye-lashes, which I was dying to wipe away.

He didn't even give me a kiss, but barged past me onto the landing. He stood sullenly by the kitchen door. 'Small wonder I look the pits. It's been a bloody, rough night.' He unbuttoned his jacket and placed it on the draining board and sat down in an old stick back chair I had pinched from a derelict house. He placed his chin in his hands. 'There can't be any truth in the story – I'd be the first to know.' He looked up at me, the sparkle gone from his eyes. 'They end up believing what they print themselves, the bastards.' Typically, he ran his fingers through his damp hair. 'Thank goodness I've got you, Millie.'

I thought he was going to cry. It made me feel so desperately inadequate. 'Would you like me to make you some toast? Or maybe a boiled egg? I could do soldiers. You look washed out. I doubt you've had a square meal for ages. It'd do you good.' I went to the fridge. 'I was right, you haven't eaten, have you?'

'No, er, not since breakfast yesterday, I think. It's been the last thing on my mind. I don't know if I could eat anything. I'd probably throw up.'

'Well, I'm making some toast for me, so I'll do a couple of slices extra, in case you feel like it.'

'Thanks,' he mumbled, his mind elsewhere.

I took out bread, butter and a pint of milk, and Paul stood up, edgy as hell and walked out of the kitchen.

He called me from the sitting room. 'I'm checking to see if they followed me.'

'Can you see anyone suspicious?'

'No, I don't think so. Hang on, a man's walking into your front garden. He's tying four dogs to your gate.' He came back and stood in the doorway, looking bewildered. 'What the hell's he on about? He's wearing a pair of weird, yellow head phones?'

I laughed. 'Oh, that'll be Pete. He's the local dog walker. The phones are for listening to classical music as he can't stand the barking. He's come to fetch Dorothy.'

'Dorothy?'

'Dorothy is a very beautiful, geriatric labrador belonging to the couple downstairs. She's an absolute darling. Pete walks her once a day in Hyde Park, along with the others.'

'Hmm, well thankfully the coast looks clear. Most of the scum were on foot because of the snow and it's too dodgy riding a bike.'

'Do you think we should go for our walk? Or would you rather we stayed here?' I asked anxiously.

'No, frankly, I don't give a toss. If they see me, then too bad. I'll deal with them. It'll do me good to get out. Thanks,' he said, as I handed him a mug of cocoa.

Ten minutes later, as we were getting ready to leave, Paul said, 'Hey, wait a minute. I've just remembered. I've got something for you.'

Oh no, it's February 14th and with everything going pear-shaped, I'd forgotten. I consider myself the most romantic, soppy cow on earth and I didn't remember. How could I be so thoughtless?

Paul took a crumpled, candy pink envelope from his pocket and handed it to me. Excitedly, I tore it open. The card was of two bear cubs holding glasses of champagne, a huge heart between them. They were cuddled up and kissing. I looked inside and the caption read, 'We love Netherfield Town Football Club as much as we love each other.'

'You're really passionate about the club, aren't you?' I asked, putting the card on the pine dresser by a fruit bowl.

'Yes, I suppose I am. It's been my life. I've followed them since my Dad first took me when I was five years old. I never thought I'd end up manager. Now look what a fucking mess I've made of things.' Again the vein flickered on his temple, his jaw tight. 'Wait. I've got something else.' He disappeared into the hall and came back holding a box. 'This is for you, dearest Mill.'

I tore off the paper and opened the lid. Out tumbled a woolly scarf and hat. Ten out of ten – you've guessed. Bedecked and bewrapped in Netherfield Town's colours, blue and white to match my complexion from the cold, we cautiously made our way to north London. The main roads were clearer, but at the end of our road Paul put on the brakes to no effect and we slid half way across to the other side, luckily with nothing coming either way. Hampstead looked like fairyland. My goodness it was cold. We started walking in the direction of Kenwood and I tried to make a snowball, only it was the wrong sort of snow and wouldn't stick.

84

After a forty-minute hike the cold was too much for us and Paul shivering and jumping up and down, made his best suggestion so far. Putting a damp arm around my shoulder, he said, 'Fancy a pint?'

He sure knows how to tempt a girl.

We crossed the road to find that nearly everyone else had the same idea. I let Paul scramble his way through to the bar while I bagged a space by the log fire, trying to thaw out. A pitiful mongrel joined me, its long, shaggy fur clogged with snow, which melted and dripped onto the flagstones.

Paul came back five minutes later with two brimming tankards of Ruddles and a huge sausage in his mouth. ''Ere, tay' is, 'an 'oo, 'ill?'

I did as I was bid. It was all of eight inches long, burnt and crunchy and I noticed he'd had the foresight to dip one end in some mustard.

I'm not saying anything.

21

Paul licked his lips and finished his beer. 'Do you think you can get the time off to go away for a few days?'

'What, is the team off somewhere?' I asked, dreading the reply, thinking along the lines of Macclesfield, Stockport or Rotherham.

'No, not the team. You and me. Together. Alone. I thought it'd be great to find some sunshine. What about Spain?'

Bugger. Back to square one. I crossed my fingers he wouldn't be considering Alicante or Malaga. Not Benidorm, *please*. Stop it, Millie.

'I know of a great place in the north, a couple of hours in from the French border. I know you'll love it. I went there once with ... with, er, friends.' He choked. 'Sorry. Bit of peppercorn. Might have been the mustard.' He cleared his throat discreetly again, searching in his pocket for his handkerchief.

He looked guilty and I wondered why. I closed my eyes. I

saw visions of a rough Atlantic coast line, turbulent surf, long empty beaches, the Empress Josephine pining for her Napoleon.

'It's on the Med. side and...'

Ah.

'Mill, are you all right? Not going to faint, are you?'

'I'm perfectly all right, it was you who...'

'What? Anyway, as I was saying, the coastline is fantastic, with rocky cliffs and secret coves and in June it should be reasonably quiet. What d'you think? Like to come?'

Oh yes, oh yes, oh YES! Did I 'eck as like. Then alarm bells sounded, properly this time. There could be *una slighta problema*. It was a hell of a long time to wait till June and disaster could strike in between. a) I could put on a horrendous amount of weight (and I've never been bathing costume friendly at the best of times), b) Paul could really get the sack, or c) the ultimate horror scenario, we could break up, because of a) and b). I tried to ignore options b) and c), plumping (note appropriate choice of words) for option a). It wasn't called the Costa Brava for nothing.

In the meantime, there was work to be done. Miracle of miracles, in spite of hovering at the foot of the table and despite their disastrous League form, Netherfield Town had succeeded beyond all expectations and had astonishingly reached the fourth round of the FA Cup. This gave Paul's future at the club a much needed fillip. It was like a fairy story. The team had sent their opponents flying like skittles – my words, not those of the media, who were disparaging and ungracious, mentioning influences like luck and rotten refereeing. Of course, as everyone knows, the best team won and the Nethers got there fair and square. The draw for the next round was to be made tomorrow, making Paul extremely nervous.

'Let me explain properly, so that you understand. Either we draw a premiership club,' he said over our habitual midnight phone conversation that week, 'and if we do, naturally we reap huge financial rewards. We're already negotiating television rights as it is and the gate receipts will be massive. On the other hand, should we draw a smaller club, the money wouldn't be anything like as much.'

This much I could grasp – I think.

Hearing that he had my undivided attention, as always, he

continued. 'On the playing side, if we get to play Chelsea, then it's a foregone conclusion we'll lose, but even if we draw Kettering for example, judging by our recent performance, the result would probably be the same.'

No wonder he was worried.

On Saturday afternoon I sat glued to my telly. Cue camera to the FA headquarters at Lancaster Gate and the gathering of the top dogs in the football parliament. At first I thought I had pushed the wrong button on the clicker as it looked as though they were playing with snooker balls in a black velvet bag, either that or Jim Davison was making a guest appearance. I switched over to BBC2. No, racing from Cheltenham. Back to BBC 1. Since there was a blond chap talking into a mike who looked nothing like John Virgo, I realised my mistake.

'Everton v Sheffield Wednesday...'

'Newcastle United v Birmingham City...'

This liturgy droned on and I was in danger of switching over to *Pop Idol* (you can tell I was desperate), when all of a sudden I heard,

'Liverpool v Netherfield Town...' followed by a whoop! Liverpool away. Even I knew that was a good one to pull out of the hat, er, bag. Having paid attention to some of the private tuition from Paul I recognised the importance of such a tie, but even I was aware that Liverpool had the advantage of playing on their own turf at Anfield. The fact that they would thrash the living daylights out of the team is academic. Take the money and run, say I.

What *is* happening to me? Is my mind being taken over by an extra terrestrial? Unless you are blind or deaf you could be accused of noticing that a smidgen more than superficial knowledge has begun to sneak in to my character relating to the old pig's bladder. Try as I might to quell any signs of conversion, I am in danger of total submission. Not that I would ever admit to enjoying a game of football, hell would freeze over first. My conundrum is as follows: I am hopelessly, head over heels, arse over tit in love with Paul and it's having disastrous side effects. Call it job interest. What's more, I am in fierce danger of turning into a manager's moll. Why, this very morning I checked my bank statement to see if it would accommodate the purchase of a sequinned, mohair sweater. To complete the ensemble, it would necessitate in the purchase of a pair of leather trou... No. Pull the communication cord and stop right there. Enough's enough. Please, I beg of you, not leather trousers. Blonde highlights in the old barnet were verboten as well, unless administered by the expert hands of Nicky Clarke. Safer to stick to the colour I was born with – at least my collar and cuffs match, which is more than can be said for Madonna.

I said *Madonna*, not Maradona...

Gawd 'elp us.

22

'Not a bad drum for a scrap metal merchant, eh?' Paul said the following Sunday as he steered between two massive, wrought iron electric gates. The car crunched on sparkling gravel as we swerved along the carriage sweep, stopping beneath a spectacular pillared entrance. All that was missing was a red carpet.

'Flippin' 'eck,' I said, gobsmacked by the ostentatious architecture. The house was rendered with pink stucco and had wooden window shutters, colonial style. The drive was punctuated with half a dozen *faux* Victorian street lamps and there was garaging for a whole stable of cars, the nearest one revealing the shimmering rear end of a brand new Bentley turbo. 'He can't have made all this from being a totter, surely?'

Paul laughed. 'No, I wasn't quite telling the truth. The Chairman owns one of the largest haulage firms in the south east. You must have seen his lorries: massive navy blue monsters with "JT Global" in gold along the sides. If you haven't already noticed them, you will now.'

I undid my seat belt and sighed. 'The boy done good, hasn't he?'

'Not half. Come on, out you get. You take the flowers for Mrs Thornton and I'll take my briefcase. I know it's a party, but I'm going to have to grab JT for five minutes. I'd rather talk face to face than over the phone.'

We'd been invited to an 'At Home' as Mrs T called it. She had planned a barbecue, but the wind which stung our faces came straight from Siberia and I hoped we'd be indoors.

'JT insists on entertaining the troops every year,' Paul explained. 'He invites the team plus wives and girlfriends, the directors and me in order to get to know each other better. Mrs T's a marvellous hostess and fantastic cook. You'll have a great time.'

We shall see. If the house is anything to go by, portion-wise I shouldn't starve.

Paul pushed the shiny brass bell. Chimes of 'Land of Hope and Glory' rang out loud and clear.

The heavy doors opened and Mrs Thornton greeted us wearing her husband's lorry livery of a dark blue and gold spotted dress and pearls the size of quail's eggs. 'Hello, Paul. Hello, er, Millie isn't it? Come in, come in, do, please.'

'How does she know you?' Paul whispered.

'We met in your Ladies' Room. You know, at the Scarborough game.'

Mrs Thornton walked in front of us and as she secured a loose pin in her chignon, she pointed to a bench in the hall. 'Drop your coats there my dears and follow me. I'm dying to show you my huge erection.'

I spluttered into giggles like a schoolgirl.

Paul cringed. 'Mill *please*,' he hissed. 'Behave yourself. I can't take you anywhere,' he said under his breath, struggling to stop himself from laughing.

'Sorry,' I sniggered, grabbing his hand for support.

Unaware of what was going on behind her, Mrs T continued with her guided tour. 'It was only finished last month and I've been busy furnishing it ever since, only my plumbago's been playing up and doesn't like being moved.'

'I'm sorry to hear you've got a bad back, Mrs Thornton,' I spluttered, hysteria only a shadow away. 'Did you lift something heavy?'

She clutched her bosom, threw back her head and roared. 'My back? Oh my dear,' she said, wiping the tears from her eyes, 'I haven't had such a good laugh for years.' She produced a lace hanky from her sleeve and blew her nose. 'Plumbago is a plant – with pretty blue flowers. Runs riot in our villa in Marbella.'

Oops.

The 'erection' was almost as big as Grand Central Station. There were enough girders and props to keep a foundry in business for a hundred years. The sliding doors to the conservatory were open onto the terrace, which was paved with pinkish marble to match the stucco. It was surrounded by a similar coloured balustrade where, in spite of the appalling weather, tables and parasols were set up. Smoke billowed from one of the largest brick-built barbecues I've ever seen in my life, where an elderly man with a chef's toque was in action with long-handled tongs. It took a moment before I recognised the Chairman of Netherfield Town.

JT wiped his brow with a teacloth tucked into his apron and caught sight of Paul. 'Morning, Paul. How d'you like your steak?'

Paul left me and went over to shake his hand. They were soon engrossed in deep conversation.

Veronica plumped a vibrantly patterned cushion on an expansive wicker chair. 'I'm delighted to see you again, my dear. You're obviously doing Paul good. He looks as though he's being fed properly at last. Known him long, have you? Have a seat and we can have a chat.'

I sank into a pile of feathered softness, happy to spend time with Mrs Thornton ('please *do* call me Veronica – everyone else does'), as, apart from Dave and Mandy, who'd obviously been to the hairdresser for the occasion judging by the absence of black roots, I didn't know anyone from Adam.

'I wonder if I might wander around your beautiful garden, please?' I asked.

'But of course. Help yourself. Take a glass of champagne with you. Mind you don't catch your death out there. It's enough to whatever a brass monkey's wotsit.'

I slipped through the glass doors and breathed in the cold air and shivered. I had the instant impression that *Ground Force*, *Changing Rooms* and B & Q had pooled resources. The brick path twisted and turned and I lost count of the statuary. The Four Seasons snuggled amongst the viburnum, Venus de Milo was armpit to elbow with the Discus Thrower, and in the distance I spotted a further four bird baths and a sundial. Bending under the low branches of a weeping cherry if I wasn't mistaken, next

90

to a topiary peacock was Mercury, the Winged Messenger. With all the flowerbeds, perhaps he was sponsored by Interflora.

'Cooee! Millie!' a girl's voice called out from behind a water feature.

'I'm over here,' I answered, 'at Victoria Falls.'

I could hear Mandy's tinkly laugh and the clatter of her high heels on the cobbles long before she came into vision.

'How y'doin'? Recovered from the quiz night, have ya? Dave and I couldn't believe you'd beaten us. And there was us finkin' we knew everyfink.'

Bless her. You'd never believe she has a first class degree in civil engineering.

'Comin' to get somefink to eat? I couldn't 'alf murder a quarter pounder.'

I followed her in a haze of Giorgio towards the house, riveted by the way in which her endearing little buttocks pinched the white satin of her Capri pants, and mesmerised by a tantalising glimpse of diamanté-studded thong. Small wonder Dave had a permanent grin. Mandy scuttled to the cold buffet. I desperately needed Paul but he was nowhere to be seen and attempting to appear as though I was enjoying myself made my jaw ache.

The team gathered around the table where Veronica and, I assumed correctly, the housekeeper, were at the helm handing out plates and cutlery.

'I'll 'ave one of 'em, two of 'em and one of 'em fings, please darlin',' a thick set man in a brown leatherette bomber jacket with knitted cuffs requested from Mrs T. Satisfied, he moved along the line helping himself to enormous spoonfuls of salad, two baked potatoes and French bread.

Veronica looked justifiably bewildered.

Paul at last pitched up and, slipping his arm discreetly around my waist, he gently tweaked a chunk of flesh. 'What the hell is he doing here?'

'Who?'

'The driver,' he said crossly. 'He should be sitting in the coach with his sandwiches. I tell you, Mill, fur's going to fly on Monday. He's just created a job vacancy.'

In spite of the grotesqueness of the house with its jumble of styles, miles of 'drapes' and sparkling chandeliers, I had to admit on closer inspection that everything was of the highest quality. Also, Veronica and JT were very kind to me, and it was obvious she had a soft spot for Paul.

Then why do they want to sack him?

Monday morning I arrived at the office to find Mary in floods of tears. I threw everything on the floor and rushed over to her desk. 'What on earth's wrong?'

'It's …. it's … it…' she gasped, great, juicy tears squirting.

I put my arm around her fearing the worst. She collapsed into my chest. 'Come on, Mary, why the screaming habdabs? What an earth has made you so upset?'

'I'm not upseeeeeeeeet!' she bawled. 'I'm so h-h-h-appy!'

Well, you could have fooled me.

She sniffed, wiped her eyes with the back of her knuckles and smiled. 'You'll never guess. It's positive. I got the results this morning.'

Oh thank you God, thank you, thank you. 'Mary, it's the best news I've heard all day.' Tears of joy sprang to my own eyes. We hugged each other and danced around the office.

'Yes, Mill,' she said, positively glowing. 'I did a test at the weekend and couldn't believe it worked, but I did belt and braces and I had the proper results from the doctor this morning.' She looked down at her desk, overcome by emotion. 'It's due in September. It must have been in my Christmas stocking from William.'

I was thrilled for her. I counted mentally and worked out it was cooked approximately six weeks ago. Oh, please let it stick and stay full term. I must admit, once she had redone her make up and lost that revolting, swollen, red nose look from crying, she did appear remarkably healthy.

She smiled at me through pale ginger lashes. 'You wouldn't mind too much if I took a rather long lunch hour today, Millie, would you? William wants to take me out to celebrate.'

'You can be as long as you like – you deserve it,' I said, meaning every word. Oh happy day.

Paul was away in the Midlands vetting future opposition so I spent the night in. I washed my hair, plucked my eyebrows and hacked away at the dead skin on my heels – and to think people pay a king's ransom for these beauty treatments. I chiselled away so ferociously at a particularly resilient piece of hard skin on the ball of my foot, that I thought I could smell smoke. Lucky old Mary. I am pleased for her, honestly, don't get me wrong, but sometimes when you're on your tod, such ebullience is hard to take. Self doubt sets in, questions are asked. All right, I am in love with Paul, so, but where will it end? It's perhaps more of a question of when rather than why. Am I in love with him more than he is with me? Is he in love with me, or is it wishful thinking on my part? I dropped the equivalent of a carpenter's rasp on the floor and opened the tube of heavy duty foot cream. We're so blissfully compatible in many respects, but we're from completely different backgrounds. We're chalk and cheese, to use the pedicure as a source of comparison. He's thirty five, going on thirty six – an eleven year age gap – and involved in a world of which I know, and want to know, sod all. Not ideal ingredients for a long and stable relationship. Perhaps I should count my blessings and make the most of it while it lusts, or go now and find someone else. The phone rang.

'Hi, Mill. I need to go to Canterbury this weekend to see my mother. I'd like you to come too.'

Ouch.

23

Six weeks and two days pregnant, Mary blew in, clad in a billowing Liberty print maternity frock as large as an army surplus bell tent under which you could easily hide half a dozen boy scouts, still with enough room to play with their woggles. She looked stunning. 'Darling Mill. I'm so happy. Everything's absolutely perfect. I can't believe it's actually happening to me, after all the trying and so on. I've been sick three times this morning all ready.'

Rather her than me. She pranced into the back room where I heard tinkling as she played around in the sink.

There was a crash of either a saucer or a cup as it shattered. 'Uh oh. Here we go again,' she cried as the loo door banged.

'You all right in there?' Poor lamb.

Mary surfaced looking peaky and plonked down in her chair, rubbing her tummy. 'Oof. I don't fancy this malarkey every day.'

From then on, every morning she would lift up her pullover or undo her cardigan and I had to feel the bump, to see if it had grown. For ages there was no change until one morning and then it grew in leaps and bounds. The day of the first ultrasound came and Mary was in a right old tiswas. She was adamant that she didn't want to know the sex of the baby.

'Look,' I said firmly, 'if it's like any of the ultrasound pictures I've ever seen in my life in magazines or on the telly, you can't tell whether it's a boy or a girl and half the time you can't tell if it's a baby.'

'You're absolutely right, of course. Anyway, they don't tell you if you don't want to know. But then...?'

'What does William think about it all? Does he want to know what sex it is?'

'Och, don't be daft. As far as he's concerned it's a boy. He's already fished out his cricket bat and put its name down for Winchester.'

That's it settled, then. Fantastic.

Do they take girls at Winchester?

24

Paul parked tidily at the far end of a cul-de-sac formed by a row of tidy Victorian workmen's cottages. 'My mother's the one at the end,' he said, pointing to a recently decorated candy pink house, with roses over the porch.

I have to admit I was nervous. This was a thousand times worse than a summons to see the Mother Superior, and I was sure I was about to be given double prep. My stomach lurched.

An antique lace curtain twitched and as soon as he rang the

doorbell, a petite, striking woman appeared at the door. For one brief moment I thought we were at the wrong house and I narrowly missed poking an eye out on a windchime hanging above my head.

'Hi, Bumble. Sorry we're a bit late,' Paul said, kissing the woman fondly, enveloping her in his arms.

I stood behind them and stared. This person couldn't be his mother. She looked more like his older sister.

Hugging him happily in return, she said to me, 'Hello, love, I'm Betty Campbell. I'm so glad Paul persuaded you to come.'

She was amazing. She only looked about forty. Far too young to have given birth to Paul at any rate. Her youth, exuberance and apparent eccentricity made him appear by far the more mature of the two. He raised an eyebrow in amusement and smiled at the surprised look on my face.

'Come in, please, the two of you. Don't want the neighbours to gossip, do we? They might think I'm holding an orgy.' She giggled. 'They all know it's once a fortnight on Thursdays.'

I warmed to her immediately.

Betty 'Bumble' Campbell was slim, neat and pretty, with plum-coloured hair, cropped short and spiked with gel, a few of the tips dyed blonde. She wore an open kaftan over black leggings and her feet were bare, the toenails painted in turquoise varnish. Padding along the tiled floor of the hall, she said, 'You two go and make yourselves comfortable. I'll make a brew.'

Paul grinned and, taking hold of my hand, led me into the front room. It was decorated like a brothel. The original Victorian anaglypta paper below the dado rail was painted deep blood red, the ceiling inky blue, randomly stencilled with crescents, stars and suns. Psychedelic posters were taped to the walls and the furniture – what there was of it – was draped with swathes of brightly coloured silk and satin fabric, spangled with mirrors. The floor was cluttered with giant cushions and heavy velvet curtains hung in the bay window, blotting out the sun. A ceramic hedgehog prickling with incense sticks smouldered in the fireplace and soft, hypnotic music played.

'Come and sit beside me,' Paul said, patting the sofa. 'And shut your mouth – you might catch a fly.'

I stumbled in the half-light. 'I'm sorry,' I said, negotiating a pile of magazines stacked on the floor. The top one I noticed was a copy of *Dirt Bike Rider*. 'I'm being so rude but I think you could've warned me. She's nuttier than my mother. Why didn't you tell me she was a hippy like Dad?'

My nose twitched. There was something else in the air apart from joss sticks and it definitely wasn't Patchouli.

'Here we are,' Betty announced, kicking open the stripped pine door before Paul was able to get up and help. 'I've made a big pot. Milk and sugar?' Casually she tapped the end of her cigarette on to the floor, rubbing the ash into an Afghan rug. 'Have I shocked you?' she laughed. 'It keeps the bloody moths out,' she wheezed in a ginny voice, coughing richly. As she pushed her ragged fringe out of her kohl-rimmed eyes, her arms jangled with metallic bracelets, which sparkled in the flickering light from a lava lamp set on an inlaid Moroccan coffee table. Her fingernails were short and stubby, painted to match her toes and I noticed she wore a Cartier watch, hanging loosely from her slender wrist. Taking a deep drag on the cigarette, which thankfully was a Marlboro light, she looked at her son with affection. 'Thanks for coming, love, so quickly. I didn't expect you to drop everything for little old me.'

'Rubbish,' Paul said, as he accepted the chipped, scarlet mug, the words 'Campbell's Soup' emblazoned across it. 'I didn't have any appointments, so it fitted in well, and also it meant I could bring Millie along to meet you. She's taken the day off specially.'

A ginger cat appeared in the doorway and licked his paw. 'Come 'ere, you old bugger,' she said and clamping the cigarette between her teeth, she clipped the tom around the ears and scooped him up in her arms. He was followed by an overweight white cat, which had one green eye and one blue. Betty took a final drag and reluctantly dropped the remains of her cigarette into an ashtray and squashed the butt. 'Deaf as a bloody post, that one, and barmy with it. But they adore each other. Says something, dunnit?'

Underneath the make up, I could see that Betty was a striking, female version of Paul, although somewhat frayed around the edges. She sat cross-legged in front of us, her slim thighs supple, and blew on her tea. Stroking the cat's head, she asked bluntly, 'fond of my boy, are you?'

I sat like a pudding, turning as red as Paul's mug.

'Give her a chance, Mum. You're – er – it's not quite what Millie expected,' he said sympathetically, adding for my benefit, 'Bumble's brains have addled over the years, haven't they, probably from one too many magic mushrooms, eh? Isn't that right?'

Betty laughed out loud, a raucous, joyous laugh, devoid of inhibitions. 'Magic mushrooms? Tell me about them. And the rest,' she sniggered behind her hand like a naughty schoolgirl. 'Actually, Millie, I'm not as daft as I seem.' She turned to face me, uttering in a stage whisper, 'I only do it because he rises to the bait every time and I love to tease him. It drives him scatty. He thinks I'm a penny short of a shilling and should be locked up and the key thrown away.'

Paul looked anxiously at his watch. 'I'm ever so sorry, Bumble, but I can't stay too long. If you fetch those papers I'll have a look at them.'

His mother disappeared into the back of the house.

'She's a one off, isn't she?' he said, with admiration.

'You're not kidding. She's so, well, so young. However old was she when she had you?'

'She's fifty-two now. I appeared on the scene when she was sixteen, following a weekend celebrating the summer solstice at Stonehenge. I was nearly christened Salisbury. At least my father had the decency to marry her and from what I can remember, they loved each other very much. I was carried around in a papoose until I was three, and hardly wore any clothes until I was five.'

'What happened?' I asked, thinking that Salisbury had a certain ring.

'He fell off the perch after Netherfield won 5-0 at home to Hereford in the Cup when I was ten. Mum's never really got over it.'

'What, your father dying?' I said, finding a space on the coffee table for my cup.

'No, losing 5-0. Mum supported Hereford.'

'You are joking, surely?'

'Course I am, stupid,' Paul answered, laughing.

'What did he die from, if you don't mind me asking?'

'Not from what you're thinking, a drugs overdose or anything like that, although it could easily have been. He had a massive heart attack.'

'Did she ever think of getting married again? She's beautiful, and it must have been hard for her being so young.'

'It was but she coped remarkably well. She wasn't concerned with being married and has always been a free spirit and had loads of lovers, even when Dad was alive. When he died, they virtually queued up at the door, as it was always open house, so she wasn't short of company.'

'Didn't your father mind, about the other men, I mean?' I asked, trying to imagine what it must have been like growing up in such an anarchic environment.

'Not really, I don't think so. He never showed it, even if he was upset by it all. He was stoned most of the time anyway.' He stroked my hair, then drank what remained of his coffee. 'She has so much love to give, you see and that's half her problem. If she wasn't so generous she'd be in a far better position now financially and if I didn't give her a helping hand, she'd be in the workhouse.'

'What, you look after her, do you? I mean, take care of things money-wise?'

'Yup, I pay the mortgage on the house, small though it is and all the bills. I also give her an allowance, sort of pocket money. If I gave her too much at any one time, she'd blow it by giving it to a cats' home.'

Betty trotted in with a pile of papers and handed them to Paul. He walked over to read them at the table in the bay window and pulled the curtains back to let in more light. There were some fitted shelves in the alcove beside the fireplace and it was only then that I could see they were decked with photographs of Paul and trophies he had won over the years. It was like a shrine.

'Come and look at the garden, love, while Paul sorts that lot out. Just grab m' fags.' She slipped her arm through mine. 'Like football, do you?'

'Bumble likes you,' Paul said as we drove through Orpington on the way back to London. 'Tell me, honestly, what you thought of her?'

I had to work this one out carefully. 'I have never met any-one like your mother in my life,' I said, slowly pacing myself. 'She's extraordinary. I admire her for her guts and for wanting to lead her life exactly how she wants. Not many people in this life manage to do that.'

'Don't be fooled. Underneath all that craziness lurks a bril-liant brain. It's hard to imagine, but when my father died, she enrolled at college and mastered in psychology.'

'Did she ever use it, practice or whatever you do?'

'No, she enjoyed the mental stimulus I think, more than any-thing. She used to dump me with the next-door neighbour to go to night classes. Apart from the degree, she is a dab hand at ceramics. You might have noticed the shed in the garden. Five years ago I paid for it to be wired and heated, and found a second-hand kiln for her. She's a natural and makes a few bob selling her pots.'

'Did she make the hedgehog, by any chance?'

He nodded.

'I could tell she's got an eye for colour. Where on earth did you get your sporting genes from?'

Paul laughed. 'We do look different, don't we? But again, don't be misled by appearances. Bumble was going to train as a ballet dancer, but met my father before she could turn pro. She also plays volleyball once a week to keep fit, but I wish she wouldn't smoke so much, that's all.'

I felt horribly inadequate. An MA in psychology, a dancer, a potter. What other talents would come to light? My Pitmans 'Highly Commended' certificate paled into insignificance in com-parison.

25

I didn't go with Paul to Liverpool for the FA Cup, much as I wanted to, since I had to stay behind and work and anyway he had enough on his plate without worrying about me into the bargain. I read all the morning papers to compare views on how Netherfield would fare. A couple were cautious. Most were crowing in advance of an inevitable annihilation of the under- dogs and others, well they laughed. I crossed my fingers and prayed for all I was worth. By my calculations they had a fif- teen to one chance and it was worth a bob or two of anyone's money. I made a mental note to drop in at Ladbroke's at lunchtime.

I closed the office later than usual for me, as a young couple turned up at ten to one and wanted to view two properties. I didn't get back to the flat until after two thirty. I have to admit that I was quite excited. Not having eaten any lunch, I turned on Radio Five and cut doorstep slabs of bread and constructed a cheese sarnie, cemented with a heap of chutney. Paul had tried to explain to me about the 'the flat back four' but, as for the offside rule, he gave up. I increased the volume.

The noise the crowd was making was unbelievable. 'We're coming home, we're coming home, England's coming home!'

I felt all patriotic and fiercely proud. The whistle's gone. Shh! Be quiet. I'm listening.

The first forty five minutes over and we've managed to hang on in there: 0-0. Not a bad start considering who it is we're playing. Bugger the half time oranges; I'm having a gin. Our brave goalie has managed to keep a clean sheet in spite of a fair amount to do in the first half. As for Liverpool's goalkeeper, I think he had time to file his nails, send a couple of postcards and phone home. It should liven up his end in the second half though, with any luck. I do hope Paul's okay...

Oh no! Liverpool have scored. From an indirect free kick. The medium wave crackled and hissed and I waggled the aerial. With my trusty Roberts half-way out of the window, I could hear the crowd going mad. 'One nil! One nil! One nil!'

I looked at my watch – another agonising twenty three min- utes to go. There's some hope left. Just one goal, lucky or other- wise, would earn a replay.

Come on you Blues, come on you Blues! You can do it. For Paul. Please. For Paul...

That's it then.

All over.

1-0.

PART SEVEN

YELLOW CARD

26

'Truly, I'm absolutely fine,' Paul assured me, sounding precisely that, which was astonishing to say the least.

To my amazement he wasn't in the slightest bit depressed, to the contrary in fact and my prepared lines of condolence and sympathy were not needed.

'Yeah, well, the lads did their best. Oh, you heard it on the radio, eh? Liverpool was definitely the stronger side, but we gave them a bit of a scare in the second half. Never mind. At least now we're out of the competition, we can concentrate on the real task and stay in the League. That's all that counts.'

For once I understood the logic and thought, how sensible. It was a terrific bonus to get as far as they had in the Cup and they had reaped the cash benefits, but now it was imperative to avoid relegation. Needless to say with only a couple of months of the season left I didn't see as much of Paul as I would have liked and thought I would devote my boundless free hours to honing the body beautiful in time for our trip to Spain.

I took up jogging. It lasted precisely two days. With a chest like mine which fights a permanent battle with gravity, bouncing around on the pavements in Notting Hill Gate produced more whistles than a consumer test of kettles. Also I got jogger's nipple. Right, thinking cap on. Aerobics? No. The ceiling in my flat is so low that it's prohibitive of jumping jacks. Join a health club? Too mean and too poor. Eat less? Whaaaaaat?

101

I stripped off in the bathroom and looked long and hard at my figure, seeking a word big enough to describe it. Junoesque sprang to mind, voluptuous certainly, but plain fat needs plain language. Squeezing chunks of fat here and there, lifting and tugging, I decided that the only piece of my anatomy with any absence of excess flesh was on the soles of my feet. I shall have to sunbathe face down.

Walking naked into the bedroom I opened the box in the wardrobe containing my swimsuits. Out sprang a leopard print, out slithered a snake and then I was hit between the eyes by an electrifying neon pink bikini. I tried it on, out of pure masochism. It was horrible when I bought it, it's worse now. Sling it. I had a certain bestial fondness for the menagerie but they were purchased when there was a little less of me two summers ago and I thought if I did wear them, I might be arrested, or at least put into quarantine. Don't chuck, but keep safely for when I have lost a couple of pounds. Pigs might as well fly and in my case they probably would. Scrabbling around underneath a couple of sarongs lay my all time fave, a one piece, black number which had cost a fortune. Superbly engineered, it gave me cantilevered breasts, a viable waist and squeezed in my backside. That in itself was worth the equivalent of a deposit on a mortgage which its purchase nearly entailed. You needed a can opener to prise it off. For a penny short of a hundred quid I could imagine I was Jane Russell. What's more, even though not in its first flush of youth, it fitted and it solved the problem of whether or not to go topless on the beach. But disaster was close behind. When I bent over there came a horrendous crrrrrrrrrraaaaaack. The rubberised fabric had perished and by checking for damage in the dressing table mirror I could see a horizontal split running across my bottom leering at me in a huge, toothless grin. I burst into tears, picked up the whole lot, threw them in the bin and then I ripped off the one I was wearing and threw that away too. Now what do I do? I sat on the floor and moped, staring at the pathetic pieces of limp lycra spilling out of the waste paper basket resembling burst balloons. There was no getting away from it, I was a touch broader in the beam this year than last.

Right, shops, here I come. Retail therapy is what is called for, big time. I went into M & S and picked out three one-piece costumes, or rather I took six off the rails, each one in two sizes. Then, back in the privacy of my own home having chosen the one I liked (or rather, the one which fitted) I could bring the rest back. Good idea? Of course it is.

Carrying my bounty, I went into Smith's to sneak a free preview at the guide books on the Costa Brava. Paul was right. The region was absolutely stunning, with hardly a high-rise block in sight and nothing like the concrete hell I imagined. Little did I know that my world was about to fall apart.

'Fancy a Donald?' a husky, male voice whispered two inches away from my left ear.

I reeled and stopped breathing. Such an expression could only come from one mouth – Rupert Holland's.

I think I'd better explain the importance of this particular gentleman in my life. Among my rogues gallery of ex's feature Nick (ex-perience), Errol (ex-periment) and – I'm almost too embarrassed to admit – Rosie (ex-tra curriculum). Last but not least was Rupert (ecs-tasy). Knowing that I looked like the wreck of the Hesperus I fiddled with my hair, wishing I had washed it. 'Oh, Rupe!' I spouted. 'You're absolutely the last person in the world I expected to bump into. What's brought you to London? New shoes? I thought you were permanently buried in muck and manure in Corn –'

'Devon,' he corrected, delighting in my confusion.

'Cornwall, Devon, same difference,' I said, wilting visibly as he stared at me with his arrogant, be-spectacled eyes, lapis lazuli blue, fringed with black lashes – indecently long for a man. He crossed his arms and leaned against a shelf of books on DIY (something he's rarely had to resort to, except perhaps on wet Mondays in August), slim and simmeringly sexy. I moved down a notch to stare wantonly at his mouth. I closed my eyes a moment longer than a normal blink and shuddered internally. Rupert had to be the greatest kisser of all time. The best. I've never known anyone who could whip up a whirlwind like him. Wasn't it Rupert who taught me that horn players weren't the only ones who could triple tongue? Hang on to your syrup – what was I doing? Rupert 'I've-got-a-big-one' Holland was homing in. I needed help – fast. I forced myself back to reality as I recalled how the bastard had dumped me. I despised him for what he did, how he destroyed my self-

103

esteem, ruined my reputation. All that I could cope with, time being a great healer or so they say, but the most serious crime of all for which I would never forgive him, was that he broke my heart. Bumping into him again after all these years was extremely upsetting and I cursed my fickle knees as they collapsed beneath me.

'Wow, it's great to see you, Millicent. You're looking fab.' He grinned disarmingly, the worst thing for me that he could do. 'Have you got five mins? Please say you'll let me take you for a drink?'

Will power at zero, pistons pumping on all cylinders, before you could say 'Shaken or stirred,' he whisked me out of Smith's and into the pub opposite. I couldn't believe the evil thoughts I was having. If the truth be known for once, I'd never really got over him, even though a fair amount of water has gone under the bridge in the meantime, to put it politely. I was stunned at seeing him again and totally disconcerted that he retained the instant knack of sending my stomach to a puree.

'You go and grab that table,' he said, pointing to a dark corner. 'I'll be back in a sec.'

I watched his tall, elegant figure swagger effortlessly over to the bar, beating everyone else to place his order, returning triumphant, armed with a chilled bottle of Lanson in an ice bucket and two fizz flutes. I noticed with increasing pleasure that the years had been kind, no, had positively improved what had already been a perfect specimen. Rich Rupert. Randy Rupert. Flamboyant, over the top and over me – or was he? Was I, for that matter, over him? Years of hollow heartache, which at the time had manifested itself in excruciating, physical pain, were rushing back to haunt and possibly destroy me. There were going to be tears before bedtime – or afterwards, if I wasn't careful. I could feel it in my waters.

27

I need you to appreciate the massive upheaval in my emotions caused by seeing Rupert again. The truth is, ours was no ordinary affair. The *liaison dangereuse* began at a dinner party some three summers ago. Rupert was there, glued to perhaps the most exquisitely beautiful girl I had ever had the displeasure to clap eyes on, whose father had the added attraction of being absolutely loaded. I was famously single, and my hosts slapped me between a thick farmer from Northamptonshire and an even thicker rugger bugger from Fulham. They were both ostensibly footloose and fancy-free and it didn't take me long to find out why. The farmer was a crushing bore and talked about nothing other than his prize Holsteins. The rugger bugger, who was reasonably good looking, apart from a rather unappetising cauli-flower ear, baled out by getting drunk before the main course and fell asleep. It did wonders for my ego, I can tell you, so I spent the entire evening shamelessly ogling Rupert, but who sadly had eyes only for his companion.

For want of something better to do as my neighbours were otherwise engaged, I drank rather a lot and ate everything put in front of me. Half way through the pudding something touched my foot. I have a bad habit of removing my shoes when I sit down and I could feel gentle but persistent pressure on my toes. 'Gosh, sorry!' I said, catching Rupert's eye, which he winked at me. I blushed. Then he did it again. Whispering something in the Hon. Abigail Wing-Reed's shell-like (the loved one's name), he stood up. I dislodged the elbow of my uncon-scious neighbour and dived under the table in order to retrieve my shoes. Having found the left but unable to locate the right, a finger prodded me in the ribs and in my haste to see who it was, I banged my head. A naughty chuckle and a cool hand helped me back to the vertical. It was Rupert.

He knelt beside me, miraculously producing my other shoe. It gave me the chance to study the back of his head, where his hair curled over his collar. I had to restrain myself from touch-ing him.

'Hoof please sweetheart,' he purred.

He was close enough for me to feel his warm breath and to count the lashes on the sexiest pair of eyes this side of chris-tendom.

My heart was in danger of doing a mischief when my foot jerked forward nearly hitting him on the nose. Expertly he slid it into the shoe and without saying a word, returned to his seat.

My mind in a turmoil, the rest of the dinner party fell into rapid decline. The rugger player woke up only to be sick in the ice bucket and was deposited unceremoniously on the sofa while someone hastily rang for a minicab. Our hosts had a blazing row with each other when the subject of children (the lack, not presence of) was raised and then things really hotted up as everyone argued over whether Tesco's was better value than Sainsbury's or Waitrose. I knew it was time to depart when the ruddy complexioned farmer asked for my telephone number. As politely as decorum would allow, I said my farewells and went to grab my coat from the hat stand in the hall.

'Midnight hasn't chimed already, has it Cinderella?' a male voice asked behind me.

I spun around as delicious tremors rocketing off the Richter scale shot down my spine, except I felt more pumpkin than Princess.

'I wonder if I might see you again.'

An explosion occurred between my minimiser bra and my suspenders. Two feet away from me stood the most delectable looking man I had seen in my life. My diary had been pitifully blank page after blank page for weeks, perhaps months and a diet of junk food and coke must have curdled my grey matter. Intellectually challenged having watched too many episodes of 'ER', knowing Mr Clooney was way beyond my reach, I was beginning to fancy my chances with Dr Greene. This person, this demi-God, this mouth-watering creature who had been entertaining the most gorgeous bird in London, was asking me out.

'What?' I asked, stunned into articulacy. 'Christ. Thank you, er, yes, thank you. That would be lovely,' I stuttered, thinking that this might be a dream, and that if I pinched myself hard enough I would wake up, alone. Praying it was really happening to me, I fumbled awkwardly with my buttons.

Undeterred Rupert leaned against the wall and chuckled. 'Here, stop dithering woman and let me deal with those. There we are. All present and correct,' he said with a satisfied smile as he slotted the top button through its hole, patting it as it shot home.

My chin wobbled. He was so *masterful*. The conversation was surreal.

'Just like a good little schoolgirl, fastened right up to the top. Headmistress will be pleased.'

I gazed at him, unblinking, trying to engrave each feature in my memory bank. Close to, he was even more devastatingly attractive, if such a thing were possible. A heavy, floppy curtain of black hair fell over his trendy silver framed specs and his beautiful, flawless white teeth grinned at me with vulpine charm. I was spellbound.

Before I fell into his arms a slobbering mess, I succeeded in pulling myself together enough to gasp, 'Thank you so much. I haven't been dressed for ages. It's usually the other way round.' My size seven feet were planted firmly in my mouth, the only plus being that they prevented a guffaw from escaping. That would have resulted in a certain death knell.

He snorted with mirth and held open the door. With impeccable timing, Ms Wing-Reed chose this moment to materialise, cosseted in shatoosh, having overdosed on Mitsoukou. She shot me a jaundiced look and clung to Rupert like a limpet mine.

'See you, Millicent,' he called out casually, his arm draped over the vile girl's shoulder, as they sashayed along the pavement to his car.

I could have spat.

When I arrived back at the flat I was in a real state. The last thing I wanted was to get involved with a two-timing bum and although I was yearning for him to call, I didn't like the scenario. It was obvious to a guide dog's blind man that Abigail had sunk her claws into Rupert right down to the bone. However, as things turned out I didn't have to wrestle with my conscience, as he didn't get in touch. Thinking it was a blessing in disguise, I was on the verge of digging out one or two names from my little black book in desperation, when, a fortnight later, the phone rang during *Sex and the City*.

'Hello, Millicent,' a male voice growled as my heart leapt from my boots to my mouth.

'Who's that?' I rasped, my vocal chords having gone on holiday.

'It's Rupert, you must remember, Rupert Holland. We met at the Dugdales'. How are you?'

Purr purr, slurp slurp. Vrroom vroooom! Of course I knew instantly who it was. I'm not that daft. There is only one person in the world I know who has a voice like a Thornton's dark chocolate truffle. 'Oh, everything's fab, thanks,' I said. 'I'd almost given up on you,' I sighed before I could stop myself. Well done, Millicent, full marks for subtlety. Bang goes the gently-gently approach.

Rupert amazingly ignored my comment. 'I was wondering, it is rather short notice, but would you like to come with me to Windsor races tomorrow night? It should be a splendid evening.'

Before you could say 'They're off!' I accepted.

The following day dragged as I anticipated the prospective pleasures. I left work early and took the tube to Hammersmith where Rupert planned to pick me up in his car, giving us half a chance to get there in time. I stood on the corner of King Street and within ten minutes he sidled up in a magnificent, gleaming Aston Martin – racing green (what else?) with a natural hide interior. We cruised west, the setting sun shining directly into our eyes, and joined the throng for the car parks. The only race meeting I had been to previously was a local point-to-point, but this was completely different. There was a real buzz. It was a perfect summer's evening, the sort you dream about when you pick up *Homes and Gardens* in January and wallow at the pictures, so cleverly orchestrated, depicting idyllic gardens, perfect picnics. England at its quintessential best.

Rupert generously handed me forty quid and together we romped through the card, ending up winning on five of the races. I preferred to use the closed eyes and wandering finger method and although this was a ploy also familiar to Rupert (but not for gambling), he chose to select his horses scientifically. He counted the jockeys as they paraded in the paddock from one to ten and started again. The horse that was in front of him on the count of six the second time around took his money – and it worked three times. Who said it's a mug's game?

We were half-way through a sizzling steak sandwich, washed down with what was to become Rupert's trade mark drink, vintage brut Lanson, when I plucked up enough courage to ask about Abigail. I had no intention of going in any deeper unless I knew that the sea was shark free, or at least with a safety net not far from shore.

'Oh darling,' he drawled, 'don't you worry about Abi. We're over, finished, *kaput*. It was on its way out the other night at the Dugdale's dreadful dinner party. It was plain for everyone to see.'

Not from where I was sitting it wasn't. I saw the look she gave me. Not entirely convinced that he was telling the truth, nevertheless my naïve heart skipped a beat.

'Yeah,' he continued, protecting his eyes from the dipping rays, 'She started bleating about marriage, kids, you know, the whole shebang and I'm afraid I turned cold at the thought.' He removed his glasses and wiped them studiously on his silk tie. Breathing on the lenses, he sighed, 'She's a dear girl, but perhaps not the brightest.'

This wasn't necessarily the reason I wanted to hear, but at least the coast appeared clear and I intended to go full steam ahead. Ahoy there!

We didn't get back to west London until after eleven, having sunk yet another bottle of poo with a couple of Rupert's pals who'd put a heap of money on the last race and won. At the time I was renting a grotty basement behind Stamford Brook which the local drunks liked to use as a free-for-all urinal and I didn't want Rupert to see my humble abode. Following my directions, he slowed down two doors away from my building and crunched to a halt as the last strains of the Intermezzo in *Cavalleria Rusticana* were being played out on the radio. As he turned off the ignition the orchestra simultaneously stopped. What timing. Typical, perfect Rupert.

Without warning, he turned towards me and kissed me. It was as if I'd been hit by a bolt of forked lightning. It was a devastating kiss, a double-99-cornet-with-extra-flake kind of kiss, demolishing reserve and good intentions in one lick. I was behaving like a hussy, a complete and utter pushover, in seventh heaven – but two minds. What was maths doing entering the equation? It knocked me for six. When I was able to surface and draw breath, I mumbled, 'Er, Rupert, I think I'd better go. Erm, thanks for a smashing evening,' abruptly moving away, my heart pounding, my lips burning, grabbing in the dark for the door handle.

It was happening too quickly. I wanted us to slow down enough to enjoy the thrill and excitement of anticipation. Well, that's what I tried to tell myself. In truth, I couldn't wait to get him inside the flat, into bed and in me.

He released me and turned towards his door. 'Not to worry, Millie, I need to get back too – heavy day tomorrow.'

Mega disappointment. Why didn't he stop me? Didn't he like kissing me? Groan. Does my breath smell? He planted a peck on the top of my head, evidently in confirmation of the second doubt.

The most come-to-bed pair of eyes I have ever seen looked darkly into my innermost person. 'Thanks for a terrific evening. We must do it again – and soon,' he said as he traced his long, tapered, winning finger down my cheek. 'I haven't enjoyed myself so much for ages.'

All back on course again. Managed to fasten lock on chastity belt, but didn't throw away the key. (If you play your cards right, Rupey darling, I'll give you the combination...) Aware I had problems of coordination, he was out of the car in a flash, holding the door for me. I stumbled onto the pavement, hiding a frustrated blush behind a curtain of hair, fumbled for my keys and gave him a glancing kiss. I missed, scoring a triple twenty in his ear, before bolting, embarrassed, down the basement steps.

'Hey, wait a mo', Millicent! Don't rush off like that,' I heard him cry.

I slammed the door a second before I gave in totally and once inside, I leaned back on it, thinking, 'Still, my beating heart...'

28

I played the virgin queen for precisely eight days and seven nights, only to succumb – so willingly, it was shameful – at midnight after a concert at the Albert Hall, behind a chestnut tree in Hyde Park. Insofar as the cast iron chastity belt was concerned, Rupert possessed a special instrument with which to pick the lock.

We strived to see each other as often as we could and I

virtually lived in his flat in Ebury Street, purely for practical reasons of course. He had a whopping 7' bed – mine was only 4'6". It was a wonderful, raging affair, when, horror of horrors, I too began to hear the sweet, emasculating *tinkle tinkle* of wedding bells and for the first time I felt a modicum of sympathy towards Abigail. Rupert, unaware of my female scheming, seemed ecstatic, alternating rampant bonking with unbelievable pampering. I had never been treated so extravagantly. He buried me under tons of Belgian chocolates, drowned me in gallons of champagne and swamped me with forests of exotic flowers and it was thanks to him I learned to tell the difference between a gerbera and a gerbil. Unfortunately, Rupert's mind went instantly AWOL if anything remotely resembling a 'serious discussion' rose its ugly head. Babies and a cottage in the country were not on his agenda. My basement area was.

I should have known better. Crunch time came one Saturday when Rupert rang to cancel a special dinner at the Ivy. I'd never been there before – up until then I didn't know anyone rich enough – and was as excited as hell as I thought, like poor disillusioned Polly did with George, that he may have chosen it with a special reason in mind. Dream on, old girl. Life isn't like that, is it?

D-day arrived and I invested in an outrageously expensive dress, all floaty and feminine, the sort I knew Rupert loved me to wear. God was being kind and for once my hair behaved itself and there wasn't a zit in sight. Something had to go wrong – and it did.

Before we closed the office that evening, the telephone rang.

'I'll get it,' said Mary. She covered the mouthpiece anxiously with her hand. 'It's Rupert,' she whispered.

Fearing the worst, my feminine antennae in overdrive, I picked up my extension. Mary looked at me, the worried expression creasing her brow, and chewed her fingernails.

Down the line poured a cascade of excuses. 'Millicent *darling*, I'm really sorry, but something's cropped up. I know you're going to kill me and I wouldn't blame you if you did, but I won't be able to make tonight.'

Silence.

'Millie, are you there, sweetheart?'

Ditto silence. I replaced the receiver, struggling with hot tears of hurt and disappointment.

'You okay?' asked Mary, gently.

'No,' I said, breathing out, my voice shaking, 'I'm definitely not.'

Three seconds later it rang again.

'Wallis and Company, good evening, Millie speaking,' I said, full of bravado, assuming correctly it was Rupert again.

'Oh, Mill, thank goodness. We must have got cut off.'

You can say that again.

'Look, I'm ever so sorry, darling, but as I said, I've got to cancel tonight. Huge prob. We've got an emergency creative meeting. One of our biggest clients has landed a day early from the States and all merry hell has broken loose. It's total bedlam here and if I'm not available to do a presentation we're in danger of losing the contract.' Pause. 'Millie, I am so sorry...'

Fuck, fuck, fuck. You can't be half as sorry as I am, mate. I twiddled aimlessly with the cord, looping it round my fingers, lost for words, those tears springing to my eyes unheeded. I tried to tell myself it was his loss, not mine. Damn, damn, damn and damn.

Mary came to the rescue. 'Do you want me to speak to him?'

I shook my head. I could read pathetic excuses at five hundred paces and I wasn't in need of binoculars to know he was lying. Not wanting to give the game away, I said, worthy of a BAFTA award, 'Yes, I'm still here,' adding for good measure between gritted teeth, 'Heavens, Rupert, don't give it a moment's thought. Of course I understand. Naturally work must come first.'

Mary walked over and handed me a fistful of Kleenex. I blew loudly into them, not caring whether Rupert heard or not.

Tough as old boots, he replied without a decent moment's hesitation. I could hear the obvious relief in his voice.

'You're an absolute treasure, Mill. I can't thank you enough. I'll be in touch. Cheers,' he almost shouted, happy as Larry the bloody Lamb. 'Not starting a cold, are you?'

This was war and the five letter word 'sorry' was beginning to feature rather too often in his Rupertoire.

But truth will always out. As luck would have it, that very evening fate declared that Polly and Susie happened to pass the

Ivy on their way back from a girls' night out at the theatre. Out of curiosity, they stopped to peer nosily through the darkened windows to see if they could spot us, as they were unaware that I'd been dropped like a hot brick that afternoon.

'We didn't know whether to tell you or not,' Polly said, looking anxiously at Susie, when they called an emergency 'ad hoc' meeting at the wine bar the next night. 'You can understand, Mill, can't you? We were in a terrible dilemma, but decided on the grounds of our long friendship that we ought to say something.' Another loaded glance from Polly to Susie, before she continued, 'They were sitting in the corner at a cosy table for two. Although we couldn't see their faces, it was too dark, we knew it was him as the buckles on his Guccis gave the game away, apart from the inch and a half of white cuff sticking out from his blazer sleeves. The lying hound was entwined with A..., Ab...' she gagged on the word, 'that frightful object. They were locked in *the* most passionate embrace, their tongues down each other's throats. We were so cross with him, we nearly stormed in and kicked him in the balls.'

Susie moved nearer to me, inches away from my face, scowling furiously. 'She was like an octopus and her arms were wrapped round his neck,' she hissed, 'it was too dark to see if her legs were, too. It was perfectly, nauseatingly, revolting.'

I was nearly sick. I begged her silently to have made a mistake.

Polly plodded on, an expert witness. 'We saw Rupert's car, you know, the Aston, parked a little further down the street. There can't be two like that in London, now can there? We double checked to make sure and yup, there it was, his personalised number plate.'

I knew it by heart.

' "RH 67" – two doors from heaven,' he liked to joke.

'The stupid prat had parked on a double yellow,' Susie said, laughing cynically. 'There was some justice after all, as he'd been clamped. We said it served him right.'

Ha bloody ha.

29

I fib when I say he didn't get in touch. He did every day, several times, for the next week. I refused categorically to speak to him and Mary fielded his calls, bless her, with economic diplomacy.

'Och, sorry Rupert, she's out on an instruction. I'll get her to ring you when she's back... What's your number?

...Och, you've just missed her.

...No, she's out at the moment having her verrucas seen to...Here, give me your number again, in case.

...I'm *ter*ribly sorry. Missed her again. She's at the VD clinic...'

He got the message.

I cried and cried until I didn't think I had any tears left. I was in total despair. If I'd had the courage I would have topped myself, but it would have defeated the purpose as I wanted to be around to see if it hurt him. I had lost what I considered to be my first real love. I dreamed I might win him back, but as he'd skipped so willingly back to Abigail's open arms – and legs – I knew our relationship was beyond repair.

I found out later from a mutual 'friend' that he'd never stopped seeing her all the time he was seeing me. The only reason I could stay so often in his flat in Belgravia was because she was over in the States on an extended modelling assignment and out of harm's way. The shit head. The only time he was telling the truth was when he had first mentioned her attempts at shunting him up the aisle, except the part he had not elaborated on was that he had every intention of going up it with her. Double, treble bastard. I was well rid of him, only at the time it didn't feel so clear cut. My wounds bled, my heart was in tatters.

A month later Mary choked on the hatches, matches and despatches in the *Telegraph*. 'My God, they're engaged.'

I didn't have to ask who.

The subsequent wedding made all the mags, from *Hello!* to *Harpers and Queen*, the golden couple. The ironic thing is that they had the nerve to send me an invitation. Needless to say I declined, having a prior engagement. As a gesture of good faith, or good breeding, however you like to look at it, I sent them a present. It was a plaster cast of the mask of Janus, the significance of which was obvious enough even for a thicko like Rupert to grasp.

What's more, Abigail thanked me for it by return, on a postcard engraved with, *'From Mrs Rupert Holland, Cullompton Manor, Cullompton, Devon. Millie, dearest, We can't thank you enough for such a thoughtful present. It'll look wonderful in our conservatory,'* she wrote in fountain pen ink, *'all a-tumble with mind-your-own-business.'*

I hate her.

I have to admit they did make a striking couple, but it only increased the agony. It could have been me in that sleek, Vivienne Westwood design in oyster silk. To tell you the truth, after all this time, I've never really got over him. In the past I've always been the one to call things off, to cool down and be the dumpee and to have the boot on the other foot hurt like stink. Added to which, you feel a complete fool when people ask what went wrong and I don't know anyone in this world who will admit voluntarily to having been given the old heave ho. Mary called it a severe case of 'pricked pride', bringing an entirely new meaning to the phrase.

And here I was, in a West London alehouse, idyllically in love with Paul and in fierce danger of being a very naughty girl indeed.

30

'Millicent,' Rupert oozed, 'you look positively luscious. You're good enough to eat. How could I have forgotten how stunningly beautiful you are?'

Harrumph. Honeyed words, indeed. 'What did you say? I didn't quite catch it.'

'I said, Millicent *darling*, that you look gorgeous, all softness and...' he sighed as he refilled my glass.

I whipped it away as he poured, splashing the contents onto the table.

'What the...?' he asked, confused at my reaction.

'You're a rotten, two-timing moral coward!' I spat at him, clenching the stem so fiercely, it snapped in two.

'Hey, steady on. What the hell's got into you? What's brought all this on?' he gasped, anxiously looking around the bar, aghast that I was creating a scene in public.

I was so angry I shook and stared at his face with fury. It was scrunched up with remorse as though I had physically slapped him. It felt nearly as good, I can tell you. All those years of pent up frustration, shame and ego-withering pain came exploding to the surface. I continued to give him a verbal lashing while he sat meekly in complete silence. Eventually, I stopped, exhausted.

'Have you quite finished? Perhaps you'd be kind enough to let me speak now, please, if you don't mind.'

'Of course,' I replied, my fists clenched so that I wouldn't punch him.

'I'm sorry, Millie, there's nothing I can say to justify what I did,' he attempted to explain, contrition setting in. 'All right, I admit it, I was a total lying bastard. I should never have done what I did to you, but matters were out of my control.' Contrition turned to wheedling. 'I don't expect you to believe me, but it's true. All I can say, for what it's worth, is I've learned my lesson.'

As I mopped up the spilled liquid, before I could prevent him, he was already at the bar buying another bottle. Did I really mean what I said? Did I really hate him as much as that, or was I trying to convince myself I did, for Paul's sake? I didn't know what I thought any longer. I sank my teeth into my lip to stop it trembling, not knowing whether to bolt while I had the chance, or to sit tight.

Before I could make up my mind, Rupert was back, already sploshing the golden bubbles into a fresh glass. 'I won't rest until you've heard my side of the story.' He wiped his mouth with a red spotted handkerchief. 'I don't know if you're aware, but Abigail lied to me, using the oldest trick in the book, saying she was in the pudding-club. Her father's a terrifying individual and threatened law suits, you name it, if I didn't do the honourable thing. A shotgun wedding wasn't exactly my idea of fun, even if the firearm in question was a Purdey. God knows why I believed her, but she had a way with me which turned me to putty. I don't know, perhaps I'm too weak.'

It's not you who are weak, Rupert, it's me. I wanted to run, to leave him basking in his misery and mistake. I didn't want to hear any more, it hurt too much. And yet, there was some invisible energy making me want to stay, to forgive him. I was being tugged in two. Why, oh why, did we have to meet this morning? Things were going so well before and now my life was like a house of cards, collapsing around me.

Rupert battled on, finding confessing as difficult as I found hearing the truth. 'You know her father owns a string of race horses? He's got them in training in Berkshire. Well,' he said, 'it so happened that a couple of his nags were running the night I took you to Windsor. I lied then about whcre Abi was.'

What a gullible dolt I was, but little did he know that God was about to land him in it.

'We moved to the West Country and Abi immediately set about decorating the nursery wing. She even went to the lengths of interviewing Norland nannies, for heaven's sake. Jesus, I was an idiot. I should've suspected things weren't right from the start. She was never pregnant, never in a million years. It was a pack of monumental porkies. I began to ask a few questions three months after the wedding, since there wasn't the slightest hint of a bump, pea sized or other.'

I began to feel sorry for him. Nobody should be misled like that, it wasn't fair, not even by Rupert's standards.

'"False alarm," she cried,' but nevertheless Abigail had captured her quarry and had become Mrs Holland for better or worse, till death do them part.

'Am I forgiven, Millie?' he asked softly, all the veneer of self-confidence whittled away.

How could I reply? I was skating on very thin ice and he retained the power to make me melt. I urged myself to leave now, while I could. To stay any longer was dangerously tempting fate. Or was it because of fate that we met again? He stroked the back of my hand, making the tiny hairs tingle, not letting me break away from his gaze. He could have parted seas with that look. My defences were coming down and I hurriedly crossed my legs so my underwear wouldn't follow suit. I tugged on my coat and picked up my shopping.

Rupert engaged an expression of disappointment worthy of an Oscar. 'You're not going, darling, are you? Please stay, we haven't finished.'

Oh, yes Rupert, 'darling', we have most definitely finished, three years ago. In fact, I don't suppose it really began. I was simply the middle course, not the whole menu. Now you're going to have to pay the bill. Service is not included.

Standing up, I hesitated a moment and looked down at him. In the grey, smokey pub light he appeared smaller, older and less alluring, or so I tried to convince myself. Whatever excuse passed through my head, it was bound to fail miserably. I had to admit defeat. He was as gorgeous as ever, always was, always would be.

'I'm going, Rupert,' I said and before he could restrain me with guile and seduce me again, I hurtled out of the bar into the street, stinging, burning tears pouring down my face. It was only the booze, I kidded myself, of course it was. Somehow I managed to get home in one piece and when I parked outside my flat I realised with horror I'd driven all the way with the hand brake on.

PART EIGHT

INJURY TIME

31

Seeing Rupert after all these years had upset me more than I could have realised. I was shattered at how easily I was swayed and overwhelmed by what had happened, or rather by what could have happened. As an antidote to my rotten conscience, knowing that I had been within a hair's breadth of betraying Paul, I devoted my spare time to putting my house in order. I had to scrub out all traces of Mr Holland. I'd had enough of going Dutch.

Paul was in a flurry of work, with cripplingly long hours, clinging on with typical determination to a job which was increasingly fragile. Telephone calls were hurried affairs and I began to snap with resentment and frustration. The only free night we planned to see each other, he called it off, saying his mother needed to see him. Worst of all, I began to compare him with Rupert, who thankfully never rang, which proved a point. With fanatic energy, I tidied cupboards, threw out rubbish, gave away to charity. My halo shone. I visited my own mother, paid bills while I could afford it and dealt with long-outstanding correspondence. I'd booked my place in heaven. I spring-cleaned my life, but somehow, the devil dust of Rupert lingered.

When Paul and I did manage to see each other, I felt awkward and all spontaneity seemed to be disappearing down the plug hole. I had done nothing wrong physically, but my feelings over Rupert remained to torment me. The worst moment came when we were in bed one night. It was late and we were both tired. We made love, but it was more of a token statement. Paul was more aggressive and silent than usual in his lovemaking and he seemed to sense that I wasn't a hundred per cent with him. I was about to get my period and all I wanted to do was to go to sleep. It had been Rupert's face I saw, not Paul's.

What gnawed at my conscience was the fact that I hadn't owned up to meeting him in Smith's. I was too frightened. Unaware of what I had done, or nearly done, Paul's concern for me was unstinting and I realised how lovely a man he was. No one was kinder, more gentle and considerate, or more loving towards me. In contrast, Rupert enjoyed the classic thrill of the chase and once his prey was captured, he lost interest. Like a cat with a shrew, he found the kill was bitter and rejected it. Rupert was merely licking his self-inflicted wounds from his mis-alliance with Abigail and I happened to be there. How could I have put my future with Paul in such jeopardy, something which was precious to me beyond words? Was it because Rupert chucked me in the first place? Why was my pride still hurt after all this time? I knew I wasn't only deceiving the one man who could save my soul but, a far greater a crime than that, I was deceiving myself.

PART NINE

EXTRA TIME

32

Although the Netherfield board was technically behind him, scurrilous rumours continued to abound and Paul sensed the sword of Damocles hanging over his head with increasing threat. 'The team's playing appallingly, with only one win and one draw in the last ten games. I've known top class managers who've been kicked out for less.'

I felt utterly helpless. I heard him sigh down the line.

'To make matters worse, the Conference is up our backsides and the only straw to clutch is that there are three other clubs in the same boat also struggling to stay in the league. I'm taking Bumble with me to Gillingham on Saturday. She might jolly the place up. I wouldn't be surprised if she dyed her hair blue for the occasion.'

I wish he'd asked me.

On the Wednesday, Mary was out at an antenatal clinic and I was trying to stay awake. The phone had been lifeless for over half an hour and no one had crossed our doorstep. My eyelids heavy, my jaw aching from yawning, I was jolted by the sudden ring of the extension on my desk.

'Hello, Millie. It's me. How are you? I'm sorry I've not been in touch since Monday. I know you of all people will understand.'

'Try me,' I said, my heart racing at hearing Paul's voice. He sounded so near that I felt I could almost reach out and touch him. 'What's the latest?'

'Everything's about as bad as it can be, frankly. The Chairman's given me an ultimatum. I feel the team don't want me to go, the devil you know and all that, but I'm almost tempted to resign instead.'

I could hear him take in a deep breath.

'The thought of being sacked is terrifying.'

Again, I felt handicapped and instead of launching into a barrage of sympathetic noises, which I feared would sound trite, I made a suggestion. 'Why don't we go and see a film tonight? I'll get a Standard and we can meet up in the West End. It'd do us both good.'

'I'd love that. I was going to do some paperwork and watch the match on Sky, but I can't face either. You choose and I'll ring you later when you know where we can meet. Speak to you later.'

So we managed to slip further into the doldrums by seeing *The English Patient*, which we both came out of in tears.

Our interlude to the 'flicks' was a one off and the club continued to make its demands on Paul's time, with a vengeance. I decided to use the evenings wisely to brush up on my virtually non-existent Thpanish. I bought the tapes and the book and settled down with a bottle of best Rioja in a gold hairnet, to put me in the mood to thrash out the language in *preparación* for our holiday, only a few weeks away. Thun, thea and thex ... thooper!

Rupert thankfully was becoming a fading memory. Learning a foreign lingo was far from an easy task and the subject matter of the first lesson defeated me completely.

I inserted tape one.

'*Nombre?*' ('Name?') a man's voice said.

'*Maria Theresa.*'

'*Señora o señorita?*' ('Mrs or Miss?')

'*Señorita a la fuerza ...*' which, loosely translated, was, 'Single, through no fault of my own ...'

The story of my life. Never mind, it might hold me in good stead should I meet a gorgeous Catalan.

Lesson two was hardly more enlightening.

'*Soy azafata.*' ('I am an air hostess')

'*Con **Ee**beria, o con **Bree**tish **I**reways?*'

This could come in very handy and then again, perhaps not. We were flying Monarch.

Mary and I were also having a hectic time. With Easter behind us and the prospect of fine weather ahead there was a plethora of properties on our books. With no shortage of buyers, we were rushed off our feet. Mary was an absolute stalwart and never complained, in spite of her burgeoning stomach, and the bell tent was filling out nicely. With all that was going on, I hardly had time to think of my own waistline and the weight miraculously began to fall off me. What a thrill it was to slip into a pair of jeans without a struggle and how easily I could put on my socks without having to sit. In comparison to Mary, I was positively anorexic.

33

'Mill, are you working next Saturday?' Paul asked me in bed, as he was watching The Premiership.

'Why?' I said in a muffled voice from underneath the duvet.

'It's the cup final and I wondered if you'd like to come with me. It'll be some occasion as it's the last one ever to be played there before they demolish the place.'

I emerged from my warm den. 'Why me? Surely you can take someone who'd really appreciate it. Who's in it?' I asked innocently.

'How can you not know, after all this time? It's between Chelsea and Aston Villa, as if you didn't know already. The Chairman's given me a couple of tickets as a reward for getting us so far in the Cup and I want you to come.'

Hmm. Chelsea and Villa, eh? Hmm. Might not be as bad as I feared.

'Okay, I'll come. Thank's very much.'

Paul laughed. 'You're so predictable. I know you'll loathe

every minute, but at least we'll be together this time – we get there early enough for lunch and then sit beside each other during the game. For once I'm merely a spectator. You might even end up enjoying yourself.'

God forbid. I opened my mouth to sp...

'Shut up a second, will you Mill? I'm trying to listen to Des.'

Oops. Sorry. Wembley, eh? I was more intrigued as to who would be in the royal box than on the pitch. 'Don't let me forget to take my binoculars,' I said out loud, by mistake.

The traffic was horrendous. The weather was boiling, way above the seasonal average and the pubs were full of supporters from both sides, happy (for now at any rate) to mingle, knocking back tankards of beer rather than seven bells out of each other.

'I don't fancy walking through this lot,' I said, as a group of Chelsea fans lurched dangerously towards us. 'I have a thing about drunks.'

'Don't worry. We've got a pass for a car park not too far from the entrance. I'll look after you.'

We climbed the concrete staircase and had our tickets checked by a cheerful girl at the door, who recognised Paul instantly. We were shown to the cavernous dining room, where there must have been several hundred people. Paul pointed across the room to Mr Thornton, the Chairman.

He was charm personified. 'Hello again, my dear. I'm delighted to see you again. I believe you got on very well with my wife, Veronica, at our barbecue. She wasn't able to come today – some charity do, or WI – so I suggested to Paul that he brought you instead. Enjoy the game!'

I didn't have much opportunity to have any further conversations, as Paul stopped and chatted with nearly everyone we met. I was quiet during lunch, too, as Paul was being bombarded by his neighbour and each time he tried to get his fork to his mouth, the neighbour asked him another question. There was no one beside me, as they hadn't turned up, and my plate was empty.

After pudding, Paul said, 'I'm just going over to have a coffee with JT. You can go outside and see the entertainment. It'll be more interesting than sitting in here. It's probably a display with the police dogs.'

Obediently, I went out into the fresh air. The noise in the stadium was deafening. Awash with the Aston Villa fans in claret and blue and Chelsea in their royal strip, the swaying of the capacity crowd made me feel dizzy. It was hard not to get caught up in the extraordinary atmosphere, when, on the far side the ubiquitous Mexican wave began to ripple its way through the stadium. Balloons were released, streamers thrown, starting pistols mingled with trumpets. A symphony of good cheer reminiscent of the last night of the Proms.

Paul joined me seconds before the National Anthem. The teams, all spic-and-span, stood in orderly rows to be presented to the dignitaries and the members of the royal family. I was proud to hear Paul sing the words, loudly and strongly. The teams were in position. The crowd hushed. The whistle blew and then with a roar the noise started again a thousand times stronger. The sun shone and I couldn't help but enjoy the emotion of being part of something so special and unique.

I won't begin to give a match report. Any of you in the slightest bit interested will know what happened. For those who don't, Chelsea won. Actually, I will allow myself one comment: it was a pret-ty bor-ing match. Yikes! Sacrilege. I shall be shot at dawn. The only real thrill I experienced was seeing Dennis Wise hold up his son, Henry, higher than the trophy. It made me feel quite broody.

34

The football season finally drew to a close. What wonderful relief. By a sheer miracle, Netherfield Town survived relegation by a winger and a prayer, to the stunned shock of everyone from players to press to public, more by default than skill. It was time for a well earned rest, but how wrong could I be?

'It's back to the drawing board for us, Mill. No time to waste. We've got a hell of a lot of work to do,' was my Paul's parting shot when I congratulated him for having kept his head above water.

'The Chairman is paying for us to go to Scotland for a few days r and r. I've got to sort out the arrangements and fix half a dozen friendlies with local clubs. Any chance you might be able to get time off?'

'No, I'd love to, but I can't,' I said, wishing I could. I think he knew all along that I'd be using up a lot of my annual holiday allowance by going to Spain. 'I'll have to give it a miss this time. Anyway, I'd get in the way. This is definitely a boy thing,' I added, laughing. 'You can let your hair down with the team. I'd only cramp your style.'

'It's a shame, but thanks for the thought. Actually, I don't know what you'd do with yourself, as we'll be playing golf and there'll be a match every evening, plus the travelling. I'll keep in touch and see you the moment we're back.'

Golf *and* football ... I could hear him say, 'Carnoustie, Troon...,' imagining the glazed-eyed look as he continued, 'St Andrews, Pitlochry...'

I was more than delighted to leave him to it.

Paul and the team left in the club coach two days later, but curiously, I received a post card from him that very morning, which I thought was extremely clever, seeing as he hadn't even left London at the time of the post mark. It depicted a saucy Donald McGill bathing beauty of massive statistics. A tiny boy stood in the shadow of the voluminous folds of her stomach.

'Has anyone seen my little Willy?' the caption read.

I took it personally, then murderously when I read what he had written on the card itself:

'Dearest Mill, surely history can't repeat itself??? See you in España!'

We'll see about that.

Hasta la vista, baby.

35

Spain beckons. Tickets and passport checked, cases packed, emptied and packed again and still bulging. Why do I even give suitcase room to something which I haven't worn for three years, for heaven's sake? What miraculous sea change will occur by switching countries? I empty everything again, mountains of fabric spilling onto the floor, only this time I worry about shoes. The list is endless: moccasins to wear on the plane, but which rub if my feet get too hot, flip flops for the beach, but they don't look smart enough for wandering around, sling backs for clubbing – you never know. You will be relieved to hear that I draw the line at gumboots. On the other hand... You will have realised by now that I am unlikely to be a modular packer. My tastes are eclectic and I'm not your black-and-white-which-goes-with-everything type of gal. I like colour and loads of it, especially when the sun is shining. I look down at the bed, or I think that's what it is, covered knee deep in clothing, as is most of the floor. Do I really need five pairs of shorts (two white and one khaki, one black and one check) and three pairs of trousers for eight days? And what about jeans? Will I get through six white tee shirts and two pullovers? What about a pac-a-mac? A cardigan? I need serious help. Is there a number I can ring in Yellow Pages for distressed packers? I nearly go and search.

Satisfied at last and having finally removed my Carmen rollers with great reluctance, I had a minor relapse and stuffed in my heated curling tongs. The case remained bulging to bursting point and I didn't dare sit on it for fear of breaking the seams already stretched to maximum. I squeezed and pushed and eventually managed to secure the zip. It weighed a bloody ton. The cost of excess luggage would far outdo the price of my ticket. Drained of energy and at the risk of slipping a disc, I lugged it into the hallway. Paul was due to pick me up in an hour and we were driving to Gatwick to catch the evening flight to Barcelona. *Olé olé olé olé*!

Unfortunately, two minutes before Paul arrived at the flat I had terminal worries about my holiday wardrobe. I undid my case for the third time and everything exploded over the hall carpet like the monster birth in *Alien*, as the door bell rang.

'What the hell do you think you're doing? Aren't you ready yet, Millie, for God's sake?' No terms of endearment, no 'Hello, darling, let me kiss you...' but, 'We're pushed for time as it is, and you haven't even started,' Paul screamed at me in a panic.

127

I sat amongst the debris and started to blub. 'I'm coming, I'm coming,' I said between sobs.

'Good, well stop mucking about and hurry up. You've got precisely three minutes, not a second longer – or I'm leaving without you.'

Many a true word spoken in jest.

Paul paced about in the sitting room, irritating me beyond belief, as I threw as much as I could back in the case.

'Please come and help me. I can't do it up,' I whinged.

'Struth, woman,' he sighed, exasperated and together we succeeded in closing the zip. My PR at zero, Paul drove like a bat out of hell, and we made the airport from the long term car park with seconds to spare. I was sweating like a pig. Once we found a trolley, we saw we needn't have worried. There was a queue a mile long at the check-in where we learned that our flight had been delayed by an hour and a quarter. There was a lot of tin to push upstairs and as we were a charter, we had to wait for a slot, allowing me time to wolf down a burger, which I regretted as soon as we were in the air. Before that, though, there was yet another very worrying moment when we thought we might not even be allowed on the flight.

'Passports?' the stewardess said, as her scarlet, inch-long talons tapped and clicked on her computer, then on her teeth.

'Passports?' Paul snarled, looking thunderously at me.

'Passports?' I repeated. 'Oh, yes, passports,' I murmured weakly, delving into my bag. Where the hell were they?

'You did bring them, didn't you? Please tell me you did.'

I bit my finger in panic, my eyes wild. 'I might have left them on the hall table...Won't keep you a sec.'

Paul's face was as tight as a drum.

'Only kidding, ha ha!' I laughed nervously, as my hand touched the friendly plastic covers. They'd slipped inside my copy of Cosmo. S H one T, that was a close squeak. Without a word of thanks, he handed them over the counter. I thought computers were meant to speed up things, progress it's called, but this took an eternity. I looked at Paul, who was pale and fidgety. I kept quiet in case he justifiably blew his top again.

'Right, Sir, er, Madam, please go to gate number 45. You'll have to hurry. They're closing in five minutes. I'll phone ahead to warn them you're on your way. Have a nice trip.'

We had to run miles, as gate 45 was virtually in Crawley town centre. There was a deathly hush as we reached our destination and having received filthy looks from the three sentinels on duty, they checked our boarding cards and let us through. We had to make our way along the whole of the plane to get to the back, which was extrememly embarrassing, as we were responsible for holding everyone up. Perspiration pouring off us, we settled in our seats.

Once I had my breath back, I had more worries to keep me busy. I am terrified of taking off, I hate landing and I don't like the bits in between. If the aircraft has the merest rattle, then I want to get off.

I know I shouldn't drink very much during a flight, one in the air worth two on the ground and all that, but I end up sinking a fair whack. I hope it will anaesthetise my terror. My rescue remedy is to study the faces of the air hostesses to see if there is any sign of fear as they dole out the tucker from the trolley. I've worked it out that if they continue to smile when I am desperately trying to keep my stomach where it should be, then all is well. If they make a sudden dash for their seats on the instructions of the pilot, then I know we're in trouble. To me air travel is an unpleasant means to an end and nothing more. Beam me up Scottie, please.

Take-off smooth, wheels returned to wherever wheels return to, climbing nicely. Seat belt sign off. Now RELAX! I look across at Paul, who is buried in the back page of the *Sun*, the *Mirror*, *Mail* and *Express* stacked on his lap. Even though I had eaten a quarter pounder at the airport, I was eagerly awaiting my tray of supper. I love those tiny pots and sealed dishes and never leave a crumb – food which even a greedy guts like me would not normally consider fit for a dog on dry land.

Paul lifted his head from the paper long enough to charm a stewardess for an extra free bottle of Rioja. 'Here, Mill, chuck your glass over. Cheers!' he said, smiling for the first time in nearly two hours.

We were more than a touch merry when we eventually landed. I left all the arrangements re collection of luggage and car to him as I was well in my cups.

Our bags appeared on the carousel remarkably fast, but there was no sign of the dreaded golf clubs. Oh yes, didn't I mention them? They are coming on holiday as well. A *ménage à trois*. If Paulie baby thinks I am going to caddie for him, he's got another think coming. I love the man, but not that much. We were still standing in the baggage hall long after the coach loads of charter passengers had disappeared.

'Might I make a suggestion?' I offered, realising that we'd been standing there like lemons for forty five minutes.

'Yes, what is it?'

'Well, you don't think it might be possible that your clubs are somewhere else? You know, a place for odd-shaped pieces of luggage? Like pushchairs? Shall I go and ask someone?'

'No. I'll go,' and off he stomped.

A few minutes later, Paul returned somewhat miffed, with his clubs slung over his shoulder. 'Why didn't you say something sooner?' he grunted.

There's gratitude for you. Eventually we collected the keys and documents for our white Seat hatchback and headed for the coast. Bravo.

In a moment of genius not often known to men, Paul had had the foresight to purchase an up-to-date map of the area. 'Mill, you'll find it in my jacket on the back seat. I need you to navigate us through Barcelona.'

Help... Danger zone. Navigate? Me? Hadn't he heard that women and maps are as incompatible as soap and little boys? Paul tangled with the congested streets, which even after ten thirty at night were as busy as the West End of London at five o'clock.

I unfolded the map. It was huge. It was also night time and I couldn't even make out whether I had it upside down or not. 'Please don't go too fast, I don't know where we are going,' I pleaded, unheard.

'Don't be daft, I'm the one driving. Hold on a mo' Mill, shouldn't we have taken that road?' he said, his head spinning 180 degrees like in *The Exorcist*.

I wrestled with the paper and hit Paul on the ear, which did nothing to improve his humour. 'Please can you stop so that we can look at it properly? The part I want is on the crack,' I cried, desperate for assistance. We were now flying up the motorway at breakneck pace, I hoped in the right direction. 'Look. We've passed the sign to Salida four times. I'm sure we should have taken the first one. We're going to have to turn round.'

Paul said nothing to appease my fears, but I saw him touch the indicator. In an uncharacteristic, unmasculine admission of defeat, we pulled into a motorway stop.

'I need a beer,' he said, taking hold of my hand. 'Come on,' and we headed for the bar.

We hadn't spoken since the last but one sign to Salida and I laid the map flat on the formica table in front of us. We were the only people there apart from a group of loud Spanish men, all drinking tots containing an unfamiliar dark alcohol. I assumed rightly that they wouldn't be much help. I fished out my pocket dictionary and flipped through the pages in the hope of enlightenment. Fuelled by a chilled San Miguel, I was even prepared to bridge the gap and ask our foreign friends to see if they could point us in the right direction. Then it struck me. I hit my forehead with the palm of my hand. 'Oh my God! Talk about stupid!'

Paul looked up at me, wondering what I was talking about.

'You'll never guess. Salida only means EXIT. It's not the name of a place after all.'

'You great lump,' he said, laughing and gave me a huge smacking kiss, much to the merriment of our gentlemen friends who at one point looked as though they might join in.

Back on the road we covered the kilometres in record time. Paul had not only been a boy scout but had also deservedly achieved the Duke of Edinburgh's gold award and was navigating to perfection. I put my feet on the dashboard and waggled my toes inside my trainers.

'Click-dunk, click-dunk, click-dunk,' went the indicator. (Salida? Ha! Now who's laughing?)

The side road was deserted. We passed through a straggly town of terraced houses, some in the process of being built from reinforced concrete, with scaffolding poles made from cut trees and not a cat or a dog in sight. Paul did stop under a solitary street lamp at one point to study the route in silence, then per-formed a nifty U-turn. We bumbled down a rutted side road, ending up at a junction devoid of signs. I didn't say anything, but I felt instinctively we should turn right. Paul switched on the reading light. Stubborn as a mule he turned left, then left

131

again, when help came in the form of the first decent set of traffic lights we'd seen since Barcelona. Huge illuminated letters indicated the way, like the star in the east, and we sailed confidently towards the coast.

The roads became single track and in the moonlight I could make out some of the countryside, which was wild and untouched. Villages appeared whose names I recognised from the guidebooks I had sneaked a look at in W H Smith's, confirming that we were nearing our destination. It made me think of Rupert. I closed my eyes and saw his face. I turned to look out of the window, in case Paul noticed. Why did I have to think of him and ruin everything?

'You've gone very quiet, Mill. Are you all right? Not feeling carsick are you?' He squeezed my hand and changed gear. 'I'll slow down a bit. These bends are a bit tight.'

It had been a long three-hour slog from the airport, including the stops, exhaustion and excitement competing brain fellows. I must have dropped off, dreaming I was on a boat, the sea rocking it in a slow, rhythmic swell. I opened my eyes, rubbed them and yawned. Thinking I must have the whirlies from the wine and the beer, the car continued to tilt and swing. Now fully awake I realised that it was the road which was turning and not my head.

'Are we there yet?' I asked, like a fractious five year old.

'Not long now, I promise,' Paul said, the patient parent.

I opened the window and was hit by the scent of pine, eucalyptus, damp night air, rotting vegetation and post sunset heat. The road snaked its way down the steep side of a mountain and then, rounding one particularly tight hair-pin bend, stretching majestically beneath us was the bay. There was a viewing area for cars off the road and Paul stopped on the edge, by the barrier. All we could hear was the *tch tch tch* of the cicadas in the branches above our heads.

'Isn't it one of the most beautiful sights in the world?'

I stared at the view. Only a few lights twinkled and the moon's reflection shone across the calm sea, like molten lead. It was paradise on earth.

'Happy holiday, darling,' he said and leaned over and kissed me, gently, tenderly.

Rupert had gone out with the tide.

36

Our hotel was at the end of a cul-de-sac. The night porter gave us our key and directions to our room, which overlooked a tiny cove with twisted pine trees reaching down to the water's edge. Exhausted, we simply scrubbed teeth and tumbled into bed. I heard us both snore.

I'm ashamed to say that after the excesses of the day before, by the time we surfaced, breakfast was a thing of the past. As midday beckoned, we took a long, hard shower and nearly missed lunch.

On the way through reception to the dining room, Paul hesitated. 'Hang on a minute, Millie. I'm going to buy some postcards, then it's done.'

I spun the carousel and caught sight of the man seated at a desk behind the counter. Speaking into a telephone, gesticulating with a tanned, immaculately manicured hand, was as perfect a dashing Don as my eyes had the good luck to behold. Endless legs, crossed at the ankles, stretched out under the desk and at the other end, an aquiline nose protruded above the proudest set of whiskers to make Des Lynam's curl up in shame.

'What do you think of this one, Mill?'

'Oh, spectactular,' I said, leering at the heavenly object as he replaced the receiver in its cradle.

Our eyes met.

'Chosen yours already, have you?' he asked, putting two back in their slots and picking out three more.

'Oh yes, without any doubt.'

'We'd better pay. You wouldn't have any change would you? I've only got notes,' he asked, checking his pockets.

I leapt at the chance to chat up my luscious Latin and impress him with my Spanish.

'Er, how much do we owe you, *por favor*?' I tried, my chest heaving and rolling my r's – spell it how you will.

'*Qué*?'

'The postcards. How much?'

'*Qué?*'

It was like walking through treacle, when, brainstorm. With triumph I almost shouted, '*Las tarjetas postales, quanta por favor?*' Where on earth did that lot come from?

'*Qué?*'

I gave up.

Paul's face was crippled with laughter, struggling to keep a straight face. 'He's having you on, can't you tell?'

'*Qué?*' I shrieked. '*Qué?*'

My admirer rubbed his moustache lugubriously and then his chin, staring at me as though I had been speaking in Urdu or Inuit. '*Es no problema, señorita. Momento por favor.*' He took the note Paul had finally extracted from his back pocket and after rifling in a drawer, he produced some coins.

Paul scooped them up, letting them fall into his trouser pocket with a jingle. I was certainly not short changed, since those dark brown eyes generously covered any deficiency. I named him Qué Guevara.

That afternoon, having imbibed the best part of two bottles of chilled Torres Viña Sol, we took a long, languorous siesta, one of the most civilised institutions ever invented by man. I woke thirsty and with a slight head.

Paul lay facing me, his blond hair pressed damply on his brow. 'We ought to go for a swim. It'll wake us up.' He stretched cat-like and walked to the bathroom.

I was tempted to call him back to bed. Instead I put on a pair of shorts (the white ones, remember?) so did Paul and we set off on an exploratory walk. The late afternoon temperature was tropical, steamy and sultry and above us the cicadas on the day shift chattered chirpily in the pine trees. Paul entwined his fingers with mine. I was so happy, happy to be away from rainy old England, happy to be here with Paul. Rupert no longer existed. Who's Rupert?

The path twisted and turned, as did my ankle, when we came upon a beach, private and away from prying eyes, accessible only by foot, or by boat. We staggered down between rocks and gnarled, exposed roots and jumped the last few feet onto clean, yellow sand. My, it was hot. I unbuttoned my shirt, the breeze catching the fine embroidered lawn, billowing it up into my face. My breasts felt heavy and full and were sticky under my bra. I wiped my forehead, moist with perspiration. Paul was sitting on a rock a few feet away, staring at me. I knew that look. I'd seen it when we were in the woods near my mother's. Great! Here we go again. *Toro! Toro! Toro!*

Some time later we flopped (Paul more so than me) in the shade of a group of sea-smoothed boulders and rested our weary bodies. I traced a heart in the soft sand.

Paul picked up my hand and kissed it. 'That was very nice, Mill. I thoroughly enjoyed that. Quite the best way to get rid of the last bit of jet lag.'

I prodded his ribs. 'I'm going for a swim.'

Not to be outdone, Paul followed me into the water, stark naked.

'Watch out for sharks!' I shouted. Regardless of anyone spying on us, I tugged off my clothing, what there was of it, and dived into the refreshing waves.

Paul swam purposefully towards me.

I duck dived underneath him, bobbing up like a seal on the other side. 'Arf! Arf!' I barked, wiping the salt from my eyes, clapping my hands above my chest as I floated on my back.

'I'm coming to get you!' Paul threatened, as he disappeared beneath the surface.

Squealing, I spun around and headed for a rocky outcrop a few yards further out, the gentle swell propelling me. The sea was crystal clear and I could see the rocks below me. Carefully placing one foot on a ledge, I felt a searing pain. 'Ouch! Bloody hell,' I yelped. Clinging onto a rock, I hauled myself out of the water and looked at the underneath of my foot. There, in the middle of my poor tootsie, as though seasoned from a giant pepper pot in an Italian restaurant, were a dozen or so black spines from a rogue urchin. 'Yeow!' I wailed again for good measure, laying on the agony.

Paul stood there dripping, casting a shadow over the injured area. 'There's only one thing to do, I'm afraid. You might not like it, but I've got to pee on it. Stick your foot out Mill, so that I can take aim.'

What? Widdle on my foot? Not on your nelly.

'Don't be such a wimp,' he laughed, brushing back a wet bang of blond hair. 'Trust me. It's an old sailor's custom.'

'Bugger the old sailor, I'm not having anyone, not even you, piss on my paw.' Never trust anyone who says, 'Trust me,' and before you could say 'Jolly Jack Tar', Paul carried out his threat with laser-like precision. It stung like mad, but do you know something? Later that night out popped the spines. You learn something every day. Someone should write a book about it.

We swam once more round the island, then headed back to shore and by the time we reached the hotel I was feeling the full effects of exposure to the sun. With most things, I tackle life head on and, true to form, yet again I'd overdone it. Having not been in anything hotter than Margate for at least two years, my old bod wasn't used to such intensity. In the cool calm of our room I fell onto the bed. 'I'm not feeling very well,' I moaned.

Paul came over and touched my head. 'Christ almighty, Mill, you're on fire.'

'One minute I'm shivery and freezing cold, then I'm boiling hot. And I feel sick,' I whimpered.

He lifted my shirt and whistled. 'You've been burned to a frazzle. You've got heatstroke. I can tell from your face. It's absolutely scarlet. Turn over,' he ordered. 'So's your back. Does that hurt?' he asked as he touched the hollow behind my knees.

'Ye-e-ess, it does,' I confirmed. 'So do my titties,' I whimpered. I twisted my sore neck so that I could see him, risking further injury in the form of a torticollis. 'Why've I got it and not you? I wore a hat and put on cream. You didn't do either. It's not fair.'

'Fair or not, it's happened and we've got to get you better quickly.' He got up from the side of the bed, opened the mini bar and took out a bottle of water. 'Hmm, there's some fizzy, no,' he said, putting it back, 'you ought to have still' and he substituted the small bottle of Fontavella for Evian. 'Here, you've got to try and drink lots of water. You're completely dehydrated.'

I sat up and started shaking again.

'Stand up for a tick and I'll help you get into bed properly.'

He pulled back the cover. My skin hurt and I tried to kick it off, but Paul was forceful and tucked it in.

'You might need a blanket. There's probably one in the wardrobe. If there's no improvement in a couple of hours, I'm getting the doctor.'

Dear Paul. He sat by me for the rest of the afternoon, bathing my forehead with a soothing, cool flannel, until I fell asleep.

I woke up alone in the dark. I turned on the light, having been woken by footsteps on the ceramic tiled floor of the landing outside our room.

Paul's caring face appeared. He looked gorgeous, already showing a bit of a tan.

'Hello, darling. How are you feeling?' He felt my head for signs of temperature. 'I've just eaten one of the best meals I can remember. You would have loved it. I had amazing gazpacho, grilled lobster, Manchego cheese and then a sort of egg custardy thing. I wish you'd been there with me.'

I groaned at the thought of food, cursing myself for having been so stupid and missing out.

'Look, I've brought you this,' he said, putting a large white plate on the bedside table. 'The head waiter was concerned when I wanted a table for one and when I explained what had happened, he beetled off to see the chef. He gave me this for you.' He lifted the silver-plated cover and revealed a selection of prepared fruit. 'If you can eat some of it, it'll do you good. Here, try a piece.'

On the end of a fork he speared a piece of sweet melon and I opened my mouth obligingly. Wonderfully soothing, it slipped down effortlessly. Then a piece of pineapple disappeared in similar fashion, then a wedge of orange. I cleared the lot. 'Thank you,' I said, gratefully, with a satisfied smile, 'I feel much, much better.' I pushed back the sheets. 'I can't believe how tired I was and I must have slept for over two hours. I'll go and do my teeth. I won't be a mo'.'

Thanks to the amount of water Paul had forced me to drink, I was feeling considerably stronger. My appetite had miraculously returned and I'd devoured my starter. We were on *demipension* after all and I was rearing to attack the main course.

Paul crawled in beside me paying great attention not to touch me in case he hurt me and lay a good foot away on his side of the bed. 'You all right, Mill?' he whispered.

'Hmm, thanks. Much better. So far so good.'

'Great. You'll be better by the morning. 'Nightie 'night then,' he said, as he turned off his light.

' 'Nightie 'night,' I echoed, turning mine on.

'Mill, what in God's name are you doing? Come out from down there immediately. You'll have a relapse.'

Wary that I might be issued with a matching red card, I took precautions. Ever the inventive one, I cried out with glee, 'Look. No hands.'

Go away, nosy parkers. Shame on you.

37

By the time the clock struck ten the next day, my sore skin had calmed down enough for me to brave the outside world. During the night, Paul had been adorable and had rubbed half a bottle of lotion into my tender parts and the other half into the skin damaged by the sun. It was a speedy cure by all accounts.

After a delicious breakfast of freshly squeezed orange juice, a bottomless cafetière and crisp croissants, we traipsed up to the hotel's seawater-filled swimming pool. Being early in the season, we missed the sun-bed battle, locating two in prime position in the shade of a cluster of palm trees. The hush was hypnotic. The only sounds were the rustling of the leaves and the rhythmic *swoosh swoosh swoosh* as a middle-aged woman swam steady lengths in front of us. From behind a straw hut a cheerful attendant appeared, bearing a bundle of fluffy blue towels. He handed us two each, one for the bed and one for after a swim. What luxury. I moved my resting place into the shade. Paul stretched out beside me and buried his nose in a fat paperback.

I dozed off.

'...To marry you...'

I was upright in a split second, quicker than a bolt of lightning. *What* had he said? Marry me? I straddled my sunbed and looked him straight in the eye. 'What did you say?' I asked.

'You didn't just ask me to marry you, did you?' I garbled, excited and flustered beyond words. 'I don't believe it! Wow! You can't possibly mean it. We hardly know each other.'

Paul responded by falling onto the floor, he was laughing so much.

'What's so funny?' I enquired, unable to see the humour in my remarks.

Clutching his stomach, aching from laughing, he spluttered, 'I didn't ask you to marry me, you clot. I simply suggested we might go further down the coast tomorrow to a pretty fishing village. It's called Tamariù.'

My jaw dropped. So, Tamariù is a fishing village. Not our forthcoming nuptials.

Paul looked at my disappointed face and creased up with another gale of hysteria. Running the corner of his towel over his eyes, he coughed twice, smothering more snorts and rolled over on his stomach. 'Oh, Mill, I haven't laughed so much in years. It hurts.'

I grunted and more than somewhat cheesed off, I wrote 'Mrs Paul Campbell' with my finger in sun cream on my chest. I'll show him, I said to myself, I'll show him . . .

True to his word, Paul organised a picnic lunch from the hotel and we drove the few miles along the coast to Tamariù, where the view made up for any misunderstanding. Snuggled between rocky outcrops covered with trees lay a sandy bay. On the hillside, bright purple bougainvillaea flashed at us, clinging to the terracotta walls of private villas. A few cafés lined the narrow promenade. The sun was hot and there was hardly a breath of wind.

We parked the car in the shade of an umbrella pine, collected our clobber from the boot and walked the short distance to the beach, passing some shops.

'Hang on a minute, Mill. I'm going to see if they've got a paper.' He vanished into the dark interior, emerging moments later with the *Sun*, a *Mirror* and what looked like the *Telegraph* tucked under his arm. 'That's good news.'

'What is?'

'The *Sun* and *Mirror* are printed out here. They're today's editions.' In his free hand, precariously he held two giant cornets.

Somehow I knew which he had bought for me. We clambered down the low parapet wall onto the sand, which filled my shoes and burned my feet, still tender from the urchin.

London seemed a world away, until Paul muttered, 'Micky Brown's been sacked.'

Not knowing Brown from Hovis, I smoothed out my towel and squidged my shorts and tee shirt into a pillow and settled down for some serious bronzing. The next half hour was interrupted with vociferous outbursts from my neighbour. I sat up and smothered myself in more lashings of factor 25 and lay back, burrowing my bottom into the sand for comfort. I closed my eyes, absorbing the warmth, like an iguana. Something tickled my ear. I turned my head to be confronted by Paul's face almost touching mine. With a mischievous glint, he planted his mouth on mine. He was a mixture of salt and vanilla, sweet and sour and divinely sexy. I was entering into the spirit of things, when he yanked hold of my arms and pulled me up. *Kissitus interruptus.*

'Come 'ere,' he said.

'But I am,' I answered, confused.

'No, *comer*. It's Spanish for 'eat'.'

The hotel had done us proud and our picnic was delicious. There was spit-roasted chicken, scarlet, sun-ripened tomatoes, a green melon cut into wedges, crusty bread, crisp, lethal spring onions as big as beetroots and a hunk of very smelly, hard cheese which proved the hit of the meal. All this washed down with a bottle of Rioja, *naturalmente*.

Stifling a burp and with a nice full tummy, I was ready for a zizz.

'I need a coffee. Want one, Mill?'

It was tempting to lie prostrate and not move a muscle, maybe even finish off that kiss, but perhaps a coffee would aid the digestion. I eased the body beautiful upwards and swathed myself in my sarong, thinking, 'Eat your heart out Cindy Crawford,' as we crossed all of ten feet to the nearest bar. It was after three o'clock but people were still arriving for lunch – Spanish time. A friendly, chubby woman took our order and returned with two small glass tumblers.

'Want a heart starter to go with it?' asked Paul, his hair sun-bleached and, if I'd had my way, sun-kissed.

140

Of course.

Paul summoned the waitress and in near perfect Spanish, a talent hitherto unearthed, requested something alcoholic, although quite which denomination, creed or colour, I couldn't make out. Swiftly, she produced a bottle from behind the chaotic bar and proceeded to pour the heftiest slugs of booze I have seen outside my mother's kitchen.

It nearly blew my socks off. 'Phwoar! What the hell's that?' I gasped, my tongue completely numb and my throat a burning furnace.

Paul roared with laughter, delighted at the effect it had on me. 'It's "Fundador". It's a cheap local brandy and it's been the cause of a few headaches in the past, I can tell you.'

Hic, hic hooray!

38

So began a love affair with Spain which was to last a lifetime, from the Catalan people and their strange language, a mixture of French and Spanish, to the exotic and yet fundamentally simple food. I discovered the delights of braised pig's cheek, *galtes*, cooked in a slow oven with thyme, carrots and onions. I tasted the tantalising flavours of *pan con tomate* – grilled bread rubbed with garlic and crimson beef tomatoes, drizzled with olive oil, sometimes with the added piquancy of salty strips of anchovy. The juicy mussels were to die for, as was the sauce, into which we dipped our bread and which trickled down our chins. Sardines were everywhere, speckled with raw chopped garlic and parsley. I loved it all. I became tipsy on strawberry cup, a dangerous cocktail of Fundador, wine, champagne and fresh fruit. We sat in the evening sunlight in the village square alongside its fortified church, in front of which sat a line of elderly, crusty, bandy-legged Spaniards, who watched the entertainment with bright button eyes and gruff humour. A Catalan orchestra played on a temporary stage, erected for a fiesta, the strange, haunting sounds from wind instruments beating a mystical, folk rhythm. We joined in, attempting to dance the complex sardana, failing miserably. This was not the harsh concrete and girder Spain of the south coast, of ex-pats and sun seekers, of new golf courses, of time share and palatial villas. This was another Spain, timeless and classy, the home of Salvador Dali and rugged coastlines. I was spellbound by the magic – heady stuff indeed. *Viva Catalunya!*

But, like all good things, it had to come to an end. I felt so at home that I began to investigate estate agents' windows, mentally adjusting the asking price from euros to pounds. We had three days left in paradise. I undid the button of my shorts and sighed with relief. All my clothes were tight and it was obvious that I had put on a couple of pounds, producing a major bout of depression that morning. We were lounging by the pool and Paul was sporting one of those goofy expressions, bewitched by a slip of a thing on his right, thinking I hadn't noticed the angle of his roving eyes through his Ray Bans. I leaned on my elbows and had a good butcher's myself. It was blonde, Swedish, about nineteen, topless and with a body thinner than one of my thighs. Enough to make you sick. At least I had a bloke with me and she only had a paperback.

As we were walking through reception to our room, my dashing don of the whiskers stopped writing. '*Ola, bon dia, señora, señor.* There is a message for you, Mr Campbell, from England. Here,' he said, taking an envelope from our cubby hole, together with our key.

Paul opened it, his jaws clenched. 'I've got to ring the club. It's a message from the Chairman.' He wrote down the number and asked for it to be dialled.

'Please go to booth number one, *señor*, it is ringing for you now.'

I studied Paul's back in the cabin and I could tell from the way he held his head and drummed his fingers on the ledge that things didn't look good. I sat in agony for ten minutes.

He reappeared, all good humour gone.

'What on earth's wrong? Has someone died? It must have been bad news.'

'I'm sorry, Millie, but I've got to get the first plane back to England. There's a crisis at the club. I'll tell you about it when we're on our way. First I have to get our tickets changed. If there aren't two places on the flight, you might have to stay here for a couple of days on your own. You'll be all right, won't you? I'm sorry, Mill, but things couldn't be much worse.'

I watched as Paul gave the information regarding his flight and ticket number, after which frantic telephone calls were made. A fax was sent and one received.

'The plane leaves from Barcelona at 7 o'clock tonight. We'd better get a move on. Oh yes, there is a place for you, that is, if you want to come with me. I wouldn't mind it if you wanted to stay.' One look at his tired, drawn face was enough.

'I'll pack. Leave it to me. It won't take five minutes.'

He squeezed my hand. 'Thanks Mill.' In silence I folded our clothes, put our wet costumes into a plastic bag and shook the sand out of our shoes. Paul left me to go and settle our account and I met him half-way, carrying our luggage to reception. There were no rows over the route this time. I drove, while Paul made calls on his mobile. A simple solution to a tricky problem, not as fast perhaps, but without incident. Luckily we left early enough and at the airport, having dropped me off with our cases, Paul was a gallant soul and returned the car back to the bay reserved for car rentals. There wasn't a kiss-me-quick hat in sight and only a few tired passengers waiting for planes to Birmingham, Luton and Gatwick.

Remarkably ours left bang on time and arrived in England five minutes early. Having rumbled the situation regarding mislaid golf clubs (which, by the way, weren't taken out of their bag), we retrieved our suitcases and caught the shuttle bus to the long term car park. I knew Paul would bring up the subject of what was going on in his own good time. We drove back to London, through dense fog in the Mole valley shrouding Leatherhead, then rain in Wandsworth.

It was nearly midnight and we had hardly exchanged two words since leaving Gatwick. Driving into my road, Paul pulled over and kissed me long and hard on the lips, tenderly and with a hint of regret.

'Please will you tell me exactly what's happening? It's driving me mad not knowing.'

'The club's about to go into liquidation, that's what,' he said, bitterly. 'The bank's finally pulled the plug on the overdraft and there's no money for next week's wages. We're in the shit.'

How I loved him at that moment. I felt utterly helpless. I wanted to hold him in my arms, to comfort him, to offer support. Before I could, Paul was up and out of the car, already opening the boot.

I stood on the pavement, feeling let down. 'Well, that's that. Thanks a million for the best holiday I have ever had.' I ached inside. 'I'm so sorry about what's happening. I wish there was something I could do to help,' I said softly.

'You're helping me by being there, Millie, when I need you,' he whispered, wrapping me in his arms. I could feel his heart beat.

He kissed the top of my head. 'I can't come in, much as I'd like to. I promised JT I'd ring him as soon as I got back, whatever time it was. I'm not looking forward to it, I can tell you. No doubt you'll have a hundred and one messages on your answerphone and I can guess mine's sizzling.'

'I understand,' I said, tears prodding the back of my eyes. 'Ring me if you need to talk. Please promise you will.'

He kissed me again, then helped me take my things inside. I watched through the sitting room window as he drove away. I hadn't switched on the light and standing behind the lace curtain I knew he couldn't see me, but he did look in my direction as he turned the car around. The room was cold from having been shut up and there was a pervading, fusty smell. I shivered. Perching on the armchair, I rewound the tape on the answerphone.

It clicked and whirred. 'You-have-one-message' it informed me courteously, Dalek fashion.

'Hello, darling. Millie? Welcome back. I've missed you. It's Mummy!' as if there was ever any doubt. 'How did everything go? Good trip, was it? How's my darling Paul? Do give me a ring when you get back and tell me all the goss. Kissy kissy.'

I decided to ring her in the morning, as it was too late to call now. There was nothing much in the post either, merely a stack of mail order catalogues (for size 16 and over – bloody cheek!) and some Tesco reward points. Had I really spent that much? No delayed Valentine cards, birthday cards in advance, premium bond win.

Nothing, zilch.

Bienvenida a la casa, Millicent.

144

39

The first thing I noticed when I saw Mary at the office on Monday was a change in her circumference.

'Hello, Millie, welcome back. You look wonderful!' she said, before I could pay her the compliment. 'It's obvious the holiday's done you a heap of good. You were looking more than a touch pasty before hand. Not enough porridge in that blotting paper and booze diet of yours.'

She was blooming, her freckled complexion strawberries and cream, her rippling, titian hair glossy as a freshly peeled conker. She waddled duck-like around the office, whistling cheerfully, dealing with everyone who came through the door as if they were long lost friends or the first people she had seen all day. She was never disconcerted with aggressive drunks, annoyed by ditherers who couldn't choose between a flat or a house, or hassled by time wasters who didn't have the money. Not even our window cleaner upset her, who spent more time occupying our chairs drinking our coffee than doing the job for which he was paid. She treated everyone with total equanimity and immense charm.

The morning sickness behind her, the new baby in front, Mary's energy was tireless. Although she had opened that account at Mothercare and a subsequent one at Baby Gap, she hadn't gone totally overboard.

'You'll never believe this but William's mother has come up trumps,' she said, stretching to reach the back of the top drawer in the filing cabinet, straining as she stood on tiptoes. 'I always thought of her as being a horrible old dragon – William's scared stiff of her, so's his father – but she's given us a mass of old baby clutter which he had as a little boy. We've got an old wooden cot, which she's repainted and restored, with a fresh quilt and padded sides, and of all things, a playpen. Can you imagine any baby of mine staying in that?' she laughed. 'What's more, she has given us a magnificent coach-built pram which apparently has trundled three generations of McCarthys around Kensington. I'll need an HGV licence to drive it. She's also thrown in a new Moses basket and a heap of other bits and pieces. It's quite embarrassing, as we'll hardly have to buy anything.' Mary fumbled in her desk drawer. 'She's also given me this,' she said as she extracted a much thumbed edition (probably a first) of Dr Spock.

'Have you thought of any names?' I asked one day, when things were quiet, toying with the teaspoon in my coffee. It had become a game. Rather than cogitate over the *Telegraph* crossword, which had become increasingly difficult of late, thinking up names proved a perfect option.

'Well, you see, sweet William is utterly convinced it's going to be a boy and I feel that it's going to be a lassie. So we have a problem. He keeps coming up with Hamish, Rory and Jamie and all I can suggest is Tansy, Lily and Nell. I think I'd prefer to wait and see exactly what I've produced before we make up our mind. What if it's a hulking ten pounder and a girl?'

I saw her point.

Everything had become anti-climactic after the trip to Spain. The good news with Netherfield was that the bank was being held at bay, for the time being at any rate. Much against his better judgement, Paul had succeeded in selling two of their best players to a first division side and had loaned a thirty year old from some club, but I couldn't remember which. He'd been a big name apparently and the hope was that he would inspire the team and lure the crowds back, filling the coffers at the same time. Although there are a few promising youngsters who've grown up with Netherfield, youth can't compete with experience and Paul was hoping he would show them the way.

We were back to the old, erratic routine of seeing each other when we could. The press was after him every day, spreading doom and gloom. There was even a hint of scandal regarding the Chairman's tax payments – or lack of – and off-shore investments, but after threatening to sue the paper in question, they backed off. Paul's hands were filled with a desperate, uphill struggle trying to get the team into shape for the season ahead, which was only days away. The sequence of disasters continued and when we didn't think it could get any worse, some boorish yobs broke into the ground the night before a testimonial and destroyed part of the pitch, demolishing the goal posts into the bargain. It wasn't an easy time for Paul.

As if his worries weren't enough, there was a disconcerting happening at the office. For the past three weeks flowers had been arriving addressed to me, but I didn't know from whom and instead of being flattered, it upset me. Mary stoically said not to worry, but I couldn't help it.

One morning there was a message attached to a dozen red roses. It read, 'From your mystery man.'

It was becoming increasingly creepy. I racked my brains as to who could be responsible when something struck a chord. I waited until Mary put down the telephone, having fixed an appointment for a valuation. 'You haven't by any chance noticed that man, have you, the one who drives a green car and buys his paper every evening next door?'

'Hm? Sorry, which car?'

'The man in the green car who parks outside the office every day. He's got bushy grey hair and thick specs. I think it's him, the phantom flower-sender.'

'I know who you mean. He looks perfectly normal to me.'

'That's the whole point,' I said, chewing my nails.

'What makes you think it's him? It could be anyone in the world. He seems harmless enough. He's too old and normal to do something like this.'

'That's exactly my point. He sort of blends in, but when I leave the office for home, whichever route I take, he's always there behind me, or beside me at the lights. I've never thought about him before, but I'm convinced it's him.' I rearranged the papers on my desk in an attempt at tidiness. 'If you don't mind, Mary, I'd like to go now, before he gets here. With any luck I'll miss him.'

'Buzz off. I'll lock up. William should be here in a minute anyway. Off you go. See you in the morning.'

I walked the fifty or so yards to my flat, feeling confident that I had possibly outwitted him. As I approached the front door, I stopped in my tracks. Someone had placed a jam jar filled with water and a bunch of mixed, simple, garden flowers. I looked around and the crescent was quiet. No sign of a green car, or the nondescript man with a shock of grey hair and glasses.

He knows where I live.

40

I hardly slept a wink that night, frightened he might try and break in. I saw strange shapes, heard noises, creatures leaping at me through the curtains, my imagination running wild. I feared the worst and predictably next morning, another huge bunch of roses arrived at the office addressed to me, two dozen in all. I felt sick. Shaking, I rang the florist's number printed on the card.

I explained the situation to them. 'I really need to know who's responsible. You must understand as it's getting beyond a joke, in fact, I'm going to call the police. Please can you tell me who it is?' I begged.

'Oh, I'm sorry love, I'm not at liberty to give you that information,' a man with a strong Welsh accent replied.

'You have to tell me,' I repeated with more than a hint of panic in my voice. 'He's following me home at night and he knows where I live.'

'Oh, that's awful, but I honestly don't know his name, look, although he's a regular customer and always pays cash, see. But listen, love, if it's any help, I think he works in the motor trade. That's all I know, honest to goodness. Sorry I can't be of more assistance.'

'Mary, I'm going next door to see John. He might know who he is.' John's the old dipso who runs the ramshackle general store and my supplier of Twix bars in bulk. Even though he's generally more than three sheets to the wind, he's always on hand and willing to help if we have trouble from the winos, if Arthur, our boy on the beat, isn't around. He was serving a customer and I took a special offer packet of digestives from the shelf while I waited. 'John, you know that bloke who comes in every evening to buy a *Standard*? The middle-aged one with glasses and the green car?'

'Yes, lovely. What about him? Not bothering you, is he? If he so much as...'

'Well, he hasn't actually done anything, yet, so to speak. I'm not even sure if it is him, but I've been getting all these flowers and whoever it is, knows where I live.' My lip wobbled. 'I'm frightened.'

'Do you want me to have a word, lovely, is that it? Leave it to me. No problem. I'll deal with him,' John said kindly, concern furrowing his brow, as he rubbed his fat, hairy knuckles, cracking them at the same time.

On the dot of six o'clock the familiar green saloon drew up outside, only this time, instead of sitting in the car after having purchased his evening paper, as soon as he was behind the wheel, he roared off. Mary and I looked at each other.

'Well, that's a development. Do you think John's said something?' asked Mary.

We didn't have long to wait as moments later he came puffing into the office and, sitting down, said, 'Well, that's him sorted once and for all. He was definitely your man, Millie. He'll never bother you again, mark my words. Before he could pay for his paper, I grabbed him by the lapels and said, 'if ever I hear you have been following that little girl next door again, I'll set the cops on you,' and off he buggered! And without paying, would you believe?'

'Oh John, I could kiss you,' I said, if only for the use of the word 'little', but I beat a hasty retreat as he smelled rather too strongly of whisky. I was nearly in tears with relief. It had been a thoroughly unpleasant experience, I can tell you, and although he didn't actually admit to John that he was responsible, we never saw him again.

QED.

41

The phone was ringing when I unlocked my flat door. I rushed over before the answerphone picked it up.

'Millie? It's me, Paul.'

I dropped my bag to the floor and sank in the armchair.

'Hello, I've just this minute come in. It's wonderful to hear your voice. How are things?'

'Oh, no worse, thank God. In fact, I wondered if you can get Mary to do Saturday for you. It's our first game of the season and we're at home. I rather hoped you might be free. It would give me some moral support knowing you're up there, cheering.'

Bang goes the shopping spree. Deep breath, cross fingers. 'Well, I was going to host an Ann Summers party, but I can cancel.'

'A what?'

I didn't elaborate. 'Of course I can change with Mary. She's a brick. No probs.' I kicked off my shoes and rubbed a sore toe. 'I was thinking. You've never met Mary, but I know she approves of you.'

'Thanks a bunch,' he said, laughing.

'Well, I'd also like you to meet William. I'm sure you'll get on, although he's not exactly sporty, as is glaringly obvious from the start. Do you think we could ask them to have supper with us, our shout? She's a bit down at the mo', feeling fat and ugly. I sympathise. There's a restaurant round the corner from where they live and it means they wouldn't have to take the car.'

'Yeah, that's a great idea. I adore pregnant women. They ooze sex.'

I rang and booked a table in the restaurant over Putney Bridge and we arranged to see them there the next night. I made my own way and my heart leaped as I recognised Paul's car parked outside. Although we spoke on the phone nearly every day, we hadn't seen each other for what seemed like ages and when I clapped eyes on him I saw how deep the worried lines of tension had become.

He smiled as I approached and put his arm affectionately around my shoulders. 'Here, give us a kiss. Mill, you look terrific and ... mmm ... you smell heavenly,' he mumbled, sniffing into my collar. 'You are an instant tonic. Sometimes I hate my job, but you'll always be there for me, won't you?'

Something shifted in the pit of my stomach and I pretended not to hear the last sentence as we headed for the restaurant. Our table was half-way along one side, with a bench against

150

the wall and two chairs. I sat on the bench with Paul opposite me.

'How've things been?' he asked, taking off his jacket and slipping it over the back of his chair.

I told him about the stalker.

'Why in heaven's name didn't you ring me? I might have been able to do something,' Paul said, deeply concerned. 'I've got friends in the Met. You are an idiot, taking the law into your own hands. It might have made things worse. Do you think he'll bother you again?'

'God, I hope not. I've never felt threatened before. It was frightening knowing someone was watching and I didn't know who. I think after the way in which John dealt with him, it's unlikely he'll be back. I certainly wouldn't. We haven't seen him since. Oh,' I said, seeing a kerfuffle at the entrance, 'I think Mary and William are here. '

Resplendent in a delicate flowery peasant dress, her russet hair pinned loosely on the top of her head and without a trace of makeup, Mary was the epitome of a luscious, fecund milk-maid.

Paul stood up to greet her, kissing her warmly on both cheeks as she introduced him to William. 'You look quite beautiful,' he said in all honesty.

'Whoof! Thanks, Paul, don't look so bad yourself,' Mary said, as she eased her bulk beside me. 'You'll have to pull the table out a bit, I'm afraid, William, as not all of me wants to get in.'

He fussed over her like a tender mother hen. 'It's great to see you again, Mill. It's been far too long. At last she's brought you out from under wraps, Paul,' he said, shaking hands enthusiastically. 'How are things at the club?'

Paul looked at me, raising one eyebrow, surprised at the question.

'William doesn't, er, follow football, do you, William?' I said, patting him on the arm, in an effort to explain the ignorance of his remark.

'Oh, sorry. Did I make a blunder?' he said, unfolding his napkin and tucking it into his shirt front, to our amusement. 'The bib? Make rather a mess, I'm afraid. Did Mary tell you we're on the look out for a house? The flat's going to be far too small for three of us and definitely a no-no if my mother

151

comes to stay. We'll never all fit. There's barely room for her broomstick.'

Mary hadn't mentioned anything about a move.

'Yes, Mill, we've been thinking of moving since I knew I was pregnant, but haven't done a heap about it, what with one thing and another. But we saw a cottage in Brook Green on Monday. It's only got a tiny garden, but it does have three bedrooms and doesn't need too much work. We were wondering if you could spare the time to go and see it, you know, check it over for us. My mind is too befuddled to see problems and pitfalls and it would be such a help.'

'Of course I will. It sounds lovely. Any time,' I said, wistfully.

We sank a whole bottle of Frascati before our food arrived, that is Paul, William and I did, as Mary was a good girl and burped her way through a bottle of Perrier. We all chose the same delicious starters from the blackboard, onion and mushroom tartlets. Then I had grilled sea bass, Paul had a steak and Mary and William decided on lamb chops. Half way through the main course, Mary's appetite went on the blink and as she knows only too well I'm never one to look a gift sheep in the mouth, she surreptitiously swapped my empty plate with hers. I devoured her cutlets as discreetly as I could and half listened to Paul and William discussing politics. Mary and I looked at each other.

In a lull in the conversation and completely out of the blue, she piped up, saying wickedly, her merry eyes dancing wildly, 'When are you two love birds going to put us all out of our misery and get married?'

That stopped them in their tracks and you could have heard a ballot paper drop. Paul's face ran the gamut of colours from white to green to grey and then purple in a matter of seconds and I was frightened he would explode as he nearly choked on a piece of meat.

'Come again?' he coughed, dislodging the culprit.

'Married, the two of you. When's it going to be?' Mary persisted.

'Er, we're not getting engaged, I mean, well, we haven't discussed it,' I offered bravely, letting Paul off the hook. 'Anyway, we've only known each other for six months. That's not nearly long enough.'

'What utter nonsense and poppycock,' she retaliated, in full

152

flow and not to be outdone, looking adoringly at her husband. 'It took darling William three whole days to ask me to marry him and even then he said he would have the first day we met, didn't you, William, but you didn't want to frighten me off! Come on, Paul, it's high time you did your stuff.'

William leaned over and kissed her on the nose. In contrast, the object of my desire was looking more uncomfortable by the minute and seemed ready to do a bunk.

'Six months is plenty of time. Goodness me, it's half a year,' Mary battled on. 'If you don't know each other by now, warts and all, then you never will,' she finished triumphantly, picking up a chop bone on my – her – plate and nibbling at it voraciously.

Paul was now laughing hysterically. 'Hey, Millie, remember Ta-*mariú*?' he asked, when he finally managed to speak, emphasising the last two syllables.

I'm afraid I didn't find it very funny. If the truth be known, I would have sold my mother to the devil, which would have been cheap at the price, to marry Paul. We're compatible, the right age, whatever that was and in love. A perfect combination. Or was it a double-edged sword? If I was really honest with myself, would I consider leaving London and traipsing after him around England wherever his work could lead him? I *like* living in the south east, that's where my friends and family are and I simply couldn't entertain the thought of living in the wilds of Lancashire, Northumberland or Yorkshire. It sounds horrendously selfish, I know it does, but deep down I'm aware of my limitations. Maybe with all the odds loaded against us we might survive a long-distance affair should he be sent away, but I doubted it. I know myself too well. Look at my semi-dormant feelings for Rupert, a case in point. I'm ashamed to say I sat there and sulked.

Mary was about to say something else when William became all husband-like and said in a slightly admonishing tone of voice, 'Leave it, poppet, look at the poor bloke.'

The 'poor bloke' had tears running down his face and looked quite mad. He picked up his napkin and blew loudly into it and wiped his eyes. 'Oh, dearest Millicent. I didn't mean to laugh, but your face. It was a picture.' He creased up with renewed mirth.

153

There was nothing at all wrong with my face, or so I thought, except it was beginning to turn puce with humiliation. The last thing I wanted was a public display of a vote of non-confidence.

Paul, sensing that I was on the verge of tears said, the laughter at last on the wane, 'Look, Mill, I'm sorry. I didn't mean to upset you. It was only a bit of fun. Here, have a sip of wine. Don't look so miserable, there's a good girl.'

Good girl? I'd show him good girl.

'Oh, Millie,' added Mary apologetically, 'it's all my fault. I shouldn't have opened my big, stupid mouth. I am sorry, truly. It's just that with the baby and my hormones up the spout, I seem to go off at the deep end sometimes. Will you forgive me?'

I muttered a curt 'yes' and helped myself to the wine, but I didn't feel like drinking it. As none of us wanted any coffee, Mary and William not drinking it any way, Paul slipped his credit card into the saucer and paid the bill.

'You okay, Millie? You look upset,' Mary said, her voice concerned.

I clamped my mouth shut as I knew the wrong words would tumble out. How I wish things had been different, but you couldn't undo what was said and done. At least her comments hadn't frightened off Paul, only made him laugh. Perhaps I should try to see the joke, too.

The McCarthys left us outside the restaurant and, having kissed them goodbye, I watched them enviously as they walked away comfortably arm in arm to their flat a few streets away.

'Come on Mill, give us a hug. I'm sorry, you know I didn't mean to hurt you,' Paul whispered in my ear, as he held me in his chunky, woolly arms.

Oh, it felt so good to be wrapped up tightly and suddenly I felt much, much better. I'm never able to stay cross with him for long.

'There, there,' he said soothingly, stroking the skin of the small of my back underneath my pullover.

Ten minutes earlier I would have accused him of being a patronising bastard, but now I relished the sentiment his words inspired.

'I ought to be going as it's getting late.' He paused, moving away slightly, lifting my chin in his fingers. 'Want to come back with me?'

154

I tugged at a loose thread on his sleeve, tempted to push it through to the other side, to hide the snag. 'No,' I said, my voice full of regret, 'better not. I'd love to, but I can see you're shattered. It's been a foul week for you and I have a feeling you'd rather be on your own. I'm fine now, thanks, the attack of the vapours is over.'

He drew me to him again and kissed me deeply, but with a tinge of sadness. Familiar, delicious tingles began to creep downwards, as I kissed him back. I was on the point of changing my mind to follow him straight round to Redcliffe Gardens, but I had a nine o'clock appointment and no change of clothes, as I hadn't quite moved my toothbrush into his flat.

'I'll give you a ring, Mill, as soon as I can. I've got a board meeting tomorrow and it could go on until well after lunch, then there's a reserve match. I'll ring you in the evening. Sweet dreams, darling. At least we'll see each other at the game on Saturday, if not before.'

Ah yes, the match. I'd completely forgotten I'd said I'd go. The sacrifices I have to make for true love. I had planned on going on a huge shopping spree, but duty called. If I so much as clapped eyes on Mr Thornton, I was in danger of saying a few home truths in Paul's defence. During the night I had a premonition of disaster, which was confirmed at two minutes past seven the next evening when, on arriving back from work, I heard the menacing tones of the phone ring. I managed to reach it before the answerphone switched itself on and gasped,

'Yes, who is it?'

'It's me. Are you all right? '

'Yes I'm fine, a bit tired though. I've just got in. We've had a pig of a day. Nothing went right and we spent the entire time chasing our tails. What's more, Mary was ratty and she's never in a bad mood. I think she's getting panicky about the birth.' I gulped, pooped from running up the stairs two at a time. I explained, 'Sorry I'm so out of breath. Hang on a sec,' I puffed, as I extricated my free arm from the sleeve of my raincoat. Then I remembered the board meeting. 'How did it go today? What did they say?' There was an empty silence. 'Paul? Are you still there? What's wrong? Was it worse than you thought?' I knew he was still on the line as I could hear the rustle of paper.

The silence was agonising, then he spoke with a voice which cracked with emotion. 'It's bad news, Mill, as bad as you can get. Even though we've temporarily pacified the bank, if we don't perform soon I'm out. Also, to make matters worse, our major sponsors have cancelled their contract, so that's a whack of our income up the spout. We were counting on them for this week's payroll. They've supported Netherfield for eight years. God only knows how we'll get another company interested with the way things are. We've managed to persuade Bryan Johnson to come on a free. He's got a healthy goal-scoring record but it's hardly enough to make a difference and I need at least two more experienced players to give us half a chance. We've got no money, we've got injuries, some long term and the team seems to have lost the spirit they had during last season's Cup run. It's going to be an uphill struggle and if we don't get our act together in the next eight days, that, my darling, is it.'

I sat there, yet again impotent and unable to offer any help or advice. I'd never heard him say so much in one fell swoop. Things were really bad. 'Oh Paul, I wish I could do – or say – something positive. You're doing a job no one in their right mind would take on and all you seem to get are knocks. It isn't fair. Surely the Chairman can find a tame friend who'll sponsor the club, even to tide you over for the next month or two?'

'It's not as easy as that. I wish it was. It's complicated and no company will want to associate itself with a club which is going down the pan. I'm not too sure I do. At least I've still got a pay packet for the time being and with the help of the couple of new players, we can try to start the new season in the right frame of mind. I'm off to Cardiff tomorrow, but I'll be back on Saturday morning' He paused. 'God, I hate hotels. I'll miss you, Mill,' he whispered.

I had never heard him so depressed, his even temperament and sense of humour were the first things which appealed to me, apart from his looks, that is. For two pins I would have driven over to Redcliffe Gardens, but for once I knew it was better not to interfere. He had urgent calls to make and also had to be away early in the morning, so reluctantly I left him to lick his wounds on his own. Neither of us was in the mood for a long conversation and we said our lacklustre goodbyes. I replaced the receiver and could feel the inevitable tears stinging my eyes. Rubbing my lids to take away the urge to cry, I remained sitting in the dark room for some time. I could offer no advice, no suggestions, nothing except listen. Unusually for me I wasn't hungry.

42

It was tipping down a deluge of monsoon proportions when I left for work the next morning, saturating, penetrating rain. Driven by a biting wind it looked as though it was there for the day. Typical August weather. All the parking spaces were taken, mostly by a pantechnicon which straddled the curb outside John's shop delivering crates of beer, forcing me to leave the car miles away from the office. Disgruntled, I skidded and splashed along the pavement, not stopping to buy my paper and dived in through the door, standing on the mat, drenched to the bone. My shoes leaked.

'Och, you poor drowned rat,' Mary said sympathetically, glancing up from her *Telegraph*, as she eyed my hair plastered to my head. 'Thanks again so much, Millie, for the other night,' she said, as I shook myself like a dog. 'It was a real treat as it's been ages since William and I have been out for a decent meal. I'm sorry I brought up the subject of you and Paul. William was very cross with me afterwards and he's never bad tempered with me unless it really matters. He could see how upset you were. I'm truly sorry.'

'Don't give it another moment's thought,' I said forgivingly, as I shook the wet from my ineffective umbrella. 'We've got an understanding, Paul and I, so don't let it worry your pretty head any more,' I said brusquely. 'I need a coffee' and without waiting for an answer I went into the back room and plugged in the kettle.

'I still think he should marry you,' I heard her say.

'Mary,' I yelled, 'That's enough.'

She stood in the doorway, her arms folded across her bump.

157

'Och, I'm sorry, but I do. You're ideally suited and he's a great guy. He's far too good to let slip through your fingers. Someone else will snap him up, to be sure and if I wasn't married to William, I'd have a go myself. So there.'

I threw her a thunderous glare and she stomped back to her desk. I stirred our coffees and ungraciously dumped hers on the desk.

Undeterred by my threats, she looked at me over the top of her half-eye spectacles. 'I mean it, Millicent, I'm perfectly serious and I won't let it go,' she smiled. 'You ought to get married and settle down. It would do you so much good.'

'I know you mean well, Mary, but I'm going to have to sit on my hands because in all the years I've known you, for the first time – EVER – I feel like thumping you.'

She shut up for a second, not entirely sure if the threat was genuine.

'Oh, you're right of course,' I said, calming down a peg, 'you always are. I do love Paul. I adore him. He's the best thing that's ever happened to me.'

'Then why on earth don't you *do* something about it?'

'How can you say that? You saw what he's like. If I so much as hint at rings, or look sideways at a church, he comes out in spots. I'm not going to jeopardise things at this stage and frighten him off for good.'

'Of course you won't, not if he's the sort of man I think he is. He simply needs to get used to the idea, that's all – like all men.'

'I wish I had your confidence. I spend so much time on my own, it gives me ample opportunity to analyse and dissect our relationship. Why does he have to do such a ghastly job, Mary? He knows I hate football. I hate everything about it, except him, of course. He's up to his neck in problems at the moment and I'm being absolutely useless.'

Mary chewed the end of her pen thoughtfully. 'It's clear you still know diddly squat about the nation's favourite game, but have you tried to like it, or to show an interest, a teeny bit?'

'I know, I know, football's terribly cool now and *everybody's* into it, but I seem to have a complete and utter mental block when he starts talking about technical things and the team. I haven't a clue who they are and by the time I get to recognise the odd face, they've buggered off to another club and I'm back to square one. I don't know which positions they play and what's worse, I've got to go to the match on Saturday. I vowed I'd never set foot in a stadium again, after the last time.'

Mary blushed, realising she had sailed a touch too close to the wind for comfort. 'I'm only rabbiting on about you and Paul because I know you're perfect together. I want you to be as happy as William and me, that's all and if I stick my beak in it's only because I care.' She purposefully snatched up a pile of papers. 'There, I've said my piece. You know I don't mean to meddle, as there's nothing worse, so I'll shut up. You have a difficult decision to make and I know you'll make the right one, without any help from me.'

I noticed with alarm that her hands were puffy. 'Mary, I wish you wouldn't worry about me. Of course I won't hold anything you've said against you. I know you mean well and if you hadn't said what you did I would have wondered why.'

Her eyes glistened and I could feel tears weren't far off for me, either.

'Thanks for being such a dear friend. You never know, Paul might surprise us all one day by popping the question. Either that, or I'll have to wait for Leap Year.'

PART TEN

SECOND YELLOW CARD

43

Before I knew it, the football season had started again with a vengeance. Summer had flown past with the speed of greased lightning and we were back to the rituals of Saturday afternoon, *Grandstand*, full time results and league tables. Netherfield Town were home to a Midlands side. I saw very little of Paul at the game – oh yes, I went – and his time, as usual, was completely taken up with the team, the supporters renewing their pressure on the board and Paul to pull a rabbit out of a hat.

'And what do they propose we buy them with?' he asked reasonably, referring to the fans' bloodlust for new players. 'Unless a fairy Godmother appears, or someone wins the Lottery, we haven't got a cat in hell's chance.'

Saturday was gloriously sunny and warm, the team done good and by the time the final whistle blew you could smell autumn in the air. You could also smell triumph. Paul not only survived the opening day of the season, but the boys hammered the opposition 3–0, which was the best result in our division.

I was sitting patiently as ever, in the Ladies' Room, when Paul poked his head around the door.

'Can you spare a minute, Mill? I'd like you to meet some people.'

I collected my things, said goodbye to Veronica Thornton and followed him out into the draughty corridor.

'We're going to their box. It's along here. They've sponsored

160

the match today and I'd like to introduce you to the boss. You could charm them and do your two pennyworth. Oh, by the way, they're insolvency practitioners.'

Talk about vultures hovering. Things did look bad.

We crept up another back staircase, along yet another corridor, until Paul eventually knocked on an anonymous door. The room was noisy and filled with smoke, and true to form, ninety per cent male. Paul took me by the hand and we eased our way through the guests. He stopped by a harassed, dark-haired man with a moustache, aged about forty five. He was wearing a black suit and a Netherfield tie. There was enough dandruff on his shoulders to fill a snowstorm toy and I practically had to stand on my hands to prevent myself from dusting it off.

'Millie, I'd like you to meet Lawrie McNee, senior partner of Broadley's. Lawrie, this is a friend of mine, Millie Palmer-Ede.'

We shook hands politely, but someone caught my eye over Lawrie's shoulder. There was a familiarity about the straight, slender back of the man in heated conversation with two others. 'Er, I do beg your pardon, I thought I saw... Sorry, how do you do?' I said, tripping over my words. 'You're insolvency practioners, I gather,' I laughed nervously. 'Come to wind up the club?'

Paul kicked me sharply on the shins, at the same time grabbing hold of my arm. Through clenched teeth he said, 'Would you excuse us, Lawrie, I've seen someone I need to talk to urgently. I'll be back in a minute.' His grip tightened and in a low, tight voice, he said, 'And you, Madam, you're coming with me.'

He pulled me away with more force than I thought possible.

When we were out of Lawrie's hearing, he said, surprisingly angry, 'What the hell's got into you, Millie? I can't believe you actually said what you did. "Are you insolvency practioners?"' he mocked, imitating my voice. 'Have you gone completely off your trolley? Are you stark, staring mad?'

Not half as mad as you, I thought. 'Oh, Paul, I'm sorry,' I said, furiously trying to back-pedal. 'It popped out, that's all. I'm always doing it – saying stupid things. You know I am. Putting my foot in it. It's like meeting a blind man,' I garbled, talking faster and faster, 'and saying, don't you think it's a wonderful sunset, or telling a one-armed man that he can do it single-handed. I didn't mean to, honestly I didn't.'

161

'Well, you might have got away with it. With any luck he didn't actually register what you said, what with the din and everything, but I do beg you in the future to try and *think* before you speak, please, for my sake, if nothing else.'

I had upset him considerably as I had committed the heinous crime of embarrassing him in front of a client. Before I could apologise further, an overpowering feeling surged through me. It was as if someone had walked over my grave and a billion watts hit home. Two feet away from us stood Rupert.

'Hi, Paul,' he said, slapping him on the back. 'Great game. You knocked the hell out of them in the second half. Congratulations. An excellent result.' He wasn't looking at Paul as he spoke, but staring at me, full frontal. 'Hello, Millie, darling. What a treat. How lovely to see you again,' he said, kissing me on both cheeks proprietorially.

Paul understandably looked astonished. 'Oh, you two know each other, do you? It's a small world. Kept that one quiet, Rupert.' He loosened his grip on my arm. 'Where did you meet, eh Mill?'

Mercifully, Lawrie came over and whisked Paul away before I had to reply. Heaven knows what answer I would have conjured up. I looked at my feet, wishing I could be a million miles away, but for once it wasn't because of the football.

'You look magnificent, sweetheart, as ever.'

He was so cool.

'Paul's the latest bloke, eh? Always was a lucky bastard. You could've done worse, I suppose. How long's this little jolly been going on?'

I looked around the room in panic, hoping to spot a familiar face I could run to for help.

'You won't escape me this time,' he said confidently, reading my thoughts.

He was so close I could smell the heavenly mix of Trumper's cologne and Johnson's baby powder. I felt dizzy. 'How ... how do you know Paul?' I asked, desperately trying to keep my voice on an even keel.

Casually he fingered the lapel of my jacket. 'Hmm, nice shmatte. Cashmere? Present from Paul?'

I jumped, as if electrocuted.

'What was it you asked? Oh, how I know Paul. Ah yes. We

162

were at ... er, I met him through the chaps I'm with today, years ago. Clients of mine.'

Something jarred. I opened my mouth, gasping for air like a stranded goldfish, confused.

'Yes, my darling?' asked Rupert, humour twisting his gorgeous mouth in a devilish grin.

'Um, I was going to say, er, mention, I didn't know you liked this kind of thing, football I mean,' I said, trying to avoid his eyes. 'I always thought you were more a rugby man.' My insides shuddered and I felt naked, vulnerable, wet.

'Oh, I am, but I'm only here because of Broadley's. Recently they wound up a client of ours. We were stung pretty heavily, I have to say. Bang went my bonus. They invited me to the game as a sweetener.' He moved perceptibly closer. 'I gather Lawrie's a vice president of Netherfield. You're right, as ever, darling,' he drawled, 'I'd rather've gone to Twickers, or at a pinch, Chelsea, but there y' go.'

For someone who normally has to staple their mouth to stop the flow of verbal diarrhoea, I became as silent as a church mouse. I looked properly at Rupert for the first time since we had bumped into each other in Smith's a couple of months ago. He was leaning against the pale, wooden panelling, his arms crossed casually across a Turnbull & Asser shirt, no tie, Gieves & Hawkes blazer, Ralph Lauren chinos and those Gucci brogues. Elegant, expensive, dangerous. He shot his cuffs, revealing square silver links shaped like computer monitors, with the logos 'Floppy' and 'Hard' engraved in white enamel. 'Do give me your telephone number, darling, please. It's been wonderful seeing you again and I want to see more of you.' He smiled wickedly. He'd lost nothing of his old charm and pick-me-up lines. Subtle wasn't Rupert's style.

Help, help, help, he still has the power to unnerve me completely. I glanced over to see if Paul had noticed anything peculiar in my reactions, but he was in an animated conversation with Lawrie, his head tilted to one side, nodding affirmatively. A sixth sense made him realise I was staring and he winked back.

I blushed. 'Wh ... what was it you were saying, Rupert?'

'Can't remember, sweetheart. Couldn't have been anything of any importance. I'll fetch us a glass of wine. I doubt very much there's bubbly. Don't move.'

I was riveted to the spot and wild horses couldn't drag me away. I chewed my nails. I should leave now and explain later.

Rupert was jostled by a group of men to his right. 'Here we are, Millicent. Get this down your gullet. Can't guarantee it's drinkable, but it's all there is. Load of cheapskates.'

I took the glass he offered, emptying it in two expert slugs. Stifling a burp, I began to tremble big time.

Rupert took my hand, a pucker of concern creasing his smooth, tanned forehead. 'Are you all right, Millicent? You've gone quite pale. Christ, you're not about to throw up, are you?' he asked anxiously.

I remembered that he was unbelievably squeamish and couldn't even cope with a child being ill, let alone a dog. I laughed internally at the memory of my first date with Paul. 'No, of course I'm not. You've nothing to worry about. It's a bit of a shock seeing you, that's all. Out of the blue. Here.' I wiped away beads of perspiration which were prickling my brow. 'I need some fresh air. Please excuse me.'

I rushed out, bumping into people in my way and stood in the drafty corridor, breathing deeply. I closed my eyes, but I could still see Rupert's wonderful face. He appeared beside me.

'Here, sit down, I've brought one of these frightful plastic chairs. Put your head between your knees. It'll make you feel better.'

You used to do that to me, Rupert, all those years ago and yes, it did make me feel better... I dug my fingernails into the palm of my hand to hurt myself. Put a sock in it Millie, will you?

'Is everything okay out here? What's happened, Mill? I saw you disappear as if the cops were after you. Aren't you feeling well?' Paul asked with concern.

'She came over all faint and needed some air, that's all,' Rupert explained. 'The room's crowded and you must admit it is a trifle stuffy in there.'

I looked wildly from one to the other, comparing them. Points, advantages, disadvantages of each clattered through my brain at a hundred miles per hour. They collided mid-stream. One tall, dark and menacingly beautiful, the other blond, kind, generous and adorable. Beelzebub and the Angel. And I fancied them both. I could no longer decide whether I was batting or bowling.

164

'If you can hold on for a bit longer, Millie, I'll take you home, but I need a couple more minutes with Lawrie,' he said apologetically. 'Rupert will look after you, won't you? You're in good hands, Mill.'

Little did he know.

'Millie, I have to see you again,' Rupert interrupted urgently in a hushed voice, stroking my face so swiftly, I wasn't sure if it was the breeze or his hand. 'I must. I couldn't leave things the way they were when we last saw each other, when you flew out of the pub. It's been driving me mad. I've rung your office ten, twenty times, but that red-headed witch you work with keeps fobbing me off with lies. You do still work there, don't you? The last thing she told me was that you were doing Voluntary Service Overseas. Hah! You doing the charity bit? Believe that when I see it.' He laughed, tossing his head back, revealing his perfect teeth, with not a filling in sight. A dentist's dream – or nightmare, depending on how you look at it.

So Mary had been fending off his calls, as she had done so brilliantly in the past. How could I not have found out? I knew she would have done it purely for my own good, but in a way I resented her interference. That was a bad sign. Rupert's rotten web was spreading.

'I had no idea that you rang,' I whispered, my stomach churning.

'Would you have spoken to me?' he asked seriously.

'I don't know. Maybe. Probably not. There's Paul, you see.'

'Ah yes, hmm, Paul. What are we going to do about him?' He touched my hair, pushing a bang behind my ear. 'Those tight little curls...'

Stop it, will you, stop it...

'I'm going to be in London tomorrow night. Ring me,' he said authoritatively. 'Here's my card, with my mobile. I'm staying at the Covent Garden Hotel. Ring me there.'

With the briefest of kisses on my lips, which burned me like hell fire, he was gone.

44

I didn't ring Rupert on Sunday night.

No, I tell a porky. I dialled the number of his hotel and put down the phone before anyone answered.

Twice.

45

Mary's tummy is of gargantuan proportions and she is having great difficulty in moving around. William forbids her to drive and since her feet can no longer reach the pedals, it's a wise precaution. I don't mind as it gets me out of the office and when the weather is as nice as it has been over the last week, the last thing I want is to be cooped up inside. Mary is over her water retention problem but she has put on an inordinate amount of weight. It suits her. I decided to make no reference to the way in which she had parried Rupert's telephone calls.

Plans have been made for her to go into hospital but she's still unsure about coming back to work after the birth. 'You see, Millie, when I've actually got the baby at home, the last thing I think I'll want to do is leave it – I would feel I was abandoning it. I want us to *bond* and be with it every minute of the day and night. The good thing is,' she prattled on, 'William no longer seems to mind what sex it is. He'll be delighted simply if it doesn't look like his mother.'

She was due to go on maternity leave in ten days' time and I wondered what I would do without her. With Paul busy and away a lot, I had time on my own, time to think and time to worry. Time to think of Rupert.

Last Saturday, when Paul drove me home, he was very quiet.

It was as if he sensed something was amiss. I tried to be bright and cheerful, rejoicing in Netherfield's success, but any comments I made fell on stony ground.

'I know you're not in the slightest bit interested, Mill, so I wouldn't bother pretending,' he said, as he took the exit off the M20. Grinding a gear on the roundabout heading into London which set my teeth on edge, he said, 'How do you know Rupert?'

I knew this question would come up sooner rather than later. I scrunched up my handkerchief in my coat pocket. 'Oh, Rupert? I knew him years ago. We had mutual friends.'

'You went out with him, didn't you?' Gear change, grind, enter another roundabout split seconds in front of a lorry.

'If it makes you feel any better, yes, we did.'

Paul frowned and looked at me, his eyes dull, twinkle gone.

'It was only for a very short time, though,' I said hurriedly. 'Nothing serious. He then went and married a girl he'd been going out with for ages and moved to Devon as far as I know. I haven't seen him for years.' (How easy it is to lie when you want to protect yourself.) It was my turn to ask questions. 'Come to think of it, how do you and Rupert know each other? He said he'd been invited by that insolvency company.'

Paul laughed genuinely for the first time since we had left the club. 'Did he now? Well, well. How the memory can play tricks.'

I didn't like his tone of voice. It was mocking and insincere. I had never heard him criticise anyone before, and I didn't like it. Could he be jealous, by any chance?

Paul flicked the indicator. 'We were at school together.'

I didn't think I could take any more shocks. They couldn't have. Rupert went to a public school, you could tell it a mile away. 'He doesn't loo...'

Paul interrupted. 'Doesn't look like comprehensive material? That's what you were going to say, weren't you Mill? For once you're very much mistaken, *old girl.*'

That hurt.

'Don't worry, I'm not offended. Far from it. Let me tell you about precious Rupert Holland.'

Why was he being so vicious? My head began to ache.

Paul slowed down to avoid hitting a cyclist up the jacksie.

'He was not only the biggest bastard in our class but also a bully and a liar and I hated his guts from the age of thirteen until we both left. I don't care for him much now, I have to say.' He turned to look at me as we waited for a pedestrian light to change to green. 'I don't care if I never set eyes on him again.'

It was too much to take in at once. For starters, I was furious with Paul for being so condescending and that really grated. So what if they didn't get on at school? It's not the first time in history kids have fought over the currant buns and free milk in the playground. Worse things happen at sea and it was donkey's years ago, after all. Also I always imagined Rupert to be considerably younger than Paul. That's not the only mistake I made.

While I simmered in my corner, Paul emitted nothing more than a 'hurrumph' for the next thirty five minutes. He drew up outside my flat, leaving the engine ticking ominously. 'Here we are Mill, hop out.' He plonked a cursory kiss on my mouth. 'I'll ring you tomorrow,' he called out as I slammed the door and he roared off into the night.

I was confused about Rupert and hurt by Paul's cruel remarks, but mostly I was terrified his feelings for me were cooling off. I ran upstairs and punched his numbers into the phone.

'...please leave a message after the tone.'

'Paul, it's me. I know you won't be back yet, but I wanted to thank you for a wonderful day. I'm so pleased I was there to see you win.' I paused, my insides in knots. 'Um, I'm sorry if I put my foot in it with Lawrie McThingy. I hope it didn't embarrass you too much. Sorry. Speak to you soon.'

I sat on the floor and hugged my knees, rocking backwards and forwards, fighting tears yet again. The path of true love is never smooth. I hated myself for being inconsistent. Paul didn't miss a trick and saw only too clearly the effect Rupert had on me. I noticed I'd not put the phone back properly, the cord caught up in my bag. I was replacing it in its cradle when Rupert's card fluttered to the floor. The engraved writing glistened in the lamplight and I ran my fingers over his mobile number. *07768 60...*

I ripped it into shreds.

46

Despite Netherfield's powerful start to the season, there was no man more worried than Paul. The local paper was having a field day at his expense and I knew that his telephone was continually being bombarded with stringers smelling bad news. One or two possible names had been linked with funding the club, but nothing positive had materialised. Straws were clutched, like a weak cross blown away from the goalmouth by a sudden gust of wind.

Never mind the football, whether or not it was because I had seen Rupert again, I don't honestly know, but a distinct chill crept into Paul's manner when we saw each other. It was something I had no experience how to handle.

I set about analysing our relationship with clinical precision. I listed the pluses and minuses, similarities and differences, likes and dislikes, pursuing triumph in preference to disaster. There is something which I haven't told you, but up until now, it had been of little significance.

Paul has been married before.

He dropped this little gem on the plane on our way back from the Costa Brava.

Half-way through my plastic meal, a thought suddenly struck me as I tackled my tortilla. 'When did you say you'd been to Spain?'

'Spain?' he asked, biting into a roll. He wiped his mouth with the blue paper napkin, biding time. 'I didn't actually.'

'What, did you go on your own, or a school trip, or something?' I persisted, as I tried to chew an entrance into an impenetrable packet of Ritz crackers.

Paul poured out the last drops of Rioja into his plastic tumbler and looked at me coolly. 'I was there on my honeymoon.'

The plane shook with sudden turbulence, or was it simply my stomach crashing to the floor in shock?

I crushed the biscuits. 'Married?' I panicked. 'You? When, for

God's sake?' I splurted. 'Lordy, that's a bit of a blow,' I choked at the understatement of the year, sweating buckets. 'But, you *are* divorced, aren't you? Why didn't you tell me before?' I felt cheated, second best.

'Oh, Millie, darling, there's nothing to worry about, honestly,' he laughed, swigging another gulp of wine.

'Nothing to worry about? You must think I'm inhuman,' I swiped. 'A wife? I don't call that nothing to worry about.' Salt started to sting my eyes. 'Did ... did you have any children?'

He sat back as far as his sardine class seat allowance would permit. 'Millie, it was years ago. It happened almost before you were born. And no, we didn't have any kids.'

Thank you God, I prayed. I folded my napkin in four, then in eight. 'How long? I mean, how long were you married?'

Unconcerned, Paul concentrated on buttering the other half of his roll. 'We were at college together. She was in graphics. We'd been going out on and off for a year, you know the kind of thing, neither of us ready to commit ourselves.'

'Yes, but you married each other,' I gasped. 'That's a commitment if ever there was one.'

He patted my hand indulgently, brushing away a stray crumb. 'Fair enough, but it wasn't at all how you imagine. She was nineteen, I was twenty. The summer had been hot, a heatwave, breaking all previous records and we were in love, I suppose. Also she was a football nut.'

That's all I needed to know.

'It seemed right at the time. How does the saying go, marry in haste ...?'

'...Repent at leisure.'

'For goodness sake, Mill, it's all over and done with. We were divorced almost before the ink was dry on the marriage certificate.' He scraped the last trace of butter from the foil wrapping and placed the triangle of camembert on top of his cracker, licking his fingers.

'Do you still see her?' I asked, dreading the reply, feeling unbearably threatened and vulnerable, the cold chicken mayonnaise I'd eaten weighing like lead.

'No, we haven't seen each other for over ten years. But we do keep in touch, Christmas and so on. Six months after our divorce, she married a friend of her parents' about twice her age who'd known her since she was a baby. She's his third wife and they've got seven kids – five from his previous marriages and two of their own.' He looked at his empty bottle of wine. 'Shall I get some more?' He stretched and pushed the button to summon the stewardess. 'There is one other thing I ought to mention.'

I didn't think I could take any more.

'I'm Godfather to their eldest, Dominic. They live on a farm in Scotland, well, it's really an estate, grouse moors, etc. I'm sure you know the kind of thing.'

I felt sick. 'What's her name?'

'Why? It makes no difference what she's called, does it?' he said irritatingly.

I needed a name so I could stick pins into the doll I was going to make out of wax. The first thing I would do on returning home was to search through his cupboards to find traces of her hair on his clothing. 'I'd like to know, that's all,' a hint of menace in my tone. I'm no saint. 'What was it, tell me, please?'

'Okay, it was Madeleine. Maddie for short.'

Madeleine, eh? Millicent? Maddie? How very convenient. He could give me her initialled suitcases. 'Tell me you don't love her any more? Please?'

'Millie, do shut up. You know what? You're becoming boring. Here, have some more wine.'

I didn't want to drink and yet I wanted to get drunk. Very drunk.

'Is that why you've never married again?' I ventured, thinking nothing could make me more unhappy.

'No, it isn't. I simply haven't met the right girl.'

47

'*I simply haven't met the right girl...*'

If anything destroyed my confidence it was those seven revealing words he uttered as we came into land. I don't blame him in a way. Now that some of the dust had settled over his

171

revelation about Maddie, I returned to writing my list. The divide between us was chasmic. For example, I was educated in a private school in Sussex, whereas Paul sowed his educational seeds at a large comprehensive in Kent, as I now know Rupert did, much to my chagrin. I grew up in a seventeenth century farmhouse with ten acres of land and my own pony, Paul in a Victorian two up, two down semi with a tiny back garden on the outskirts of Canterbury. At last two points in common: our mothers lived on their own and we each had a flower child for a parent. Hardly enough on which to build a future.

I turned to a second page. I left school at eighteen after having taken (and failed) my A Levels, Paul left after his 'O's, passing in nine subjects. He then went on to college and took his 'A's which led him to a degree in Physical Education in the Midlands. I butterflied from job to job in London, with no proper training behind me, having a whale of a time, but Paul buckled down to an FA coaching course while he taught PE in a minor public school in Kent. He was offered and accepted a post on the coaching staff at Netherfield Town, the team he has followed all his life. His dedication and application didn't go unnoticed and in a short space of time he became assistant manager. The rest is history.

I read what I'd written again searching for inspiration but found none. Depression hit rock bottom. The telephone rang. 'Hello, I've missed you so much,' I said, scrunching up the list in my hand, aiming it at the fireplace.

There was a moment's silence, before a thousand calorie, velvet voice said, 'I've missed you too, Millicent, more than you care to know.'

I drew in my breath.

'By the way, I'm sorry to disappoint you, it's not Paul, my dearest, it's Rupert.'

I sank into the armchair. The hairs on the back of my neck tingled. 'Where the hell did you get my number?' I asked crossly.

'Yes, I'm well, Millie, thanks for asking,' he said sarcastically. 'Your number? Your mother gave it to me.'

'My *mother*?' I asked in disbelief.

'Yes, she was very obliging. Such a kind woman. I asked

172

directory enquiries for her number when they told me you're not listed. I was quite flattered, she seemed to remember me very well.'

Oh yes, she remembers you all right. How could she forget? She'll tell you about the sleepless nights spent sitting on my bed as I cried, wishing I was dead after you chucked me. She remembers...

'Look, Millicent, I'm in town tonight. I have to admit I was rather upset you didn't call when I was last here and I wondered if we could meet up. Maybe for a meal. For old time's sake?'

I was about to be thrown to the lions and I was happy to dig my own grave. Recently Paul had been piggy and distant and I was still smarting over the fact that he'd been married before and not had it in him to tell me until our holiday. I needed to assert myself. I sat up straight in the chair, holding onto my stomach for strength. 'Yes. I will. Where?' I uttered before I could stop myself. I must be stark, staring mad.

'Great. I knew you would.' The sheer gall of the man should strangle him.

There was still time to back down.

'I'll come and pick you up at your flat. It's the one off the Portobello Road, isn't it? Top floor? Twenty minutes. By the way, don't dress up.'

He could have me naked on a plate the effect he had on me. My heart was beating so fast I could almost hear it. I knew I should ring him back and cancel. I stared at the phone, then my watch. In less than a quarter of an hour he would be here. I stood up, feeling dizzy. Then sexy. Then achingly longing.

That evil voice in my head whined, horns rampant, cloven hooves prancing, *'there's nothing wrong in going out for a simple meal with an old friend, is there?'*

I had to eat, after all. I ought to ring Susie, or Polly, or both, for advice, but there's no time. I rushed into the bedroom which looked as though I'd been burgled. I shook the duvet and fluffed the pillows. Picking up two pairs of knickers from the floor, I stuffed them under a cushion. Opening my wardrobe, I couldn't stop the excitement mounting in my throat. I hadn't felt like this for ages and it was exhilarating.

I grabbed a pair of black trousers off the rail, relieved that they didn't need ironing, then took a matching cashmere roll neck from the shelf and my black ankle boots. I looked like the Milk Tray man in drag. As I was buffing the toes of my shoes on the back of my trouser leg I caught sight of my face in the bathroom mirror and guilt stared back at me in spades. I scowled, sucked in my cheeks and scrubbed them with blusher. I snapped shut the Bourjois case and unscrewed the gummy cap of my mascara. The final touch was a smear of gloss on my lips.

The doorbell rang, the sudden, shrill sound making me jump. My heart thumping for all it was worth, I twisted my hair into a pony tail, hastily securing it with a scrunchy and prepared to let the devil into my home.

Get thee behind me Satan, I whispered as I turned the handle.

He did – four hours later.

PART ELEVEN

RED CARD

48

I tripped over my wet bath towel, swore under my breath and deftly toe-poked it behind the chair. Pausing a second, I tried to calm myself. Aware that my eyes were bright – 'hard', my mother would have said had she seen me in this state – I ran my damp hands along my hips and released the latch.

'Hey babe, you look as though you've lost weight,' was Rupert's opening gambit.

I'd done it on purpose, choosing black, to create exactly that effect. Conniving trollop.

'I'm ready. Let's go, shall we?' I wasn't going to invite him in for a drink first. I needed to get into neutral territory, but on my own terms. 'Where's the Aston?' I asked outside, momentarily disappointed at not seeing it parked in the crescent.

'The DB7? Had to sell up, I'm afraid,' he explained. 'That's my run around, over there, the white one.'

He pointed to a none too clean 'S' reg Audi, a large dent rusting on the passenger door.

'Thought we might go to Geale's for fish and chips. Maybe have a bowl of fried clams first, between us, for starters. Bit of fun, slumming it and all that.'

I had a distinct feeling that he might have fallen on hard times. Maybe Abigail was proving expensive. Actually, I was pleased he'd chosen Geale's, as I was so nervous I couldn't face the thought of eating fancy, fiddled-with French food. What's more we walked, as the restaurant was only five minutes' away.

Throughout the evening, Rupert was a perfect gentleman. He wined and dined me, flattered me, pampered me. '...You haven't changed a bit... If there is one thing I'll always remember, it's your eyes... God, you're gorgeous... Aren't the clams brill?'

He was fun and made me laugh, something which Paul hadn't been of late, and I was enjoying myself. Expertly, he cast his net and I fell shamelessly straight in to the middle, offering no resistance whatsoever. He was charming, gentle and irresistible. So what, I hear you say? For once in my life I was relatively sober, as I'd been wary and rightly so of drinking too much. Immoral superglue stuck me to my seat and my last line of defence crumbled when he helped me put on my jacket. It was the way he touched the collar, with a possessive, confident hand. I knew then it was too late.

49

I suppose you want to know what happened, although I'm sure I don't need to spell it out in letters ten feet high. Your suspicions about my character are right. I'm a slut, a tart, a mess.

Oh yes, we made love, if you can call it that and it was probably on the cards after the initial sip of wine. It was back home, in my flat, in the bed I share so blissfully happily with Paul, in the same sheets, his sweet smell on the pillow. Rupert was exactly how I remembered him: a considerate, energetic and unselfish lover, but it wasn't Paul. Nothing can compare with him. What on earth could I have been playing at? Not only had I let myself down, but I had cheated the one man I truly love. It took a swift, greedy bedding with Rupert to prove that simple fact. I felt cheap, a fool, tatty. I had behaved like a common prostitute and I wasn't even being paid.

When it was all over, I turned away, full of self-loathing, any thought of further physical contact with Rupert repulsive. 'I

176

want you to go, please, now,' I whispered into the pillow, full of remorse and trying not to cry.

He propped himself up on his elbow and looked down at me. 'Eh? What was that?'

'I want you to go.'

'But it's fucking one o'clock in the morning, Mill, for Christ's sake,' he said petulantly, like a spoilt child whose exasperated parents had removed the batteries from his Game Boy.

'Will you go, please? Now. I don't want you here.' I couldn't stand his company a moment longer. I'm sorry, Paul, so sorry...

He looked astonished at first, then hurt, then resigned. 'Okay, if that's the way you feel, it's fine by me,' he said, sucking in air through gritted teeth. He kicked back the crumpled quilt and picked through his clothes mingled with mine on the carpet, in the same way our legs had been minutes earlier.

In his haste, he put his boxers on back to front. Scowling, he ripped them off and put them on the right way. 'Where's my bloody sock?'

I trembled as I watched him dress, feeling alienated, dispassionate. In other circumstances the situation would have been hilarious.

Rupert jolted me back to reality and gave me a cursory peck on the cheek, his breath unpleasantly stale. 'I'm off then, Miss Grumpy Goody Two Shoes, obeying instructions,' he said sarcastically, his mouth curled in a sneer as he pulled on a loafer. ' 'Bye, Millicent. It was lovely to see you. We must do it again,' he added, stifling a yawn, '*On se téléphone, oui?*'

He hesitated for a moment in the doorway and settled his glasses on the bridge of his nose with his index finger. With the shadow of stubble accentuating his fine cheek bones, he still had the knack of looking wonderful. His shirt collar was casually unbuttoned and his silk tie hung limply round his neck, the brass buttons of his blazer glinting menacingly. He scooped up his keys and loose change from the chest of drawers. 'I'll see myself out,' he muttered, unable to disguise the bitterness – and unless I'm mistaken – a certain sadness in his voice. Rupert, who had virtually never experienced rejection in his life, appeared to be genuinely hurt.

For one split second I felt sorry for him, but not half as sorry as I felt for myself. Perhaps it's unjust to trowel all the blame onto him, after all wasn't I the one who agreed to see him in the first place? We used each other, it was as simple as that. I never heard him leave, as I was crying too loudly. My coupling with Rupert may have been a seminal experience, but at last I had laid a ghost.

I wouldn't be surprised if you find it difficult to believe that I was prepared so willingly to risk destroying my relationship with Paul by sleeping with a rat like Rupert. Think about it. Imagine yourself in the same situation. Rupert is a rascal and his *raison d'être* in life is to bewitch and entrance the whole of womankind. For him, it's not simply notching up another ring on the bedpost. He genuinely adores women. You could weigh the same as Frank Bruno since he stopped boxing, be unfit and forty and he would treat you as if you were the most precious thing on earth. Who could resist such charm? Perhaps if you understood my current frame of mind you may feel at least some sympathy for me. I don't ask for forgiveness, for you to condone what I did. I abhor my conduct. I want you to see things from my point of view, that's all. You can wrinkle up your nose in disgust, become po-faced and holier than thou, but have you never indulged in something which you may regret for the rest of your life? I'm only human. There is nothing more I can say to justify sleeping with Rupert. The more I thought about what I'd done, the worse I felt.

PART TWELVE

PENALTY SHOOT-OUT

50

The office was empty, the lights off, when I arrived at nine the next morning, Mary nowhere to be seen. I needed her there, to talk to, to be reassured that what I had done wasn't life threatening and that one day I would be forgiven – that is, if I could ever learn to forgive myself. I wondered briefly where she was, but I was so self-obsessed in what had happened over the last twenty-four hours, that I'm ashamed to say, I gave it no further thought. My only comfort came in the shape of a bumper-sized packet of Jammie Dodgers and a spot factory in a polystyrene cup of hot chocolate from the sandwich bar next door.

It wasn't until around eleven, that I was shaken out of my contemplative stupour.

It was William. 'Oh Millie,' he breathed, panting down the phone, 'I'm sorry I've not been in touch before. You'll have to forgive me. Mary's gone into labour.'

Oh Lord. I sat up quickly at the news, spilling the drink down my front. I rubbed the stain, only making it worst. 'That's wonderful news, William. When did it all start?'

'You'll never guess in a month of Sundays. It was hysterical. The old girl's waters broke by the fish counter in Tesco's last night of all places and I had to rush her into hospital. I nearly had to pile her into the trolley with the organic veg! There's no sign of anything major happening yet, so I skived off to have a snifter and give you a tinkle.'

'Oh, that's fantastic. Give her my love and lots of luck – to you both. I hope it doesn't hurt too much. Keep me posted, promise?'

I heard him cough discreetly.

'Are you sure you're all right, Mill? You sound a bit offish. Not sickening for something, are you?'

Thankfully he ran out of money before I could answer. I said a hundred prayers that all would be well. At half-past six William phoned again.

'It's...' he shouted, followed by silence. 'They've...'

'Come on, Billium, take a deep breath. What's happened? How's Mary?' I asked, as if talking to an idiot.

There was a lot of sniffling and snuffling on the end of the line. 'Sorry, Millie, I'm all emotional, overwhelmed that's all. Everything's fine. Perfect in fact. We've had...' and another onslaught of sobbing hit my ear.

I waited patiently until he was able to compose himself.

'Oh lordy, Mill! It wasn't a boy and it wasn't a girl. We've had twins!' he shrieked.

It was impossible. They couldn't have. It would have shown up on the scan.

'They're *wonderful* Millie. Absolutely heavenly. A perfect brace. Did I say we had twins? We're going to buy a puppy for them, to grow up with. Oh my goodness, I must get back! One of each, eh? Fancy that. Did I tell you?'

I gulped back the tears, from happiness, relief, with one pang of jealousy and two pangs of envy. To hell with work, I locked the office and went and bought all the roses in the bucket outside the florist's, plus a bottle of champagne and belted hell for leather to the hospital. I hadn't a clue which ward Mary was in but everyone fell over backwards to be helpful.

'Oh yes, let me see now, Mrs McCarthy,' said the nurse, as she consulted her book. 'Here we are. The darling twins. Room 24.' She smiled at me. 'They're beautiful!'

I had to restrain myself not to sprint down the corridor. I peered through the glass window and saw William holding Mary's hand in such an adoring manner that I hesitated, thinking it might be better if I came back later, but they saw me.

Beaming as though his face would split in two, he called out, 'Don't stand outside, Millie. Come in and look!'

180

I stood in amazement. Beside Mary the babies lay in identical cots, making soft gurgling noises.

'Hello, Mill,' she said in a hushed voice. 'Aren't they scrumptious?'

I couldn't reply straight away, as seeing the tiny mites all bundled up in blankets took my breath away. At last I managed to say, 'Congratulations. I'm lost for words.' So as not to show that I was about to burst into tears, I walked over to the sink and put the roses in the basin, my eyes filling at the same rate as the water from the tap.

Mary smiled. 'Oh, my sweet, you're crying. Please don't. I'm doing fine and so is William and so are the bairns, although I'm not quite up to running the marathon yet. They've got all their fingers and toes and everything where it should be, particularly where the wee laddie is concerned,' she added, giggling like a ten-year-old.

As my emotions had become public knowledge I blew heartily into a Kleenex and sat down in the chair on the far side of the bed. Although a vision of happiness, on closer inspection I could see how exhausted Mary was, with deep, smudgy bruises under her eyes, which were severely bloodshot.

'You've noticed my dracula peepers, eh? Well, they tried to pump me with chemicals and the such like, but I wanted to do it my way.' She shifted in the bed, trying to find a comfortable position. 'To my cost. Never mind, the battle scars will fade. Next time, though...' Sitting up, she winced, as both William and I did. 'Actually, between you and me, it's a bugger. I reckon they used a cheese slice. I can't believe I actually produced these two little monsters. Did William tell you they weighed over five pounds each?' she said in amazement. 'That's four thumping bags of sugar. No wonder I couldn't move.'

We all laughed.

'Come closer,' said Mary. 'You can touch them, you know. They won't bite.'

I leaned over the cots and saw two minute heads, covered by doll sized bonnets.

'They were strong enough not to go into an incubator, although it was touch and go with Wilfred,' William added proudly.

Wilfred?

'Did you say Wilfred?' I ventured, hoping I had misheard.

'Yup, that's right,' laughed Mary. 'We've called the wee boy Wilfred and the little girl Elsie. Wilfred and Elsie McCarthy. There. Isn't that splendid?'

What had happened to Rory and Jamie, Lily and Nell? I tried to identify which was which.

'Underneath the titfers, Wilfred's the baldie and Elsie has the ginger mop in case you were wondering. Oh and we'd like you to be Godmother – to both, if that's all right with you, of course,' William said puffed up with pride, 'Job lot, eh?'

That did it. I could no longer contain my tears and they positively gushed. I couldn't speak as the scalding tears cascaded. William, who I noticed was not as dry-eyed as some men might be, came to the rescue and handed me the tissue box, grabbing a fistful himself.

'There there, it's all right, Millie. It's quite normal apparently. *Post partum* emotion and all that,' he stuttered, embarrassed, 'no point in keeping a stiff upper lip, when one's amongst friends.'

Mary gazed lovingly at her husband. 'We always wanted you to be Godmum, but when we had twins we were in a pickle. William had the brilliant idea and suggested you could be Godmother to both. Please say you will,' she implored.

I looked at the family which had suddenly doubled in size. What kind of an example would I set? I crossed my fingers. 'Yes, I'd love to. I feel very honoured.'

We hugged each other and cried together, which set off the babies. The rumpus alerted the nurses.

I stood to one side as they attended to Mary.

'You could probably do with a cup of tea, Mrs McCarthy? And something to eat. You must be famished after all that effort, even for hospital food.'

'Oh, yes please. I could eat a horse.'

I doubt that horse would be on the menu, but come to think of it, anything was possible on the NHS. A stiff drink wouldn't go amiss and I nearly suggested whisking William off to the nearest boozer. 'I think I ought to be on my way,' I said, seeing how close they were and I felt like a gooseberry.

'Thanks so much for coming,' Mary said. 'We haven't asked how Paul is. We saw the result on Saturday. Tell him well done from us.'

'Thank you for the flowers and the champagne,' I heard William say as I closed the door.

On the way out, I grabbed a Standard, dropping the coins in the slot. I unfolded it, to be hit between the eyes for the second time in my life by the following headline, **'CAMPBELL SACKED'**.

What a day.

51

In a foul, black mood, with a pounding headache, I turned on the bedroom light, knowing I had a face like a split pit boot. I hadn't the strength to make the bed after I'd kicked out Rupert. It was all I needed. I was jealous of Mary, disgusted with myself and feared I could never face Paul again. In anger, I tossed the pillows onto the floor, ripped off the duvet cover, then chucked everything into the washing machine. Normally I use an eco-friendly, cool wash. Today I added double bio and set it to 90 degrees. To hell with the environment. I didn't want a single trace of Rupert to remain. I watched as the drum began to churn, when the telephone broke my trance.

It was Paul. 'You've seen the news, then? The board's finally given in to the pressure, so I'm out.'

'I thought after Saturday's result they'd keep you on. Why do it now, when things are looking up? It doesn't seem fair.'

'Fairness doesn't come into it. We're on the verge of bankruptcy and that's the way it goes. They've put the coach in charge of the squad until they can find some poor sod to take my place.'

'What do you think you'll do now?'

'Well, seeing as they've sacked me so early into my contract, I'm due a fairly hefty whack in compensation, which'll tide me over for some time. I might go away.'

Paul go away? I couldn't bear it. I tried to sound calm. 'It wasn't your fault. Even I know that the team hasn't been playing well, but you weren't the cause of the sponsors leaving, or the problems with the bank, were you?'

183

'It's not like that, Mill. They need a whipping boy and since there's no money in the kitty to mastermind a quick fix, it's the manager who carries the can.'

I heard him breathing heavily.

'I'm sorry, I've been going on about my problems as usual. How are things with you?'

I told him about Mary and the babies.

'You'll make a perfect Godmother,' he said. Then, in a business-like tone, he added, 'I must go. I'm meeting with my solicitor in half an hour. I'll be in touch. Be sure to give Mary my love when you next see her.'

Despondently, I ran the messages on the answerphone. There was a typically garbled message from Susie. I rang her at the flat, but it was engaged. I needed someone to talk to. I rang Polly. I told her everything.

'My God, Mill, I don't know how you do it, really I don't. You've got perhaps the two best-looking men in London running rings around you and you're sitting at home on your backside moping.' She paused. 'You were a good girl and used a condom, didn't you?'

A what? Icy fingers trickled down my back. 'Er, yes, of course we did. I'm not that stupid.' Oh Christ.

'Good. Anyway, when you've made your mind up which one you're going to back, do me a favour and let me know. I can tell you that I certainly wouldn't kick Rupert out of bed, that is if I could get him into it,' she said, with a wicked laugh.

I went to the hospital after work the next evening to find Mary sitting up bright as a button, with one infant plugged in. She radiated happiness. I crept in as quietly as I could, making sure I didn't bang the door. I leaned over the bed and gave her a kiss and sniffed in the sweet scent of new baby.

'There's no need for hush,' she said brightly, 'they seem to sleep through anything. Let's hope it's like that when we get home. The dulcet tones of the Hammersmith flyover will be the acid test.'

I wasn't going to worry her about Paul's problems, or mine for that matter, being too ashamed to mention it. I moved the black leatherette chair closer to the bed, 'Mary, can you explain something which has been troubling me all night. I've been racking my brains and can't work it out. How on earth, with all the technology they can lay their hands on, can they let you wade through nine months of pregnancy and think you were expecting only one and not two, babies? It doesn't make a blind bit of sense.'

Mary chortled and kissed the head of the infant at her breast. 'It didn't to us either, I can tell you. When I assumed all the agony was over and the midwife yelled at me not to stop, that there was a queue to get out, it gave me the fright of my life. Apparently, for the first time in the history of the hospital, the day I went for my scan was the day the machine went on the blink. They're hanging their heads in shame and they're petrified we might sue. That's why they're being so nice. They even gave us this private room as a further sweetener.'

Mary looked lovingly at the nuzzling baby and stroked its tiny head. I couldn't tell which it was, so simply referred to 'it' as being too adorable. She was taking to motherhood like a duck to water. I suppose coming from a large family herself, having twins out of the blue was not too daunting a prospect. She lifted the small person over her shoulder, its tiny, perfect feet and hands moving this way and that, while she rubbed its back. I was itching to hold it, but didn't dare ask.

Predictably, Mary read my thoughts. 'If it wasn't because of the fact that his supper would probably be chucked up all over your cardie as soon as you held him, I'd pass Wilfred over. Unless you want a badge of honour, of course. Better wait a second or two for him to perform.' She continued to pat and encourage as I watched, awestruck at the brand new life only hours old she held in her arms. 'Here you are, Wilfred, little darling. Off you go to Aunt Millicent.'

Oh dear, that's what I am, is it, maiden Aunt Millicent? Heaven help me. It made me feel about a hundred and ten. Cautiously I took hold of the wobbly object, terrified I would drop it. He was so light, so fragile and in the palm of my hand I cupped my Godson's head. It was not much larger than a cricket ball and about as red and wrinkly. Emotions of deep, primaeval love flowed through me, jostling with a mingling of regret, sadness and that lingering sour, vile whiff of jealousy. Paul, I thought, Paul and me, Paul and babies. What I had done with Rupert could have seen to that vision of paradise. I placed the little person back in his cot and tucked him in. 'Have I done it properly?' I asked, anxious that I might have damaged him in some way.

'Oh, yes, that was perfect. You'll make a marvellous mum,' Mary said as she busied herself ready to feed Elsie. With a clattering and chattering, William came bounding through the door like an over enthusiastic puppy, or at least, I think it was him, due to the fact that he was smothered in flowers.

'Hello darling. Hi Mill,' he cooed, through mammoth bunches of freesias and delphiniums, dropping flowers left, right and centre. He kissed his wife with passion and sat on the bed. Elsie was guzzling as though petrol prices were due to go up at midnight and didn't bat an eyelid as her father stroked her head.

'I think I'll leave you two to it. I've got some telephoning to do.'

'Thanks for calling in, Mill. I should be out tomorrow, with any luck. Remission for good behaviour. Oh, if you're speaking to Paul, give him our love.'

I rang Susie as soon as I got back, expecting to get her machine, or at best an engaged tone, but after the second ring to my surprise, she picked it up.

'Mill, I'm sorry I haven't been in touch. You know what it's like. It only seems like yesterday I was reading the Sunday papers, and now it's...sorry, anyway, Polly has told me *all* about it. You old scallywag.'

Great. So much for confidentiality. Was nothing sacred?

'Tell me, was it as good as the old days? With golden bollocks, I mean?' she asked. 'I'm simply dying to know.'

I didn't lower myself by replying.

'I'm sure you'll bring us up to date in your own good time.'

I heard the glugging sound of liquid being poured.

'Hmm, I've just got a glass of wine. Just got in. Lovely. Where were we? Oh, yes, we both heard the news on Capital about Paul being sacked. That's *awful*. How's he taken it?'

She ignored my silence.

'Why don't we meet up and have a chin wag? It'll do you good, white *whine* therapy and all that.'

186

I looked at the time. Quarter to eight. There was nothing in the fridge and sure as hell I couldn't find the energy to phone for a take away. I wasn't hungry but I could murder a drink. 'Okay, you ring Poll and I'll be there in twenty minutes. If you're there first, order a Pouilly. Second thoughts, make it two bottles. This is serious. I feel like splashing out.'

'Haven't you done that already, you old slapper?'

I was able to park outside, which was an added bonus. I couldn't cope with wandering around the block to find a space without double yellows.

'We're truly sorry, Millie,' said Polly, as I sat down opposite them. 'What's going to happen now, do you think? I fear you've really cocked things up this time.'

I hadn't got a clue whether she meant with Paul or Rupert. I stuffed my nose into my wine glass by way of escape. Cowardly as ever, I hedged my bets and waited.

'Will he be taken on by another club, or is it the wilderness *ad infinitum*?'

'There's nothing on the horizon. He'll get a fair amount of compensation, but that won't last forever and knowing what a sensitive person he is, he'll end up horribly depressed. I pray he gets an offer from somewhere – and soon. That's the only way he'll survive.'

'But that might mean he's sent miles away. Would you go too? You know what you're like about leaving London,' Susie said, always the first to hit the nail on the head.

'I simply don't know.' It was the first time I had told the truth in forty eight hours.

A subdued trio, the Pouilly didn't do the trick and we left long before the place became busy. I picked up some fish and chips on the way back to the car out of habit, eating them morosely as I drove. Not the freshest, they were flabby and lifeless, as I was. The high street shops were already full of Hallowe'en trappings – it was only the first week in September for goodness sake. I passed one window at the lights displaying grinning pumpkins.

I didn't grin back.

I'd become a miserable old git.

187

52

In Mary's absence I'd been helped – and I use the term loosely – by a succession of temps ranging from bad, to very bad to appalling. With Mary looking less and less likely to return to full-time work, I thought it would be a good idea to employ someone to take her place permanently.

During an unaccustomed lull in the conversation at the wine bar one Friday night (Paul was on his way to Wales to see an ancient aunt, via Wrexham) Polly, ever the philosopher, said, 'Mill, I've been thinking. You've got a job and a man who's jobless, I've got a job but am manless and Susie is manless and jobless. Now, there's a fine thing, begorrah, bejasus.'

'Indeed it is,' I said. 'Ever considered estate agency?'

The long and the short of it, once my absentee boss approved my suggestion, was that Susie started work with me on the following Monday morning. After Mary's departure, at last I had a soul mate again, alongside whom I could cope better with my frustrations, home and away.

The following weekend she was doing the Saturday stint, so I was free. Paul asked me to go to Suffolk to get away from the tension, the bitterness and the lack of job offers. Fresh sea air might blow away some of the cobwebs. I knew I needed, although he didn't, a fresh start. Who knows, we might even catch crabs in Walberswick.

We drove up the A12 on the following Friday night and, with the help of a guide book, found a quaint 'restaurant with rooms' tucked away in a village near Wickham Market. It was a rambling old house made up from two cottages, slap bang against the church. When we were taking our cases out of the boot I couldn't fail to notice Paul's golf clubs lying expectantly at the back. *Plus ça change...*

We were shown to our room via endless creaking staircases and corridors and crept into bed immediately. We lay there wide awake, the curtains drawn.

'I want to see the moon,' Paul said as I lay peacefully in his arms. 'You never see a proper night sky in London with all the light pollution.'

He had opened the windows wide before getting into bed and we couldn't hear a sound. No traffic, no drunks, not even a cat. Then an owl hooted. It took a little while to adjust, but we filled the time before falling asleep as best we could and I realised I hadn't entirely lost my sense of humour.

The next day, after a pantagruelian feast of porridge and best Suffolk bacon, we headed towards the coast. East Anglia. People only go there to go there, if you see what I mean. It's not a short cut to anywhere, it stops at the sea and it sticks out from the rest of England. There were few people about, mostly locals, as it was the end of the season, all the grockles having returned home, their children back at school for the autumn term. We walked along the shingle beach, searching amongst the pebbles for cornelian, or maybe a stray doubloon. We studied the cliffs at Dunwich to see if they eroded before our eyes. Later, we slurped two dozen oysters sitting on barrels in a ramshackle café, and drank rough, draught ale in an unspoilt pub, listening to the seafaring gossip at the bar. Rupert, at last, had become a distant figment of my imagination.

Rupert? Who's he? Never heard of him.

Reluctantly, we left after lunch on Sunday in an attempt to avoid the worst of the traffic. The rain, which had been threatening all day, finally fell and, in spite of our early start, the roads were clogged. The weather deteriorated to a pea souper fog, and I was thankful I wasn't driving.

Eventually, Paul dropped me off at my flat. 'Mill, there's something I have to say.'

My heart stopped and the oysters slopped about unnervingly. Could he have found out about Rupert? Nobody knew but Susie and Polly and they would never have split.

He looked pale and serious. 'I wanted to tell you in Suffolk, but I didn't want to spoil our weekend.' He played with the car keys, jangling them along with my nerves. He cleared his throat. 'I've been offered a job.'

'Why, that's brilliant,' I said, a fraction too quickly, the relief spreading all over my face that his worry didn't concern Rupert. 'Where is it? In London?'

He looked upset that I hadn't been troubled by his announcement. 'Er, not exactly. It's in Cheshire... And I'd like you to come with me'.

Nothing could have prepared me for that piece of news. I flopped back in my seat, not knowing what to say. Cheshire. It couldn't have been worse. 'But...' I began, intending to bluff my way through a refusal to budge.

'No buts,' Paul interrupted, 'of course you need to think about it, Millie, I realise that. It's a huge commitment. For both of us. It won't be easy. I'm clearing my desk at the club tomorrow and have to be in the north by next Saturday. They're officially handing over the job as manager to me on Monday, when there'll be a press conference. It's up a division, which is great, so I can't possibly refuse.' He looked at me pleadingly. 'Only, if you don't want me to go...'

The padlock on my mouth had been fastened, locking my teeth together, trapping my tongue in a scold's bridle.

'No. Sorry. I'm not being fair. Don't make any decision now. Sleep on it. I'll ring you tomorrow...'

I was completely stumped for words. Rupert had been blasted out of all existence, thank God, with these developments. The man I loved more than life itself was asking me to go and live with him and I was letting him down. Paul must have sensed that my reply would be negative; perhaps that's why he asked.

He kissed me gently. 'Have a think, Millie. I've got a new chance, a likelihood that I might achieve something, to make my mark. It's too good an opportunity to miss.' A lighter tone came to his voice. 'Believe me, it's not all doom and gloom, factories and rain, or so the tourist brochures would have us believe. You could even take up riding again, like you've always wanted to.' He turned away. 'I've a strong chance of success, which is what really matters. Please give it your best shot.'

Silently, I opened the door. 'I'll think about it, I promise.'

Please don't do this to me, Paul, I begged. I didn't know what to do.

'Fine, I won't put you under any pressure. I respect that any decision you make will be the right one.' He joined me on the pavement. 'Here, let me give you a hand with your case.'

I felt an utter shit.

190

'I'll ring you in the morning.' He kissed me on the nose. 'Thanks for a great weekend. I'm sorry if I've spoiled things. It seems to have become a habit of mine recently,' he conceded gloomily.

Life is a bitch. I didn't ask for these complications. I want everything to fall into place, with no demands so we can all live happily ever after. Where did I get that idea from? Walt Disney? I didn't sleep much that night, but when I did I dreamed of road maps and motorways, criss-crossing with juggernauts in murky rain, industrial zones and ghastly shopping malls. In desperation the following evening, I rang my mother, needing to hear her reliable, sensible counsel.

'Now that you've got that off your chest, Millicent my girl, the most important thing is, did he ask you to marry him?'

I chewed my hankie.

'I take your silence as a "no",' she said, philosophically. 'In that case, it's up to you, but if you really love him you'll be prepared to go to the ends of the earth to be with him, whatever it entails. Nothing in the world would prevent you from doing that if that is what you feel in your heart of hearts. If you can't make those sacrifices, then the time simply is not right. Sit on it for a while and see how you get on when he's gone is my advice.'

Wise old bird. Oh, the relief of having the responsibility lifted from my shoulders. I decided to stay put. My decision completely floored Paul, who'd been convinced I would be packed, ready and waiting.

The disappointment in his voice cut me to the quick.

'Of course I understand, Millie,' he said bravely, clearing his throat. 'Let's see how the land lies when I get there and you can let me know if you change your mind. It's a bit of an unknown quantity at the moment, I'll give you that. I won't pressurise you further, I promise.'

My God, I felt a heel. Once again that night I played my plus and minus game, only I couldn't think up any pluses. Paul = Cheshire = the unknown. Rupert = London = trouble. Why is my brain – my heart – still programmed to tune into him? A leopard doesn't change its spots and he's made absolutely no contact with me since that fateful night. I should know better and be grateful for small mercies.

My lack of support for Paul stared me in the face. I am a selfish pig. 'I need more time,' I beseeched.

In an attempt at being more positive, I went back to the local library, and fished out anything available on the Manchester area. It must have something going for it. Turning the pages of an AA guide, I was soon absorbed, and it didn't look half as bad as I had originally feared. It was simply ignorance on my part, that's all. I closed one volume and picked up another. A wave of anxiety came over me again, instantly annihilating any tenuous element of hope. What would I do there? It has the highest rainfall in the United Kingdom, it's cold and I wouldn't know anyone other than Paul. I love my flat in London, my friends are there and my mother is within easy reach. To uproot from all this to the ends of the earth was a terrifying prospect. I stood up and shoved the books back into their slots and as I banged the last one home, I accepted I simply couldn't do it. I had to take the bull by the horns and put Paul out of his misery before I changed my mind.

Although it was only twenty to five, I poured myself a stiff drink and dialled the all too familiar numbers. 'It's me,' I said unnecessarily when he picked up the phone on the second ring.

'Hi, sweetheart. How are things?'

'Okay.'

'Great. I hope you've some news for me. I could do with it. Have you had time to think?'

'I have to tell you the truth and you're going to hate me.'

'I could never do that, not in a million years.' He sounded worried. 'What is it, although I don't think I need ask.'

I nearly put the phone down, unable to continue.

'Millie, I can't go on like this, hanging on by a thread. It's tearing me apart.'

'Well,' I said, my voice trembling, tears not far away. 'I can't come with you. It's nothing to do with you, or the way I feel about you, I promise. I'm sorry, but my life is here, in London. For the moment at any rate.'

Paul didn't make a sound.

My tears started in earnest. 'Can you forgive me, or at least try to understand? Paul? Say something, please.'

When he did reply, his voice was shaky and I knew I had

192

shocked him to the core by the stark finality of my answer. It wasn't his normal voice, but cold and distant.

'Of course I understand, Millie. You're not cut out to be tied to the sort of life I lead. How could I have ever thought you'd give up everything to bury yourself here, with me? It's a different world from the one you're used to. It wouldn't be fair. You'd be lonely and isolated. You've done the right thing. We have so little in common.'

I thought he had said all he had to say and was about to speak in my defence, when he said, 'But I love you and I don't know what I'm going to do without you.'

To complete my desolation, he started crying.

I was stunned. That was the first time Paul had actually told me he loved me, the three words I had dreamed of hearing him say, prompted and cajoled him into whispering in my ear and he had chosen to say them now. I soldiered on, relentless in my task of self-preservation. 'Please, please forgive me.'

There was no reaction.

'I love you too...'

'Right,' he said, matter of fact to hide the hurt, his voice razor sharp. 'That's it then. I'll be leaving tomorrow evening so I don't know if we can meet to say goodbye.'

'I have to see you. I can't let you go like this,' I pleaded.

'Millie,' he sobbed, 'I need to see you, too.'

He put down the receiver.

53

The following morning, before he left London for a new career and a new life, Paul came to say goodbye. It was the first time he and Susie met. After only five minutes, he said nervously, 'I'd better get going. I've got a long drive.' His face was paler than vellum.

Susie disappeared discreetly into the back room on the pretext of washing up. Paul stood and took me in his arms. I had never felt so alone and helpless.

Holding my face in his hands he kissed away the salty wetness. 'Please keep in touch, Millie. I don't know how I'm going to cope without you beside me. I shall pray every night that you might change your mind.'

Before I could do or say anything, he was gone. I stood there shaking, holding back a flood worthy of Moses.

Susie poked her head round the door. 'Are you okay?'

'No,' I wailed and rushed out into the street to call him back. I screamed yes, yes, I'm coming with you, I'll go anywhere, to Timbuctoo, anywhere. Please wait for me. Take me with you ... please.

But I was too late.

He was nowhere to be seen.

54

Looking back on the time since Paul left, I shall never know how I survived, or how Susie coped so admirably with my black moods. I moved, spoke and did everything on cruise control, unaware of the weather, the time of day, the year, or the month.

Did I say month?

What's the date? It can't be the sixteenth? Oh no... Where's my diary?

We're not the sixteenth already, are we? We can't be, it's impossible. I checked the date on the *Telegraph*. Yes, there it was as bold as brass, definitely not the fifteenth, nor the seventeenth. It's the sixteenth.

And I'm ten days late.

But there is one tiny problem. Who is the father?

I've already used the fifty-fifty but I've got two lifelines left. Do I ask the audience, or do I phone a friend?

55

During my lunch break, I strode purposefully into Boots on Notting Hill Gate to buy a pregnancy testing kit. I didn't dare tell Susie of my suspicions for fear of too many probing questions. I didn't feel or look any different, but I knew it was happening, as I'd already done a test at 5 o'clock in the morning, watching riveted as a clear, blue stripe appeared as if by magic. I sat on the loo and imagined I was beginning to feel sick. I felt my boobs and they were as they were the day before, or were the nipples slightly sore?

Sure as eggs is eggs, I didn't want 'it' to be Rupert's, but if 'it' was Paul's, then I felt I'd been reprieved. Only, under the circumstances, how could I tell him? Consumed with fear, hand in hand with a growing thrill, I wondered what to do.

I told the girls.

'You're not going to get rid of it, surely?' asked Polly bluntly, as I sipped a mineral water.

'Of course I'm not,' I snapped. 'How could you possibly ask such a question?' I looked from one to the other and said seriously, 'It's probably not much bigger than a pin head, but it's real. Part of me. Yes,' I paused, 'I'm definitely going to have it.'

Susie waved to the waiter for another bottle of wine. She stared at me shrewdly and leaned forward in her chair. 'I must say, you don't look any fatter. Are you throwing up yet?'

'Suse, don't be so crass,' Polly said, coming to my defence.

'No, thank God, it's too early, I think, although I feel foul all the time and my tits started to tingle this morning. I'm tired too, but perhaps that's because I'm not sleeping.'

'I'm not surprised,' both Susie and Polly said together, simultaneously clamping their arms across their chests.

'Have you told Paul?' Their faces were intent and concerned.

'No,' I said, my eyes stinging.

'Why are you looking so miserable?' Polly said, pouring some wine into their glasses. 'Paul told you he loves you and if you spring it on him during a good moment, he'll be thrilled, I'm sure.'

Susie nodded encouragingly, then a cloud crossed her face. She looked anxiously at Polly. 'Er, it is Paul's, isn't it?'

I shut up like a clam.

'Tell us, please Mill, that it *is* his?'

I pulled out my hankie and twisted it and turned it, knotting the end, then untying it. I banged my fist on the table. 'I don't knooooow...' I sobbed.

'Oh my God. It's Rupert's,' said Susie.

'I don't know whose it is,' I cried.

'Houston, we have a problem,' joked Polly, in an attempt at making light of the situation. 'Look, you two, we have to take things bitty by bitty. Namely one, you're up the duff, at the moment that is. As a matter of interest, how far gone are you?'

'I've calculated about six weeks, maybe a couple of days more, maybe less, depending on whether it's ... Rupert's or Paul's...'

'Phew, thank God for that.'

'What do you mean?' asked Polly.

'Well, at least they're *close together* – you know,' she hissed, 'so neither will be any the wiser, once Millie makes up her mind, stupid.'

I felt increasingly like a slab of meat being dissected during an autopsy and The Thing growing inside me was becoming more unreal. The longer I left it, the harder it would be to back out. I stood up. 'I'm off.'

'What?'

'I've had enough. I'm going home.'

'We haven't overstepped the mark, have we? You're not cross with us, are you Millie?' Polly said, nervously twiddling her fringe.

'No, of course I'm not cross with you. Quite the opposite. I'm poleaxed, that's all. I want to have a bit of time to myself, to sort things out. You know how it is. I've got a lot on my mind.'

'You take care, now,' Susie said, patting me affectionately. 'If you need anything, anything at all, ring me – or Poll – we want to help. We're on 24 hour call-out, you know that.'

'You won't do anything silly, will you, Millie? Promise?'

'No.' Only chuck it in, that's all.

196

They turned to each other and Polly said, 'Before you go, we want to say something. We had a brief chat, Suse and I, while you were in the loo and, well, if it helps, we'd like to do all we can for you, Mill. Sisterhood and all that crap.'

I had to smile. They were the most unlikely pair of fairy Godmothers this side of Hollywood.

56

Paul telephoned me the next evening and for one moment I nearly pretended to be my answerphone, but couldn't remember how the beep went.

'I can't tell you how much I miss you, Mill. I'm settling in okay, but I could do with you here. It's lonely at night and I miss your funny face.'

I fought back tears.

'I know I shouldn't ask, I promised, but have you thought about it any more, about coming up here? Not permanently, of course, but maybe for a weekend, to see what it's like. I won't force you to go to a match,' he said, with a hollow laugh. 'Please say you'll come.'

The absence of commitment on my part weighed like a lead balloon. I would never, in a million years, trick him into thinking the baby was his simply to suit me, when it could equally be Rupert's. I hated myself. I cut short our conversation on the pretext that I was on my way out. I could feel his hurt from where I was sitting.

I kept all Paul's messages on the answerphone so that I could listen to his voice over and over again when I couldn't sleep.

My situation seemed hopeless. I had made my bed and now I had to lie in it.

57

I'm two months, three days pregnant and I feel like death. I can't stop being sick, I don't want to eat anything and I've got seven zits on my chin. I've lost count of those on my forehead. So much for the glow of motherhood. Instead of producing a bump, I've lost about half a stone, which under normal circumstances would have cheered me up. It's Wednesday and it's wet. Susie's out on an appointment and I'm struggling with a load of filing which neither of us wants to do. I thought it would take my mind off things.

'Hello, excuse me,' a soft voice said behind me, 'I wonder if you could help.'

A ravishing, waif-like being stood in the doorway, her blonde hair glued to her head from the rain. She was carrying two heavy Sainsbury's bags, bulging at the seams with vegetables and a French stick.

'I do apologise, I didn't hear you come in. Please, take a seat.' I slammed the drawer of the filing cabinet and went to my desk, pointing to the empty chair, relieved to have an alternative to the tedium of tidying endless pieces of paper. 'What exactly are you looking for? Was it a flat, or a house?' I asked, searching for a pen.

I stared at her. There was something strangely familiar about the way her neck arched as she deposited her shopping on the floor.

'Actually, I'm looking for a one bedroom flat,' she said huskily, unbuttoning her dripping mac, 'It's for me, on my own. Nothing big.'

I couldn't take my eyes off her.

She frowned. Then a look of recognition swept across her own face. She placed a tapered, unvarnished fingertip to her throat. 'My goodness, you're M-Millie, aren't you?' She blushed, embarrassed. 'I'm sorry, no, of course you're not, aren't... Sorry. I'm mumbling. I didn't mean to be rude, but for a split second you looked like someone I met a long time ago.'

I knew exactly who she was. It was Abigail. Rupert's *wife*. The word stuck in my throat. It had to be her, I knew it was, although she looked completely different from the last time I saw her. All the glitz and glamour had been washed away, her face bare of make up. She looked about eighteen. A tired eighteen.

'Abigail? I don't believe it. What on earth are you doing here? Where's Rupert?' I must have touched a nerve as she winced painfully.

'There's no reason for you to know, but we've separated, um, that is, er, we're half-way through a divorce.' Her eyes welled with tears. ' "Irretrievable breakdown of marriage",' she whispered.

I could have hit myself. Why hadn't Rupert mentioned it? 'Oh, I'm sorry. I didn't mean to be so tactless. Nothing changes. Usual clumsy me, I'm afraid. It flew out, as it always does. It was the surprise at seeing you,' I stammered. 'What on earth went wrong between you? I thought you were so happy together.'

'Oh, practically everything, you name it,' she said, her face pinched and nervous.

I opened my drawer and took out a handful of tissues, which she accepted gratefully. 'Look, I can make us a coffee and we can have a chat. I'm not exactly rushed off my feet, as you can see.'

'Yes, thank you,' she sniffed bravely, 'I'd like that, but I'd pre-fer tea, please, that is if it's not too much trouble.' Her eyes glistened. 'I'm not in the way, am I, holding you up or any-thing?'

I felt a real hypocrite. 'No, of course you're not,' I replied as I tinkered in the kitchen. I leaned against the sink, willing away a dangerous wave of nausea. Please don't let me be sick, not with Abigail here. With a bit of persuasion, I managed to get it under control. What a nightmare. 'Here you are. Do you take sugar? There's a biscuit tin somewhere.'

'No, no thanks, no sugar.' She blew on the steaming tea. She appeared so fragile, as though she was made of spun glass.

'I'm sorry to hear you two have split up. You were made for each other.'

She looked me squarely in the eye, but with no sign of

malice. 'I knew all about you and Rupert, of course. He told me everything.'

Everything? Oh, help.

'He informed me in that delightfully casual way of his the night we got engaged, "to clear the air", he said. I nearly backed out then. Perhaps I should have, but I loved him so much and I thought he'd change. The fact that he told me proved something, didn't it? His excuse in telling me was that we would never have any secrets from each other. Can you believe it? I was about to marry someone who'd been having an affair while going out with me. Oh – I'm sorry, I didn't mean to be so tactless.'

My face must have given the game away. 'No, I'm all right, I wish it hadn't happened, that's all.' You're not the only one who suffered, mate.

She clenched her knuckles and I thought she might break the handle of her cup. 'You have no idea how jealous I was of you. I could see at once what was going through Rupert's mind when we met at the Dugdales'. It wasn't the first time he'd had a wandering willy, so I should have been warned.' She ran her hand unabashed under her nose, laughing nervously. 'Do you remember what a fuss he made putting on your shoe, pretending to be Prince Charming. It was utterly puke-making. I should have killed him then.' Her voice softened and her grip on her cup relaxed. 'You were so beautiful and wild – and fun. Everything I wasn't. I admired you.' She bit her lip. 'He used to call me Black Ice when he was cross.' She looked down at her wet feet, her blonde lashes sweeping across her cheeks. 'He said you couldn't see it, but you knew it was there.' She was exquisitely beautiful, like a waterlogged angel.

'Oh, Abi, if only you knew. It wasn't nearly as bad as you think. Rupert didn't love me, not for one minute.'

'Perhaps, but did you love him?'

I hesitated before replying. 'Yes, if I'm being honest, I did. For a time, anyway, or I thought I did. You have to realise that I couldn't believe someone as gorgeous as Rupert was giving me a second glance, let alone a first one. I was flattered. It was a challenge, I don't know. Perhaps it's never happened to you, a *coup de foudre*, or should I say, a *feu de paille*. It burned itself out before it began. Maybe it was a last fling before he married you, a swansong, I don't know. All I can say is I've never pinched anyone's bloke before, knowingly that is and I'll never do it again.' One look at her sad face meant I had to fib, for her sake. I was beginning to feel hot. 'I didn't consciously two-time you – he told me you'd bust up. There was no way I'd ever embark on an affair if I knew there was someone else involved. You'll have to trust that I'm telling the truth, whatever Rupert told you.'

'It's ironic, really. Although you slept together I believe you.'

I promised to go to church for the next six months and to say a thousand hail Mary's on my knees, in sack cloth and ashes, whatever it might take to absolve my misdemeanours.

'I'm sorry, Abigail,' I said, embarrassed, 'I can't turn the clock back sadly. I wish I could. Doing the wrong thing and hurting people seems to be what I excel at. I hope you can forgive me, that's all.'

'It's all right. It was an accident waiting to happen.' She smoothed away a hair caught in her lashes. 'Do you want to take down my details?'

58

'...Hello, Paul Campbell.'

'Hi, it's me. I'm not interrupting am I?'

'Darling Millie, if you call buttering a piece of toast busy, then I am. It's great to hear from you. What are you up to?'

My insides turned wobbly at hearing his voice. My whole body was trembling through nerves, excitement, I don't know. That old familiar, nice sick feeling resurfaced. 'I'm not up to much, either. I'm running a bath, preparing for another lively evening at home on my own.' I twiddled the cord in my fingers. 'Your clockwork hippo fell off the rack into the bubbles and I needed to talk to you, that's all.' Oh, please don't let me cry... 'To see if you're all right. I wish you were here,' I whispered.

Paul didn't reply immediately. Then I heard a crunch down the line. He was eating.

'Hmm,' crunch, 'Hmm, sorry, missed that. What d'you say? I was thinking of coming up,' chew, 'to London this weekend,' swallow. 'Will you be around, or were you going down to your mother's? I'd love to see you. Any chance?'

Switching the receiver over to the other ear, I sat and picked up a pencil. I began to doodle.

'No, I've nothing planned. I'll be here,' I said, my tone non-committal.

'You sound less tired, Mill. That's good. I worry about you, all alone in your little flat. You seem happier. You haven't won the lottery, have you, or had a pay rise?'

'There's small hope of either, but I have had some news.' I sucked the end of my pencil. Should I tell him I was pregnant? No, not now, not on the telephone. It would scare him off. I was too terrified how he might react. I needed to do it face to face.

'It must be something big – you sound different from the last time we spoke.'

'Big's the word, but I would rather put it on hold until we see each other.'

'I can't wait,' he said. 'Let's try and sort out something definitely this time, please.'

I knew what he must be thinking, and hated myself for raising his hopes. I gnawed my knuckles to stop myself from sobbing out aloud.

'Millie? Are you still there? Mill? Answer me. Please. Ans...'

59

I fell asleep in the armchair. I had cramp in my leg, pins and needles attacked my feet and my neck seemed beyond repair. I untangled my tortured limbs and checked the time. Half-past eight. I felt so tired, as if my bung had been taken out. I heard a faint beeping sound, thinking it must be someone's burglar alarm further along the crescent, but on picking up my slipper which had fallen off, I realised it was the telephone. I hadn't replaced the receiver properly. At least it prevented Paul from ringing back. I switched on the answerphone as added protection.

To make matters worse, my bath water was stone cold. What a waste. I have never been more depressed. I realised I couldn't face Paul, not tomorrow, not next week, not next year. Never.

'I'm afraid I'm not here to take your call. Please leave your number, date and time of your call and any message and I'll get back to you as soon as possible.'

'Hello. It's me, Millie... Erm... I'm afr... I'm sorry, but I don't think I – I don't want to see you... Sorry. Can't explain. I'm sor–'

60

'Grief, girl, you haven't told him, have you? I can see it a mile away.'

Polly had succeeded in getting me to emerge from my self-imposed purdah only when she agreed to meet me in the greasy spoon opposite her office to satisfy my worrying craving for fried bread.

'Now let's be honest with each other. What's the betting on the baby being Rupert's? You're not still hankering after him, are you, after all he's done to you?' she asked candidly, not beating about the bush.

'No, of course I'm not.' I looked at her imploringly. 'I would give anything for it to be Paul's, you know that.'

'Right, now we've got to think up plan A. Pass me the sugar, would you, please?'

'Here you are. Oh, I nearly forgot. You won't believe it, but Abigail – you know, Rupert's wife, came into the office yesterday when Susie was out.'

'That's a blast from the past. What did she have to say for herself?'

'For starters, you'll never believe it but she and Rupert are getting a divorce. She's so different from how she was. I nearly didn't recognise her.' I shovelled some spilt sugar into a pile on the table with my spoon. 'She's managed to hold onto her looks, unfortunately, and she wasn't wearing a scrap of make up. She wants to buy a flat. Quite a come down for her I should think.'

'Abigail was always too good for him. Oops, sorry, Mill, done it again, but for the time being we've got to concentrate on your little problem, because it's not going to disappear overnight.'

'Yes, you're right.'

'First things first, you've got to tell Paul, willy nilly.'

'I can't, Polly, I just can't. What can he do about it, for goodness sake, with me stuck in London? Particularly if it isn't his.' I picked up a crust in my fingers. 'He'd kill me if he ever found out.'

'He should bloody marry you, that's what, if you ask me. Even if it isn't his, it is all but, considering the time you've been together. It would only have been a matter of time before it happened between you anyway.'

'Yes, but...'

'No buts about it, he should be told. He has every right. He's a responsible guy and would stand by you, even if he knew the truth, I'm positive. Also he has the advantage of advanced years to appreciate fatherhood, hasn't he?'

'He's not as old as all that,' I grumbled, 'you make him sound like Methuselah.'

'And what about your Ma? Has she got any clue at all as to what's happening?'

I began to feel sick at the thought of confessing to Ma, the childhood fears of receiving a ticking off never far away. 'She doesn't know either. She hasn't guessed yet, I don't think, as I've not put on any weight, although she kept on giving me odd looks when I saw her last weekend.'

'Well, knowing her, it won't be long before she smells a rat. You've got to involve her, Mill. She is your mother and she might be able to help.' She poured more sugar into her coffee from the chrome-topped dispenser. 'By delaying things it'll only complicate matters.'

I ran my fingers over the angry lumps on my face. 'If Paul sees me in this state, I'll lose him altogether. Look at me. I'm a massive walking carbuncle.'

'Okay, so you've got spots. So what? It's not the end of the world and they'll go in time – if you stop bloody picking them, that is. Anyway, if he comes to London, you can plaster your face with guck.'

I touched a throbbing, emerging pimple at the side of my nose. 'Do you really think that'll work?' I asked pathetically.

'Of course. Once you're over the three month hump, you should start blooming. Take Mary. Even she was an absolute fright for the first few weeks.'

'Paul did mention once that he found pregnant women sexy. He didn't mention spotty ones.'

'Right, now we've got the wretched acne sorted, we need to deal with your barnet, which really is cause for concern.' She tentatively picked up a lank wing, rubbing it between her thumb and index finger with a look of disgust. 'Hmm, when was the last time you had it cut? Or washed it, come to that? And was it done by a professional, by any chance? Looks more as though it's been hacked by a combine harvester with blunt blades.'

I booked an appointment for the next day.

'Fort you'd left the country, darlin',' Edie said, a mouth full of pins, as she wrapped me in a floral cape and pushed a pink towel into my shirt collar. 'We ain't 'alf got our work cut out 'ere, haven't we just? Goin' anywhere nice?'

I shut my eyes and let her get on with it. Dear Edie was somewhat over enthusiastic with the hose and drenched my sweater under the layers of towel and gown, choosing to do three washes as against the normal two. She was a good judge.

'Fink I found somefink livin' in 'ere,' she said, squeezing the water out before tucking me up in a turban.

There was something curiously perverse in the treatment Edie administered and her scissors seemed to be fired with rocket fuel. I felt more like a mongrel in a poodle parlour than a human coughing up nigh on forty quid to have my hair tamed. Maybe I should have gone to the poodle parlour – I was already in the doghouse.

''old still while I shove the velcros under the 'ood. There. In you go darlin'. That's dunnit.' She swivelled the thermostat on the dial and dropped it in my lap. 'DO Y' WAN' A MAG' OR SOMEFINK?' she shouted in my ear. ''ERE YOU ARE, LOVE. THESE SHOULD KEEP Y' QUIET.'

I accepted the latest copies of *Hello!* and *OK!* Having digested the revolting recipes (a hundred things to do with a mushroom) and wandered through Anthea Turner-Bovey's ghastly wedding photos and Joan Collins' wigs, I turned casually to the section of black and white photographs towards the end. What I saw nearly made me throw up.

There, in the top right hand corner beside a picture of Jamie Oliver arm in arm with Gary Rhodes, was a picture of Paul.

61

He was standing very close to a girl. She was young and pretty, with urchin cut hair. Judging by the freckles on her *retroussé* nose, she was probably a redhead and she was gazing up at Paul as though he was the most important thing in the world. And what, I hear you ask, was he doing? Grinning, like a cat who'd got the cream, that's what.

I must have screamed out loud, because Edie came rushing over. She turned off the drier, her face creased with worry. 'Are you all right love? You look as though you've seen a ghost.' She felt my hair under the hood. 'I fink you can come out now. You're cooked.'

I didn't wait for her to brush my hair, or style it. I simply asked her to remove the rollers and I paid in cash, leaving her a massive tip because I couldn't wait for the change – or explain my strange behaviour – and ran to my car. I collapsed on the steering wheel and shook convulsively. Paul had met someone else.

A tap disturbed my wild thoughts and a traffic warden's face peered through the window. 'Is everything okay, Miss?' he asked, tweaking his Hitler whiskers.

I wound down the glass, touching my tangled mess of curls, stiff with setting lotion. 'Yes, thanks, everything's fine.'

'Are you sure? You look a bit on the upset side to me. Anyway, you'd better move sharpish, or I'll have to give you a ticket. You'll be into the Penalty zone in thirty seconds.'

62

'Hello, can I speak to Millie, please?'

'Yes, who's calling?'

'It's Abigail, um, Abigail Holland.'

Susie clicked the button on the exchange on her desk. 'It's Abigail. For you.'

'Hi, Abigail, how are you?' I asked, nodding my head to Susie to say that I was okay.

'I'm fine, thanks Millie. I wonder if I could come and see that one bedroom flat in Colville Terrace this morning. I've got some time off and I could be with you in just under an hour.'

'Sure,' I said, opening my desk drawer and rummaging in the muddle of paper clips, rubber bands and Twix wrappers, 'I've got the keys – somewhere – hang on a mo'. Suse, you don't know where the keys are to the one bed in Colville Terrace, do you? Ah, hang on a sec, here they are. That's fine, Abigail, see you soon.'

'Well, she's obviously serious about leaving Rupert, isn't she?' Susie confirmed.

'Yes, I think she is, only there was something in the way she talked that made me wonder if there wasn't more to it than meets the eye.' I looked at the clock above Susie's head. 'I've got time to grab a sandwich before she comes. Shall I get you one from next door?'

Abigail blew in with a flurry of autumn leaves, a soft, camel-coloured pullover complementing her peachy skin, her stick-like frame poured into a pair of black suede trousers, and a tweed jacket. She looked as though she had leaped directly off a fashion plate in *Country Life*.

'I'm sorry I'm late. I had to wait ages for a bus.'

Abigail slumming it on *public* transport?

'We've got plenty of time and I haven't got another appointment for a couple of hours. I can make us a cup of tea if you like.' I desperately wanted to pump her for more info about Rupert.

'Thanks, that'd be great.'

'Mill, I'd better be going now myself, or I'll be late for my appointment,' said Susie, looking anxiously at the darkening clouds through the window. 'Do you think I need a brolly?'

'Better take it in case, oh by the way, this is Abigail, Susie. Susie, Abigail.'

'It's nice to meet you. Must fly. Byee,' she said, giving me a quizzical smile.

'She seems nice. Gorgeous looking and fabulous hair. Is it real?' asked Abigail.

'It certainly is. Now, let's see, here are a couple of new properties which came in this morning. I was about to post them to you, but have a look and see what you think, while I make a pot.'

I left Abigail reading the details, and leaned against the lavatory door. I felt like death warmed up. I didn't know how long I could keep up my act. 'Here you are, milk no sugar, that's right, isn't it?'

'Um, thanks, you've a good memory.' She removed her jacket and stretched gracefully like a cat to hang it over the back of her chair.

I noticed she wasn't wearing her wedding ring.

She smiled openly. 'It's really nice bumping into you again. No, don't look at me like that, I mean it, honestly,' Abigail added kindly. She tipped her head to one side. 'Are you all right, Millie, you don't look very well. Are you sure you can take me to see this flat? I don't mind leaving it for now.'

'I'm pregnant,' I said, before I could stop myself.

'Wow! That's fantastic. I'm so pleased for you.'

'Don't be,' I said somewhat ungraciously, 'It's not as simple as that. There are one or two complications.'

'Oh dear, I'm sorry. Aren't things going to plan?'

'Not exactly, I'm afraid.'

'But the baby's all right, isn't it?'

'Oh, yes the baby's fine, as far as I know. There are other problems.'

She picked up her cup. 'Is he married?'

'Something like that,' I answered a bit too sharply. I didn't want to talk about it.

Realising her mistake, she said, 'I'm sorry, Millie, I didn't mean to pry.' She blinked away a renegade tear, and said quietly, 'I wish I had a baby.'

'But I thought you had, or were going to,' I said, surprised.

'Me, a baby? Whatever gave you that idea?' she asked, trembling slightly, spilling tea in her saucer.

I leaned back on my chair and eased my sore stomach. 'We were all under the impression that you and Rupert had to get married. That's the yarn he spun for my benefit, at any rate.'

'Is that what he said? The lying hound. Of course I wasn't pregnant. I'd never do anything as tacky as that in a million years.' She wiped her eyes with a small, lace-edged handkerchief.

I could smell lavender.

'Daddy always accused Rupert of being a mythomaniac. No way could I have been expecting a baby, certainly not with him at any rate.'

I began to shake inside. 'What do you mean, not with Rupert?'

'You couldn't make another cup, could you, please, Millie? That one didn't hit the sides and I haven't eaten a thing all day.'

I went into the back and refilled the kettle. My heart was thumping. I didn't wait for the tea to stew and poured out what looked disgustingly like cat's pee. I put the cup in front of her. 'Here, have a biscuit,' I said, pushing the tin towards her. 'Please tell me, Abi, there isn't anything wrong with Rupert, is there?'

She bit into a squashed fly and her eyebrows shot skywards. She ate hungrily, licking the corner of her mouth. 'He had mumps very badly and glandular fever when he was twenty and was really, really ill. The end result is that dearest, darling, macho Rupert fires blanksh,' she revealed, her mouth full of biscuit, sending a spray of crumbs across my diary. 'Oopsh, shorry!' she apologised, wiping them away with the back of her hand.

I stared stupidly at her, the magnitude of what she had told me beginning to sink in.

'He's ninety-nine point nine per cent sterile.'

The blood rushed to my ears, pounding like waves. Sterile? Rupert? I can't begin to tell you the relief I felt at that particular moment. It positively soared through me, breaking the sound barrier. That meant my baby had to be Paul's. Oh joy of joys. My God, I'm a lucky bugger. I don't deserve it. Then I thought, poor, blameless Abigail, but I'm afraid my sympathy didn't last long. Selfishly I realised that Paul need never know about my, er, little hiccup with Rupert, and I could take my horrible secret to the grave, which is probably where I'd end up if he ever found out the truth.

I took a deep breath, suddenly ashamed of my evil thoughts, when ecstasy at the realisation that I was off the hook took over from any feeling of remorse. It was all I could do to prevent myself from hugging the girl.

Desperately I tightened the muscles around my mouth to stop myself from laughing hysterically. 'Well I'll be ... That has to be the saddest thing I've heard. (May I rot in hell). You poor darling. (Stop now, before you get struck by lightning.) I had no idea. (But I do now.)'

Abigail's periwinkle blue eyes filled with tears. She has to be the only person in the world, apart from Gwynneth Paltrow, who can look even more gorgeous when they're crying. 'When we were first married,' she sighed, wiping away a drip, 'we were desperate to start a family, but nothing happened. Month after month went by and regular as clockwork, I got the curse, so Mummy made me have all the tests under the sun, thinking it must be me. In the end they found out there's absolutely nothing wrong. To the contrary in fact, I'm as fit as a flea and all the doctors said I am extremely fertile and sent me packing. They told me not to try so hard and that it was bound to happen naturally.' She began to blush, her huge eyes tragic. 'Now you know the truth. The irony is that it's Rupert who has the problem. You know how proud he is. The mere hint that his bits and pieces might not be quite up to par made him flip.'

'Did he do anything about it?'

'At first he refused, denying all responsibility and insisting that the doctors had misread my results.'

210

'Have another biscuit.' Abigail had absolutely no inkling what her confession meant to my future. 'What happened?' I asked, mopping up stray currants from the bottom of the tin with a wet finger. 'What on earth made him change his mind?'

'It was simple,' she answered, gulping down her tea. 'Hmm, lovely.' She dabbed her mouth delicately. 'He wanted a son, a mirror image, someone who would reflect his own glory, to show off to his friends. To play rugger with.' Her face began to crumple, but she managed to stem the flow of tears. 'I know it sounds callous, but Rupert is wonderfully vain. He's the only man I know who carries a compact mirror. He doesn't care who knows it, the privilege of the beautiful, I suppose. But he is so good looking – he is, isn't he?'

'I don't think I've ever seen anyone as perfect,' I answered truthfully.

She moved her cup around in its saucer and smiled secretly. 'Mummy used to say he had PGL.'

'PGL?'

'Pointless Good Looks. A mini replica of himself was a tremendous lure. For both of us, I suppose, if I'm honest with myself. I also wanted to see what I could produce. Anyway, he booked himself into the hospital on the QT, only telling me when it was all over.'

I found it hard to imagine Rupert closeted in an NHS loo fingering a copy of *Men Only*, knowing instinctively he would have achieved a better result with the *Ferrari Owner's Handbook*.

'When the results arrived, they showed he had a virtually non-existent sperm count. Not one wiggly worm was worth its weight. Nothing. The fact is,' her face contorted dangerously, 'Rupert can't make babies.'

I felt like abandoning my tea and opening a bottle of champagne. Here was my guardian angel, blown into my office by chance, my saving grace and I wanted to kiss her. I pinched myself till it hurt, to stop myself from grinning. 'I'm so sorry,' I managed, my voice cracking, 'it must have been awful for you. What are you going to do?' I should have been drowned at birth.

She gave a shallow laugh. 'You only have to look at me to realise that my modelling career is well and truly over. I look a fright. When Rupert and I split up, Daddy wanted to buy me a house in Chelsea, but I've changed a lot over the last couple of years. I don't need Manolo Blahniks nor Prada bags, I had enough of them when I was working.' She smiled at me. 'You would have had a field day at our local Oxfam. They couldn't believe what was in the bin liners when I dropped them off.'

How sweet she could have considered that they would in any way fit me.

'You haven't lost your looks. If anything, you're more beautiful than ever. Sort of ethereal.' I could afford the odd compliment. 'But if you've given up modelling, what are you doing?'

For the first time her face lit up with genuine excitement. 'Please don't make fun of me, Millie, but I work at the hospital where Rupert had his tests. I'm training to be a paediatric nurse. I want to look after the cancer babies.' She lifted the lid off the biscuit tin, grabbing the last Garibaldi. 'May I? They were delicious. So was the tea. Thanks for listening, it's been such a help to talk to someone who understands.'

I nearly said the same thing to her. 'We'd better go and see that flat, before it's sold to someone else. I'll get my coat.' She took hers and slipped her slim arms through the tailored sleeves. 'There are no hard feelings, are there, I mean about me and Rupert?'

'No, of course there aren't. It was such an age ago. As a matter of fact, I'm really happy we bumped into each other. It's done me the world of good.'

I held the door for her and dropped that latch, knowing that Susie wouldn't be long. 'Tell me, when does your divorce come through?'

'The divorce? Quite soon as a matter of fact, well, the decree nisi that is. Unbelievably we've been able to agree on most things. My solicitor says he's never handled such an amicable settlement – there've been no battles over houses, contents, dogs ... children,' she said in a hushed voice, 'or anything.' Her eyes filled with tears again. 'I wonder sometimes why we're going through it.'

'You're still in love with him, aren't you?' It had been staring me in the face. We reached my car and I unlocked the passenger door to let her get in first.

Buckling her seatbelt, Abigail broke down completely. It upset me to see her in such a state. I might be an egotistical bitch at times, but I'm not totally heartless. Between sobs, she said, 'Yes, you're right, I do love him.' She blew her nose on the only dry corner left of her hankie. 'I always will, in spite of everything. He was my life.' She gave a hint of a laugh. 'You must think me mad, but then nobody's perfect.'

Her unconditional forgiveness was sobering.

'I'm not the best person to give advice, as you've probably gathered, but I know true love when I see it. Even when Rupert and I were seeing each other, I always felt an overpowering impression that you were never far away. He let slip a couple of times and called me Abi. How's that for undivided attention? I bet he never called you Millie.'

That revelation cheered her and she laughed. 'No, he didn't as a matter of fact.' She blew her nose and the shutters descended again. 'Do you think he might still want me? Enough to try again? It seems so silly to sever everything when we haven't really had a good bash at it. I think I would adjust to no babies of our own. We could always adopt, or maybe try that business where they use a needle to remove a sperm from his balls and inject it into an egg, on a saucer. It's worked for other couples.' Her face became serious, her bottom lip trembling dangerously. 'Oh, Millie, I don't want to lose him. Not again.'

I slowed down and turned into the Portobello Road. 'You won't, I can bet on it, but you've got to tell him the truth. The first thing is to stop this stupid divorce. The only people getting any rewards are the lawyers themselves. Tell him you love him and see what happens. I'll keep my fingers crossed.'

'You've been so kind to me.'

'Yes, well, in the meantime we'd better see this flat, but somehow I don't think you'll be looking for one on your own. I'm prepared to put good money on it.' I parked half on the pavement outside the converted terraced house. 'Here, take the key and go on in. I'll join you in a sec. Got to lock the car.'

I couldn't resist it.

I punched the air victoriously. What a goal!

63

'You ... have ... one ... message.'

'Millie, it's Paul. Is everything all right? I've been trying to reach you since the other night, but you're never in. I've phoned your mother and she hasn't heard from you for three days. I'm really worried. Please ring me as soon as you get this message.'

I didn't.

64

The spots are on the march and no new zit has reared its ugly head for a week.

I've picked the scabs off the others.

65

Although tempted to ask Mary if she was prepared to recycle her bell tent, this morning I purchased my first proper maternity dress. I went into Dorothy P's and bought one in denim, a white t-shirt to wear underneath, giant pants and a pair of plimsolls. I'm beginning to look the part. In the changing room, I caught sight of my tummy and I was shocked at how round and comfy it looked. You'll be relieved to hear, I've stopped being sick.

Oh yes – I've told my mother.

Knowing the truth about Rupert only makes matters worse. I'd left it too late and Paul has met someone else.

I've decided to go this one alone.

66

'Er, Mill, have you seen this, um, this by any chance?' Susie was waving a copy of the infamous magazine.

'Yes, I have, as a matter of fact,' I said very quietly.

'Why didn't you say anything?'

'What was there to say? He's found another bird. There's eff all I can do about it.'

She put her arms around me. 'Come here and have a cuddle. It might not be as bad as it appears, you know. The camera does lie.' She walked back to her desk. 'Have you any idea who she is?'

'Of course I don't,' I snapped unreasonably. 'Do you think she's pretty? She's hanging onto Paul as though she owns him. He doesn't look too unhappy, either,' I added miserably, sitting in my chair with a thump. Chewing my nails, I pleaded, 'What am I going to do, Suse? What's going to happen to me?'

'There's not a lot you can do, my love, short of sitting tight and getting on with your life. Either that, or you'll have to confront him sooner or later.'

'But why does he have to find someone else so quickly? I can't stand the thought of him with her, or anyone else.'

'It was bound to happen, as you and I are only too aware. You wouldn't go with him, which is fair enough, and I understand your reasons, but a gorgeous bloke like Paul, on his tod, miles from home? You must have realised something like this would happen, didn't you?'

'I know, but when you see it staring you in the face, it hurts.'

'Of course it does, and I'm sorry if I was harsh. I didn't mean to be.' Susie came round to my desk and looked at my diary. 'You've only got one appointment this afternoon. I'll shut up shop for half an hour and I'll do it. It's only around the corner. You go home and have a rest, you look as though you need it. Put your feet up with a good mag – er, a book.' She manhandled me through the door. 'Now go, off with you. I'll deal with everything. Oh yes, by the way, the hair looks fab.'

67

I was exhausted. I slept on and off for most of the afternoon, a heavy, dreamless sleep. I tidied the bed and, rather than get dressed, I put on my woolly tartan dressing gown. The kettle having boiled, I poured hot water onto a tomato and basil cup-a-soup and stirred the liquid, squashing the lumps against the back of the spoon. With my free hand I opened the paper to see what was on telly. Scanning BBC1, I was tempted by the holiday programme, until I saw which area they were promoting: Barcelona and the Costa Brava. There was *Emmerdale* on the other side and as I never watch it, there seemed little point. I'd never pick up a twenty year plot in twenty minutes. I was tossing up between Channel Four news or listening to the radio, when the doorbell rang. It was seven o'clock. Wondering who it could be, I pushed the intercom. 'Hello?' I asked, hoping it wasn't a charity seller, as I'd got no change, only a fiver.

A man's voice answered. 'Millie, can I come up? It's me.'

It was Paul.

I put my soup on the hall table, shaking like a leaf. I couldn't not let him in, could I? What on earth was I going to say? Angrily, I thought he's got a nerve coming here, after being photographed with that ... person. He must have known everyone would see it. Hesitantly, I pushed the button to let him in the front door.

He looked worried and older. 'Hi, Mill. It's all right if I come in? You're not getting ready to go out,' he asked, looking at my dressing gown, 'or expecting someone?'

'No, come in. I was going to have an early night,' I said curtly.

There was a cool rush of air as he brought the outside cold in with him. I shivered. He stood awkwardly on the landing and stared at me, his face white as a sheet.

I twisted my fingers in and out of each other, digging any nails I had left into my palms. I was terrified by his expression of disbelief.

Stony-faced, he said, 'You're pregnant, aren't you?'

It scarcely shows. How could he tell? I sat on the hall chair, my legs giving way. 'How did you guess?'

'I know you like the back of my hand.' He leaned against the wall and sighed, his face tight and sad. 'You've changed, some-how, you're different. I felt it on the phone the other night. Don't ask how.' He began to pace up and down, looking at me every now and then but with no recognition. 'I – I can't take all this in. It's come as a bit of a shock.' Accidentally, he knocked a watercolour off kilter. 'This is too much,' he said, trying to straighten it with a trembling hand. He turned around and faced me. 'Whose is it?'

The tone of despair in his voice cut me to the quick.

'I presume it's Rupert Holland's,' he said, his eyes flashing angrily. 'It's his, isn't it?'

His reaction was far worse than I had feared.

'There's no point in lying to me. I know you've been seeing each other.'

'How?' I asked in a frightened voice.

'He came up to Manchester last Saturday with Lawrie and he had great pleasure in telling me he'd taken you out.' Tears glistened alarmingly. 'My God, Millie, what the hell have you done?'

I was speechless. It was all going horribly wrong. Then I remembered the photograph in the magazine. How's he going to explain that one? It made me feel stronger, for a brief moment, at any rate.

Before I could attack, Paul said, 'Where is he then? Lover boy? Buggered off and left you in it, has he, eh? It's what he usually does. Can't say I'm surprised.'

I pulled at the tassle on the end of my dressing gown cord, unravelling the thread. 'No, it's nothing like that. It's not Rupert's baby.'

He looked genuinely surprised. 'Now there's a funny thing.

Not Rupert's? Pull the other one. Then who the hell's is it? Some other poor sod's?' He scratched the corner of his mouth in disbelief. 'You have been busy.'

Wretched tears started and I could feel my nose swelling and going red. I knew I looked hideous. 'It's yours,' I choked, 'it's your baby.'

'For the first time in my life I simply don't believe you,' he said bitterly. 'I think I'll leave you to it,' he said, brushing past me into the hall, sending my soup flying.

'But what about the photo of you and that girl?' I cried out, but he was already half-way downstairs. I heard the front door bang.

68

I don't know how long I sat huddled on the landing floor. I stood up, cold and stiff. In utter desperation I rang Mum. 'I need you, Ma,' I sobbed, 'can I come home, please, now?'

Two hours later I parked in my mother's drive. She was standing at the door in her pinnie, grey-faced and worried.

'Oh, Millie darling, what a mess,' she said, kissing me. 'Come in and tell me everything. I've put the kettle on.'

It was an impossible task. I was crying so much, I doubt she was able to make head or tail of anything I said.

'Of course he knows it's his, darling,' she said, pouring me a second cup of tea, 'Any fool would realise that. He's coming to terms with the shock, that's all, you'll see.'

I was humbled by her total faith in me. I had failed to mention Rupert. We were startled by the shrill ring of the telephone. It was late and nobody rings my mother after 7 o'clock if they want a coherent conversation unless it's an emergency. It could only be Paul.

'I'm going to take it in the sitting room. You don't want to speak to him, do you?'

I shook my head.

'You sit here while I deal with him.'

I heard Ma's voice, firm and authoritative. '...No, I'm sorry, you can't. No, I don't want to get her. She's very upset. I've sent her up to bed so it will have to wait until tomorrow.' There was a brief pause. 'Yes, I'll pass that on, all right, goodbye Paul.'

'How was he?' I asked as I blew my nose in one of Dad's old hankies.

'Well, to be honest, he sounded dreadfully upset. Did you want to talk to him? Did I do the wrong thing?'

'Oh, Ma,' I said, feeling the warmth of her comforting arms around me, 'No, you were perfect. Did he say anything else?'

She pulled away slightly and smiled enigmatically, smoothing away my fringe. 'No, he didn't darling. Time for bed.'

69

I returned Paul's call as soon as I woke up the next morning. It wasn't even six o'clock, but I didn't care. 'We need to talk.'

'Right. I'll come down to London tomorrow night. I'll be with you at six thirty.'

PART THIRTEEN

HOME WIN

70

He arrived at eight, after a dreadful drive south through end-less roadworks and an accident involving a jack-knifed lorry, which spilled a load of frozen chicken all over the M1. He looked exhausted and I noticed he had lost weight. Darling, dar-ling Paul. I wanted to cling to him, never let him go, tell him I loved him and repair any damage I may have done, but I had to wait. Timing was imperative.

He stood in the doorway, holding a bunch of freesias and a bottle of champagne. If he had come intending to fight, then these weren't the usual weapons. He kissed me politely.

I crossed my fingers and prayed that we would be celebrat-ing in a few minutes. I turned off the bright central light in the sitting room, the warm glow from the side lamps softening the deep lines in his face.

'We're in a mess,' he sighed, flopping in the leather armchair he liked to sit in. 'Who's going to start?'

The proverbial bull in the china shop, I launched for the jugular. 'I saw your picture in *Hello!* Who was that woman you were with?'

'Oh her,' he said, grinning. 'It's amazing, I can't believe how many people have seen it. Fame at last.'

Eh?

'Grief, I was only standing beside her for two minutes, when

220

this photographer bloke came and took the photo. What's more, they cut off her husband.'

Husband?

'She ... she's married, then?' I stammered, my heart pounding, 'I thought you and...'

Paul had the decency to burst out laughing. 'I can see it all now. You didn't think that she and I... We... Oh, Mill, you are a clot. I don't even know her name.' His face became serious again, the shutters descending, undermining the small amount of confidence I had scraped together.

'What are we going to do?' I asked, unable to hide the hurt and fear in my voice.

He parted a stray curl away from my face. 'I don't know, Millie, I really don't.' He stood up. 'Come on, let's open that bottle of champagne, or maybe you'd better not, as you're...'

'Paul, it is yours. What do I have to do to convince you I'm telling the truth?' I said, my heart hollow and aching.

He walked into the kitchen and I watched as he undid the foil on the top of the bottle. 'One drop won't do any harm. Hurry up with that glass, it's going to spill all over the place.'

I felt as though I was in some strange dream. 'I saw Abigail yesterday,' I said casually, mopping up the mess with some kitchen paper.

'Abigail? Rupert's wife?'

'Yes, she came into the office looking for a flat. They're getting divorced.'

'I'm not surprised. She's far too nice to be mixed up with a bastard like him. Oh, God, sorry,' he said, as my face crumpled. 'Didn't mean that to sound the way it did. What did she have to say for herself?'

'Rather a lot as it happened. You know she was never pregnant when they married? Rupert made it all up.'

Paul drank half his glass in one go. 'Did he now?' he said, looking me straight in the eyes, his expression sombre.

'Yes, but that's not half of it. She'll never become pregnant, or not with Rupert, I should say.'

'What do you mean?'

I played my ace. 'Because he's sterile.'

Paul coughed and walked over to the window. 'I see,' he said, 'how very convenient.'

221

'Don't say it like that, please. You make me sound so hard.'

He turned around to face me, his eyes glazing with despair. 'Millie, I don't know what to say.' He put his champagne glass on the window-sill. 'Come here.'

I was frozen to the spot.

He moved a step closer. 'Don't be silly. Come and have a hug. I need it.'

I rushed into his arms and could feel his heart beat as I slipped my hand inside his jacket. He had been sweating and his shirt was damp under the arms. 'I don't know how to explain what I did, with Rupert, I mean. It was as though it wasn't me – it was another person, I don't know.' I raised my head, bumping it on his chin. 'Can you understand? Haven't you ever done anything foolish in your life? Something you hate yourself for?'

'Probably, I can't remember. Anyway, it's different for a man.' He stroked the back of my neck under my hair. 'You know, when Rupert told me you'd seen each other, insinuating the worst, it wasn't the best bit of news I could wish to hear, believe me. If I try hard enough, I suppose I can see it from your point of view – I'll have to. It'll take time, that's all. I can't blame you for trying it on with him again. He's a good-looking bastard, always was and I'd been a shit to you over the last few weeks. I was half expecting you to meet someone else and then when I had to go to Manchester, well, that clinched it.' He let me go and poured some more champagne into his glass, returning to the leather armchair. 'I wish it had been anyone but Rupert, that's all.'

I put my hand over the top of my glass as he offered me the bottle. 'Better not.' I crawled over and positioned myself on the floor between his legs. I touched the reassuring warmth of his dark green cords and rested my head on his knee.

'I reckon we've still got something worth working at, don't you, Mill? If we try hard enough to put this business behind us, that is.'

I bought time by drinking the last drops of champagne. The bubbles fizzed down my nose. Never in my life have I been more nervous. I took hold of his hand, kissing the fingers individually and whispered, 'Paul, I love you. I never loved Rupert, it was, oh I don't know, he was so persuasive. He

222

could charm the birds off the trees.' I held my breath. 'It didn't mean anything. Can you ever love me again, the way you used to?' I felt his body go tense, each muscle taut as a drum.

Then he made a strange noise. I shall never in my life forget the expression in his eyes.

'Oh, Millie, Millie, Millie,' he said, 'Love you? Love you? How can you ask such a stupid question? I've never stopped loving you, never. Ask your mother. Ask Susie and Polly. Ask Mary. Ask the postman.'

I wasn't sure whether to laugh or cry again. Through kisses and hugs, I managed to say, 'It must have happened while we were in Suffolk, you know, the baby.'

Paul smiled at the memory. 'How far gone are you?'

'Three months. You're lucky you didn't see me ten days ago. I was like Spotty Muldoon's sister.'

Paul hauled me up onto his lap and kissed me. Wiping a stray tear away from his cheek, he said, 'Dearest Mill, I can't tell you how happy I am. This has to be the best moment of my life, well almost. Netherfield staying in the Third Division was better than winning the Pools.' He grinned, his eyes bright and sparkling. 'I can't believe it. My God, a baby.' He parted the folds of my dressing gown. 'Can I touch?' He put his hand tenderly on my stomach and an electric shock passed through my body. 'Have you felt it move yet?'

I couldn't help but smile. 'No, in the books I've borrowed from Mary, it says you don't feel anything until at least four months, but I'll know it when I do. It's bound to be wearing football boots.'

His cupped a breast in his hand. 'Do you think these are going to get any bigger?' He kissed it, tickling a nipple with the tip of his tongue. 'I hope so.' Gently, he drew the sides of my dressing gown together. 'There is one small thing. I think we should get married?'

Married?

Yes, yes, YES! Manchester here I come.

I wasn't able to say anything because I was convulsed in tears of sheer joy.

'I'll take that as a yes, shall I? Now that's settled, we'd better get a move on. You go and call your ma, while I ring mine on my mobile. It's going to be tough telling her she's about to be a grandmother.'

It wasn't quite the proposal I had imagined, but in an obtuse way it was even more emotional. As he kissed my forehead, my eyes, my ears, anything within reach, I raced through the agenda: pack up the flat, give in my notice, tell Mary. No, tell Mary first, then Polly and Susie, then give in my notice. They'll have to be my bridesmaids. Oh goodness, I'm never going to get myself organised in time. I'm going to have to write lists.

71

'Where are we going to live?' I pondered, in the middle of writing envelopes.

'At my place, of course. There's plenty of room. You'll love it, I know you will.'

Inspired by a whirlwind of energy, I worked round the clock packing, telephoning and on occasions being perfectly objectionable. The mothers of the bride and groom spent the following fortnight in an absolute frenzy activating the Kent and Sussex grape vines.

'I don't want a big wedding, Paul, I couldn't bear it. I'll spend the whole day in tears. Also it seems a bit silly when we could put the money to far better use. What do you think?' I asked, as I folded an old utility blanket into a box.

'Hmm, hang on Mill, move your backside, I want to see who's on top of the leader board. He's unbelieveable. Tiger's leading by eight shots. Shit a brick, he did the first nine in 31. Hm, sorry, what did you say?'

'The wedding, idiot. I don't want a big do.'

Click, clunk, over to teletext. 'Whatever you want, darling. It'll be fine by me.' Pause ... 'M & S down another three pence. I ought to buy some more and average. Remind me tomorrow.'

I looked at him blankly.

'Double up and halve the buying price.'

Realising that Paul's concentration level was less than a courting shrimp in a rock pool, I continued to carry out most of the planning. Neither of us wanted to push the boat out when it came to the wedding, but thanks to Ma and her networking we received a mass of presents. Also his mother was brilliant. She sent me a huge bundle of baby clothes she had knitted herself, all in bright reds, yellows and greens. There was even a minute pair of pixie boots she'd sewn from felt, with gold bells on the toes.

We drew up a very short list of guests, comprising only immediate family. Susie and Polly leaped at the chance of acting as my witnesses and I arranged the special licence at the register office.

As the day drew nearer, I would have given anything to be put under a total anaesthetic until such time as the deed was done, the ring on my finger and the guests departed, not that I'm a party pooper – you should know me well enough by now.

'I rather like the idea of nipping off to Gretna Green, without telling anyone. The old anvil and all that. It would be so romantic to elope, don't you think?'

'Knowing your mother, she'd be horrified, anyway, it's an excuse to buy a huge hat. Same goes for mine, although it won't be quite as traditional.'

I could just about squeeze into my one posh frock that had enjoyed many an outing, but Ma insisted on taking me out to find something more suitable.

'I'm not having my only daughter getting married in an old dress,' she cried, adding dramatically, 'like Orphan Annie!'

'Does my tum look big in this?' I asked the eager assistant, confident of a sale.

'You'll have to get a bigger bouquet, that's all, dear. It looks loverlay.'

The only one I remotely liked which didn't make me look like a great dollop of meringue or like a python having swallowed a sheep was duly packed in tissue.

'I'm afraid we won't be having an actual honeymoon,' Paul dropped into the conversation one evening as we were watching the video of *The Sound of Music* for the eleventh time. 'We're away this Saturday. Occupational hazard.'

Captain Von Trapp was in the middle of his first kiss with Maria and I was in raptures.

'We'll catch up on one later, I promise.'

I was far too busy drooling over Christopher Plummer.

Two nights before our wedding, Paul went out for a meal with a couple of friends, while I sat on my own at home with a lamb chop for company.

Susie rang just as I had finished my last solitary meal. I ran into the bedroom and picked up the receiver, looking excitedly at my wedding dress hanging on the wardrobe door. She had offered to spend the evening with me but her father wasn't too well and she wanted to nip home to check up on him. Anway, the three of us had already celebrated together two nights before.

'Don't want you pitching up at the register office looking a wreck,' Polly had said wisely.

'Sorry I took so long to answer, Suse, I was washing up,' I said down the phone.

'Right, Millie, I had to give you a call. Promise me you'll do at least one traditional thing when you get married?'

'What on earth would that be?' I asked dreamily as I fingered the folds in the soft fabric. 'Well, you have to hold a bouquet. It's essential. It's traditional and when you throw it away at the end, with any luck I might catch it – or Poll.'

'I wasn't going to bother,' I grumbled gently. 'It's a waste of money.'

'Rubbish. Anyway, your mama always has masses of flowers in her garden. Ask her to make one. You know she'll come up trumps and it'll please her you've asked.'

So that's exactly what I did. Ma rushed round the garden at dawn on the big day, braving a sharp frost in her flanalette nightie and wellingtons, mixing miniature irises with bits and pieces from the greenhouse and delicate fronds of maidenhair fern. It was the prettiest posy I had ever seen. Jane Packer had better watch out.

When Paul staggered in after midnight only two sheets to the wind, I had already been in bed for half an hour, reading, and watched him stumble about the bedroom, tripping over his clothes, trying hard to look sober.

As he turned off his light, he said, 'By the way, I've seen Tom's new girlfriend.'

Tom was going to be his best man, an old friend from University days whom I had yet to meet.

'What's she like?'

'Well,' he hiccupped, 'my advice would be, don't stand next to her in the wedding photos.'

72

I barely slept a wink the night before the morning of the day which would change the rest of my life. Paul snored loudly and persistently and I thought candidly of our life ahead together. I swivelled the ring on my left hand which Paul had presented to me just before we left for Sussex.

'Here,' he said, embarrassed, 'I've got something for you.'

I glanced up from the current edition of *Brides* magazine and put down my cup of tea. 'What's that?'

'It's something I should have given you before, you know, when we decided to get married, but I've only just been able to get hold of it. Here, shut your eyes and put out your hands, er hand,' he corrected, laughing, as though I was a child.

Something light touched my palm and on opening my eyes I saw a small, faded red leather box. Gingerly, I undid the clasp and lifted the lid, revealing a ring. 'Oh, Paul, it's beautiful. Far too beautiful for me,' I gasped, overwhelmed. The diamond in the middle was massive. It had a deep blue sapphire either side and they were set in what I strongly suspected was platinum. 'This didn't come out of a cracker, did it?'

'Nor from the pawn shop. Stop mucking about and put it on. It should fit, or I hope it does.'

I struggled with the tears. I wish I wasn't so soppy. 'Please would you put it on me? It would bring us luck if you did. Please.'

Paul prised the ring out of its box and slid it over the fourth finger of my left hand, his own fingers trembling. It was the perfect size. 'How did you kn...?'

'I pinched one of your rings from your dressing table and tried it on. It went as far as the first knuckle on my little finger, so when I took the ring to the jewellers, they were able to adjust it. Are you sure it fits properly?'

'Oh yes, it's as though it was made for me,' I answered, turning my hand this way and that to catch the light. Wait till the girls clock this, I thought. 'You haven't told me where it comes from.'

He looked across at the terrace of houses opposite, then turned to face me. His face was in shadow, but I could see the expression in his eyes. 'It was my grandmother's ring. It was passed onto Bumble when she became engaged to my father and it was always going to be mine, provided I found someone suitable.'

That was a strange thing to say. 'But how come you didn't give it to Maddie? Surely it should have been hers?'

Paul came and put his arms around me and snuffled into my hair. 'Well, yes, I suppose by rights I should have given it to her, but there was something about her Bumble didn't like, although she never told me at the time. I have to say that she didn't hesitate a split second before fishing it out for you.'

PART FOURTEEN

PROMOTION TO THE PREMIERSHIP

73

Our wedding day was the happiest, although probably the most lachrymose day of my life, apart from an incident which could have spelled disaster. It occurred when Ma was clearing away the breakfast things.

'Botheration and flip doodle!' my mother exclaimed, the nearest she ever got to swearing.

Things must be serious. I stopped loading the dishwasher. 'What's the matter? Have you cut yourself?'

'No, I'm being a silly old woman that's all. I've spilt the salt. Whoops! Over the shoulder it goes. Don't take any notice. I'm a bit cackhanded today, that's all.'

The ringing of the telephone interrupted. I took the receiver from the extension on the wall, near the larder. 'Hello?'

'Is ... is Paul there, please?' asked a husky woman's voice.

'Er, yes, he is, but he's busy at the moment. Can I take a message? Who's calling?'

'Um, is that Millicent – sorry – Millie?'

Who was this strange female ringing Paul on his wedding day? 'Sorry, but I didn't catch your name. Who did you say was calling?'

There was a slight pause and when she spoke again it was with less authority. 'Um, can you tell him Maddie Buchanan called, please. I wanted to wish him luck.'

Maddie. Cheeky so-and-so. I began to shake.

'Is everything all right, darling? You've got your funny look.'

I shook my head, indicating I wasn't sure and Ma continued to stare at me, her expression full of concern. I cleared my throat. 'Ah, Maddie, yes, it's me, Millie.' I pulled at the twisted phone cord. 'Paul's caught up, as I said, but I'll tell him you rang.'

'Oh, thank you,' she gushed, sounding suddenly quite human. 'I hope you don't mind me calling, but I did want to let him know that I was thinking of him – of you – and to wish him all the best. Second time lucky and all that! I hope I didn't worry the life out of you, butting in like this.'

'No,' I said, lying through my teeth, 'Not at all. It's very thoughtful of you. Thank you. I'll pass it on.'

'Good. Thank you. Actually, we're flying down south in the not too distant future. Would it be too awful if we looked you up? I know it sounds daft, but I'd very much like to meet you. From what I've heard you'll make Paul far happier than I ever did. Well, I'd better ring off. I'm sure you've got a hundred and one things to do. *Ciao!*'

I replaced the receiver and scowled. *Ciao*. I hate it when people say that.

'Hi, my darling child bride, who was that?' Paul asked, appearing in the doorway. He was wearing Dad's old robe, a habit we'd never had the heart to discourage and was cuddly and adorable. 'Anyone important?' he repeated, as he kissed me, ruffling my hair.

'It was a bit of a shock, as a matter of fact. It was your ex-wife, of all people, ringing to wish you – us – luck.'

He scratched the side of his nose. 'Well, that's really decent of her. Typical Maddie. Must have taken quite a bit of courage, don't you think?' He put the kettle under the cold tap and turned it on full blast, splashing water everywhere. 'Did she leave a number, by any chance?'

I removed the tablecloth and shook it out of the window. 'She mentioned something about coming to see us. They're coming down from Scotland in a couple of months.'

'Great. It'll be nice to see Gerald again. He's a good man and I haven't seen Dom for ages. He must be quite grown up. I've not been a very good Godfather and it'll enable me to catch up on lost time.'

Ma looked harassed. 'Stop wasting time gossiping. You two had better put your skates on. Look at the time and I'm not even dressed. Nor are you. Hurry up! The cars will be here in ten minutes.'

'My God, you're right. Help. Paul, I know it's bad luck to see me in my dress, but you'll have to do it up for me. I can't reach the buttons. Quick!'

Ma wore her mink coat. ('To hell with the antis,' she challenged, 'it's both warm and practical.') As for my mother-in-law, well, what can I say. Bumble bless her, turned up at the register office decked from head to toe in silver leather astride a Triumph 'Bonneville' T120, painted in its original livery of grenadier red and Alaskan white. My father would have killed for such a beast. She swung her legs smartly over the bodywork and parked alongside the main door between a pram and a pushbike. Unclipping her helmet she tossed her hair (which she had dyed to match her catsuit) and pulled a magnificent emerald green Kashmiri shawl from the saddle bag and, with all the panache of a bullfighter performing a veronica, flung it over her shoulders. Then she extracted what looked like a headband with plumes and nestled it amongst her hair. She looked sensational. A roadsweeper leaned on his broom and whistled appreciatively as she bent from the waist to unbuckle her heavy duty boots, swapping them for a pair of snakeskin numbers with spine-chilling stiletto heels.

'Right, Daphers,' she said, smiling broadly through vermilion lips at Ma, whose own mouth was wide open not only in astonishment, but I reckon also with admiration, 'Let's get this show on the road, shall we? Where are the little buggers?'

The ceremony was clinically brief, the way I wanted it and the reception chaotic. I almost ended up not married, as I was unable to say Paul's name. I tried twice, shaking so much from nerves and with the added hindrance of a parched throat, no sound came out. The registrar waited patiently. At last I managed to gasp, 'Paulenrycamel...'

'That'll do dear.'

74

'Do you love me, darling?' Paul whispered in my ear, rocking me gently in his arms when we were alone at last in the kitchen, my mother having taken Bumble to look at the greenhouse. 'Honeshly and truly, till death ush do part?'

He was nicely sloshed. We both were.

'I love you thish big,' I confirmed, flinging my arms as wide as I could, sending the cafetière crashing to the floor. 'Now look what you've made me do.'

'Drop it,' he giggled, 'but you've already done that. Gi's a kiss.'

75

Oh, I do like being married, but please don't get carried away by the sentimentality of it all, as I shall bring you down to earth for a brief moment, which in my mind sums up the male of the species. For our wedding night, on the excellent recommendation of Tom, the best man, Paul had booked us in to the Spread Eagle Hotel in Midhurst. Tom thought this was hysterically funny, but the staff at the hotel had heard the story a hundred times before. We bolted upstairs to our room, pissed as newts, to find a magnificent four poster bed and all the trimmings, exactly as it should be for two hundred smackers plus VAT a night. Having unpacked, I went into the bathroom, determined to do a Wonder Woman act and reappear seconds later scantily clad in diaphanous silk. I hurried a touch with my toilette. I left on my mascara, switched off the light and padded across the deep pile carpet and stared in amazement at Paul. There was my husband of ten hours, forty three minutes and fifty point two seconds lying across the bed fully dressed, the television clicker in his hand. The screen flickered in the soft light, which moments earlier I had bargained on being the basis of a mega-seduction.

'My darling?'

'Shh, Mill, can you be quiet for a mo'? I'm catching up on the goals.'

I can't repeat the words I used, or this book would never pass the censors. Suffice it to say, Paul never saw those highlights, not that night, at any rate. I moved the goalposts. And do you know what my sweetheart had the cheek to say? Let me tell you.

'It is my job, you know, Mrs Millicent Campbell, it is my job.'